Joshua Wolfe walked slowly, steadily, toward the building. His hands were at his sides, well away from the holstered sidearm.

Inside the building, he *felt* the great Lumina, a deep hum beyond hearing, a glow beyond vision. It swirled in his mind like a maelstrom, pulling him toward death.

He tried to take its power, failed. Another was blocking him, one closer, more familiar with the Lumina's power.

Aubyn.

He *felt* her waiting for him, an antlion deep in her pit, a spider waiting for the web-twitch. She was reaching for him, for his mind.

He entered the huge circular room, looked around. There were two mezzanine balconies above, then the diffused crystalline light from the faceted-glass roof. To one side was a large reception desk of exotic woods. No one was behind the desk. There was a body lying near one wall, a gun lying not far away. The air smelt as if lightning had struck nearby not long ago.

A woman waited in the center of the room.

She appeared unarmed.

"The crystal," Aubyn said, "what I've heard is called a Lumina, is mine. I found it. I killed for it. This is my world, and soon I'll be ready to reach out for more."

By Chris Bunch
Published by Ballantine Books:

The Shadow Warrior
THE WIND AFTER TIME
HUNT THE HEAVENS
THE DARKNESS OF GOD

With Allan Cole:

The Sten Adventures
STEN
THE WOLF WORLDS
THE COURT OF A THOUSAND SUNS
FLEET OF THE DAMNED
REVENGE OF THE DAMNED
THE RETURN OF THE EMPEROR
VORTEX
EMPIRE'S END

THE FAR KINGDOMS
THE WARRIOR'S TALE
KINGDOMS OF THE NIGHT

A RECKONING FOR KINGS
A DAUGHTER OF LIBERTY

THE DARKNESS OF GOD

Book Three of *The Shadow Warrior*

Chris Bunch

A Del Rey® Book
BALLANTINE BOOKS • NEW YORK

A Del Rey® Book
Published by Ballantine Books
Copyright © 1997 by Chris Bunch

All rights reserved under International and Pan-American Copyright Conventions. Published in the United States of America by Ballantine Books, a division of Random House, Inc., New York, and simultaneously in Canada by Random House of Canada Limited, Toronto.

http://www.randomhouse.com

Library of Congress Catalog Card Number: 97-80361

ISBN 0-345-38737-6

Manufactured in the United States of America

First Edition: December 1997

10 9 8 7 6 5 4 3 2 1

* CHAPTER ONE *

A Federation battlefleet whispered through subspace. In a compartment aboard its flagship, the *Andrea Doria*, two men stared down at Joshua Wolfe's body. One was a fleet admiral, the other a Federation Intelligence executive.

A third man wore coveralls and combat harness. He sat in a chair, a blaster held casually in his lap.

"How many safeguards does he have?" Admiral Hastings asked.

"Every damned one we could build into his mind, sir," the second man, Cisco, answered. "He was one of our best before he turned renegade."

"You think you'll be able to get what you want without killing him?"

"We have to," Cisco said grimly. "FI doesn't have anything else."

The first man pursed his lips. "Well, you built him, you ran him, so you'd *better* be able to peel him like an onion."

"Yes, sir. I've already got our best psychs on standby."

The admiral left the compartment without responding. Cisco took something from his pocket and examined it. It was a gray, featureless stone with a few bits of color in it. "Stay dead like that," he said softly. He put it away, then swung to the guard.

"How much longer are you on shift?"

1

"Two hours and some."

"Stay careful," Cisco warned. "We don't really know what we have here, so don't get casual."

The guard stared at Cisco. "Yes, *sir,*" he said, putting heavy emphasis on the last word. Cisco nodded, then went out. The hatch slid closed.

"Yes, *sir,*" the man said again. "Yes, sir, Master Cisco, large-charge spymaster sir."

He glanced at Wolfe.

"Guess I oughta kick you in the shins a time or two, eh, since shit always flows downhill, huh?"

*

The man tightened the black band around his biceps, then pulled the small lanyard. The bell from the ancient ocean-ship *Lutine* clanged three times through the high-ceilinged, wooden-paneled chamber.

By the third peal, the room was silent.

The man cleared his throat.

"The Federation exploration ship *Trinquier*, overdue on planetfall for three weeks, is now considered lost.

"All Lloyd's carriers involved with this matter are advised to contact their policies' beneficiaries."

*

Another continuum . . . red spray across the stars, connecting them, holding them, blood-syrup of death, nothing living but a single invader . . .

Joshua Wolfe, between death and life, felt the touch of the alien and pulled back in horror.

The drug Cisco'd shot him with still washed through his system; nothingness clung.

Cisco has the Lumina. I am naked.

Defeat.

No. You had strength before. Find it now. The Lumina gave you nothing but kimu.

Joshua struggled, fell back, floated away once more.

Time passed.

Once more a bit of life came, angry, yammering.

Rouse yourself. Now. There will be no time when we reach Earth. You must strike first.

No. Easier to drift, to drown.

Images came, went, like old-fashioned photographs looked at casually, then cast into a fire, twisting, warping as they vanished:

The corpselike face of an Al'ar, grasping organs blurring through a series of strikes. Then the alien stopped, waited for the young Joshua Wolfe to echo his movements. The Al'ar was named Taen.

. . .

*The hissing, invisible **kill-barrier** in the prison camp, not far from his parents' graves.*

. . .

The Al'ar, about to open the scoutship hatch, whirled, but not in time, grasping organs coming up, but late, too late as the death-strike went home. The dirty, ragged boy pulled the corpse away and clambered into the ship, went to the controls.

He sat behind them, stared at their utter alienness, felt fear shake his spine. He forced himself to breathe, as he'd been taught, then remembered all he'd learned, all he'd been told, from any prisoner who'd been inside an Al'ar ship.

Tentatively, he touched a sensor. The hatch behind him slid closed.

He touched two more, and the panel came alive; he felt the shuddering of power behind him.

A cold, hard smile came to Joshua Wolfe's lips.

. . .

Joshua wore the uniform of a Federation major. Behind him were ranks of soldiers in dress uniform. A general held an open velvet case with a medal inside. His words were "highest traditions of the service," "without regard for his own safety," and "refused to recognize the severity of his wounds, but insisted on returning to his weapon," and so forth.

They had little meaning to Wolfe. All he heard was death and killing.

. . .

Joshua, wearing fighting harness with blaster ready, cat-paced through the empty streets of Sauros' capital. But there was no one to kill. The Al'ar had gone, utterly vanished.

. . .

The face of the man who called himself Cisco, saying there was yet one more Al'ar, and Joshua was to hunt him down.

. . .

The last Al'ar, blurring out of concealment, striking at Joshua.

Taen.

. . .

The shadows of the Al'ar Guardians, telling him why they'd fled their home-space for Man's universe, showing him the invader Joshua's man-mind could only see as a ravening virus, devouring world after world, system after system, jumping across and filling the spaces between them.

. . .

The emptiness in the Al'ar ship where the great Lumina stone had hung before it was stolen by a shadow drenched in blood.

. . .

Taen, as the Chitet bolt took him in the back, slumping in death.

. . .

Death . . . that welcomed.

It would be very easy to let the animal-mechanism shut down. Nothing was ahead but pain under the not-gentle hands and tools of the FI interrogators.

Death.

Defeat.

The red crawl of the "virus" would continue through another galaxy and on and on.

Wolfe stirred.

Can you reach out? Can you find anything? The Al'ar Guardians?

Nothing.

Something came, or rather returned to him. An echo, far worlds distant.

The ur-Lumina he sought?

Nothing once more.

Again. Feel for anger, feel for fear, feel for those who hate you, who want you.

Another flicker, far distant, a man who hated with a white-hot heat, remembering the woman Joshua had freed and returned to her lover, now her husband.

No. Not him. Not Jalon Kakara.

A red-orange sear of flame, stone pinwheeling up as the Occam *smashed down from its orbit into a dark gray palace, the frantic yammer of a world whose leader had almost died.*

The Chitet.

He felt *them.*

Looking for Wolfe, looking for the Great Lumina, cult-mind sweeping, hunting.

Then the drug took him back down into its embrace.

*

"This is utterly absurd," Cisco said in a near-snarl.

Hastings looked at him coldly. "Orders are orders, and these certainly are from an unimpeachable authority."

"Sir," Cisco began, "this makes no sense. We have

Wolfe secured. I can't think of anything anybody's got that could ruffle the *Andrea Doria*'s hair. So why the hell are we ordered to divert and transfer him? We're only, what, half a dozen jumps from Earth now? Utterly no sense whatsoever," he said, ignoring the mindcrawl suggesting a reason.

"Consider an explanation, mister," Hastings said. "We're well within the bounds of the Federation. I hardly think even your Chitet would try to grab him here. We beat them, remember? We drove them away. They aren't anything to worry about, at least not for us. Once you have your spy debriefed, it'll be a simple matter for the police to take care of matters.

"You're being paranoid, Cisco. I'd rather suspect Com-FedNav wants to keep my battle group close to the Outlaw Worlds, rather than have us waste the time and energy to go all the way back to Earth, dump off one man, and then jump back out here.

"The pickup group specified in the order seems more than large enough to keep a countergrab from happening."

"Admiral Hastings," Cisco said, "you saw what the Chitet had around that fortress. That was a goddamned battleship!"

"An old battlecruiser, actually," Hastings corrected. "I think you're being a bit hysterical, Cisco. Don't forget the orders are not just for Wolfe, but for you and your entire team to transfer as well. But I'll give you this. When we rendezvous with the other ships, if there's any irregularity, I'll refuse to turn him—or you—over to them. And I'll reauthenticate the original orders with ComFedNav right now. Does that satisfy you?"

Hastings glowered at the FI executive.

"No," Cisco said. "But that's the best I'll get, isn't it?"

*

Four ships waited—one frigate, one armed transport, and two sloops—as the Federation battlefleet emerged from the nowhere of N-space.

"This is the Federation Naval Force Sure Strike," came the com from the *Andrea Doria*. "Challenge Quex Silver Six-Way."

"*Andrea Doria,* this is the FNS *Planov*. Reply Cincinnatus Yang."

"That's the correct response, sir," the watch officer reported to the *Andrea Doria*'s captain. "And I checked the Jane's fiche. That's the *Planov* onscreen. Current Nav-Registry still carries her and her escorts as being in commission."

"Tell them we're beginning the transfer," the ship's captain said. She turned to Admiral Hastings. "Sir?"

"I see nothing wrong," the admiral said. "Cisco?"

The agent's eyes flickered. "There's nothing apparent, sir," he conceded.

"Do your people have the—package ready?"

"Yes, sir."

"You may begin the transfer, then," Hastings told the ship's captain.

*

"Ready?"

"Ready, sir," the senior FI tech reported to Cisco.

"Get him on board."

The tech triggered the antigrav unit, and the bubble stretcher holding Joshua Wolfe lifted off the deck. Two men steered it through the hatch of the *Andrea Doria*'s shuttle; the other seven men in the FI detachment followed.

Cisco gestured at Admiral Hastings, something like a salute.

"See you on Earth," Hastings said in response, without returning the salute.

Cisco nodded and boarded the boat after his men.

Hastings waited until the shuttle lock slid shut, then he grimaced in distaste to his aide. "The air's better when the spooks are gone," he said.

The young blond woman grinned at him. "Guess it's nice Earth's a decent-sized planet, sir."

Hastings guffawed and clapped his aide on the back. "Let's get up to the bridge and make sure they're well on their way."

*

The *Andrea Doria*'s shuttle nosed up to the *Planov*'s stern, and a cargo lock yawned between its twin drive tubes. A mag-probe touched the shuttle's nose and drew it inside the transport.

"We have your ship," the com crackled. "Unloading."

Ten minutes passed.

Hastings looked sideways at the *Andrea Doria*'s captain. "Very slow, even if they are unloading flatlanders. Your boat crew needs drill."

"They'll get it, sir," the officer said, anger touching her voice. "My apologies."

"This is the *Planov*," the com said. "Loading complete. Stand by."

The armed transport's lock opened, and the shuttle slid out, tumbling. There was no sign of its drive activating.

Abruptly the *Planov* and her three escorts vanished into N-space.

"Courteous bastards," the aide murmured, but Hastings' attention was on the monitor and the slowly revolving shuttle.

"Something's wrong," he snapped. "Captain! Send a boarding party to the shuttle!"

"Yes, sir."

"Have them armed!"

The captain's face flashed surprise for a bare instant. "Sir!"

*

Ten suited men floated around the *Andrea Doria*'s shuttle. Two hung near the craft's nose, two near the drive tube. The other four clustered around the airlock. All had heavy blasters clipped to their suits.

"No external damage to ship," the team's leader, Sergeant Sullivan, reported. "No sign of lock damage."

"Cleared to enter."

Two men braced on either side of the lock, weapons ready, while the leader touched the lock door sensor.

The outer lock door slid open.

The leader, with one other man, went inside. "Cycling inner lock," he reported.

Static snarled, then:

"Son of a bitch!"

"Report!"

"Sorry. This is Sergeant Sullivan. Everyone on board's dead! Unconscious, anyway!"

"What about the prisoner? The man in the stretcher?"

"No stretcher, sir. Wait a minute. One of the women is sitting up, sir. I've got my outside pickup on."

Very faintly the men on the bridge of the *Andrea Doria* heard:

"What happened?"

"Gas ... They were waiting for us ... gassed us ... didn't give us a ..."

Then silence. Sullivan's voice came:

"She's passed out, sir."

*

"Well?" said the woman with alabaster features fine enough for a museum.

"Pretty standard, Coordinator Kur," the medical tech said. "They first hit him with Knok-Down, maybe a more concentrated blast than normal. Then they kept him under, almost to the point of needing a life-support system. Suppressing conscious thought, pain, and so forth."

"Any damage?"

"I assume you mean mental. Probably none."

"How long to bring him out of it?"

"Three, perhaps four hours."

"Summon me when he's fully conscious."

*

Wolfe opened his eyes slowly. The compartment around him swam, then steadied. He was in a comfortable bed. The air smelled of disinfectant. He felt ship-hum in his bones.

Sitting in a chair beside him was a woman wearing conservative, dark clothes, almost a uniform. She was perhaps five years older than Wolfe, and he found her beautiful, in a chill, forbidding way. *Like a statue,* he thought.

Behind her stood two men, also wearing dark clothes. Their hair was close-cropped, and they might have been brothers. They each held blasters aimed at Wolfe's chest.

"Welcome, Joshua Wolfe," the woman said. "I am Authority Coordinator Dina Kur. You are now in the hands of the Chitet."

* CHAPTER TWO *

Wolfe eyed the two men with guns.

"Honest, I *really* appreciate the rescue," he said. "So you won't have to shoot me more than once or twice to make sure I'm beholden."

"There is no point in facile cleverness," Kur said. "Let me put it to you clearly. We are aware you seek the stone called the Overlord Stone or Great Lumina, as do we.

"We consider you our most dangerous enemy, since you have circumvented our plans on several occasions, including the destruction of an entire Chitet mission and its ship on the planet of Trinité; then you severely damaged a patrol cruiser of ours in your escape. We are also aware of your hijacking of the patrol vessel *Occam*, and using that ship in an attempt to murder our Master Speaker, Matteos Athelstan. Under normal circumstances, you would be immediately put to death for crimes against the Chitet and, ultimately, the future of humanity. But these are not normal times or circumstances.

"You also, in the company of an Al'ar, purportedly the last Al'ar alive, investigated a certain area where the Great Lumina had been, and where we had set alarms. I was aboard the *Udayana*, and followed you to the abandoned planetary fortress where you held off our forces until the Federation could arrive. Our cause gained many

11

martyrs that day. What happened to the Al'ar who was with you?"

"He is . . . gone beyond. Dead," Wolfe said.

"So we assumed, and that made your continued existence, as long as you do not further jeopardize the Chitet, essential, at least for the moment," Kur said. "He was killed, and you were taken by the Federation. We were informed by reliable sources you were being returned to Earth as a captive, so evidently those you thought to be your friends have changed their positions. Or you have.

"Regardless, you are going to assist us in our quest, Joshua Wolfe."

Her voice had remained utterly, inhumanly cold. "Our Master Speaker is aboard this vessel to ensure that all goes well, and that we will be successful in recovering the Great Stone the Al'ar called the Overlord Stone."

"I *am* going to help," Joshua agreed.

"Don't play me for a fool, Joshua Wolfe," Kur replied. "I'm not going to listen to nonsense about a sudden realization of the truth of our beliefs. We are not on the road to Damascus, nor are there many visions in N-space."

"Oh, but I am going to cooperate," Wolfe insisted. "For I already know how to find the Chitet—sorry, the former Chitet—who murdered eleven men and women and stole the Great Lumina. But I'll need your resources to recover it."

Kur stared at him, without blinking. "This decision is well beyond me," she said. "I must consult with Master Speaker Athelstan."

*

Wolfe 'freshed, ate, and slept, feeling the last of the drugs wash out of his system. He asked if he could work out, and his request was denied, without explanation.

His guards were changed every hour, and never varied

their routine. They sat, eyes fixed on Joshua, never answering anything he said, nor volunteering anything of their own.

Two ship-days later, Authority Coordinator Kur returned. With her were three Chitet. Two were men, average looking, calm-expressioned. One wore a close-cropped beard. The third was a small woman who, in another setting, might have been considered quite pretty.

"Master Speaker Athelstan wishes to speak with you," Kur announced. "Now, listen closely, Joshua Wolfe.

"Your life is important to you, I assume. It is also important to us, at least until we have fully exploited you and whatever knowledge you possess.

"You will continue to be watched by gun-guards such as those who have been with you since your capture. It is known that you're a master at most forms of combat, armed or otherwise.

"We have also heard stories which appear preposterous about your other abilities, which I assume you acquired from the Al'ar at one time or another.

"We can take no chances, Joshua Wolfe, even if it means sacrificing whatever leads you might provide toward the Overlord Stone.

"These three are an additional safeguard. They are Guide Kristin," Kur indicated the woman, "and Lucian and Max." Lucian was the bearded one. "They are among our most highly trained security specialists, and have formerly been assigned to the private bodyguard of Master Speaker Athelstan, so you should respect and be wary of their skills.

"You do not need to know their family names. Kristin speaks for the team. They have orders to kill you if ordered, and if anything, I repeat anything, appears wrong, to destroy you instantly, without waiting for a command from Master Speaker Athelstan or myself. Remove your tunic, please."

Joshua obeyed. Kur stepped out of the room again, and returned with a small flat black case.

"Put your hands in front of you," she ordered. "Guards, each of you stand to one side, so you have a clear field of fire. If Joshua Wolfe attempts anything, kill him."

The guards obeyed. Kur took a flesh-colored pouch with thin straps from the case. "Turn around," she ordered. She touched the object to the base of Joshua's spine. It felt cold for an instant but quickly warmed. She ran the straps around his waist, touched them together, and they joined seamlessly.

"Replace your clothing," Kur said. "That object, as you can probably surmise, is explosive. It is phototropic, and will gradually take on the coloration of your skin, though you should exercise care about disrobing in public, because the camouflage is not perfect.

"The charge is shaped, so someone standing next to you when the device is detonated would be unharmed, and only momentarily deafened.

"You, on the other hand, would have your spinal cord shattered. If you attempt to remove the charge, a signal will be sent to the operator, and he or she will instantly detonate it."

Joshua sat down, leaned back. It felt as if he had padding against his spine, no more.

"The woman or man controlling the detonator to that device is watching a monitor at all times, a monitor carrying your image," Kur said. "You do not need to know how far away the operator is, nor even where he or she is, nor where the monitor is. If you are moving, one of these three will have a tiny camera concealed about his or her person. If you are in one place, the camera will be hidden there. It might also be more than one camera, so there's no point in finding and destroying one single pickup.

"If the operator sees anything amiss on the monitor, or if you vanish from its screen . . ."

"Quite clever," Wolfe said. "I see you three are now my closest and best friends."

"That is an excellent way to think," Kur said. "Now, Master Speaker Athelstan awaits."

*

"You were once in possession of a Lumina," Athelstan said, stating a fact, not a question. He appeared in his fifties and could have been a successful merchant banker. Wolfe had seen him once before, on a vid interview. He'd ascribed the glitter in the man's eyes to camera flare. There was no such excuse now.

There were three others in the compartment, which was soberly but richly paneled: Kur, Max, and a Chitet in his early thirties who was Athelstan's aide.

"I was," Wolfe said. "The Lumina was originally purchased by one quote Judge end-quote Malcolm Penruddock of Mandodari III, stolen from him by a spec thief named Innokenty Khodyan. I recovered the gem on a warrant, and Khodyan got dead in the process.

"I interviewed Penruddock about his interest in the Lumina—"

"At the behest of Federation Intelligence," Athelstan said.

"It was . . . and also for my own interests. But your Chitet killed Penruddock and his wife before I found out very much. Almost killed me."

"He did not deserve the Lumina," Athelstan said. "He'd been quietly approached to sell it, but refused. That left us no other course."

"Must be nice to be sure of who deserves what and

when. And that's not quite how it went," Wolfe said calmly. "Credit me with a bit of intelligence. You first commissioned Innokenty Khodyan to steal the Lumina from Penruddock, using a fence named Edet Sutro as a cutout. You killed him on Trinité. For a group of people who think themselves philosophers, you sure trail a lot of bodies."

"Nowhere does it say philosophy cannot resort to direct action to accomplish its goals," Athelstan said. "And our goals are great, encompassing not only the salvation of humanity, but enabling it to reach the next level of evolution as well."

"There was a Chinese once," Wolfe said, "who said, 'Those who would take over the Earth and shape it to their own ends never, I notice, succeed.'"

"Lao-tzu lived long before the Chitet," Athelstan said. "And there were those of his time who came very close. Buddha. Confucius. The group of Jews who created Jesus. Mohamet . . . But there's no point in this sparring. I assume the Federation has the Lumina."

"They do."

"Does that cripple you? What powers did the stone give? We have one, but none of our savants have been able to do more than the most minor trickeries with the object."

Wolfe's eyes flickered. *So they have one now.* "I can still find the Mother Lumina for you," Wolfe evaded.

"How? We have searched hard for it, for almost seven years without result."

"Obviously you were looking in the wrong places," Joshua said. "And you didn't have a ferret with sharp enough teeth."

"I agree. The facts dictate the truth." Athelstan's head bobbed slightly, as if he'd just recited a prime canon of his faith. "Tell us how to look, and we shall."

"Not quite that easy," Wolfe said. "If I just tell you, my continued existence, as your knob-rattler Kur has pointed out, would become a little redundant. So even if I knew, exactly, I wouldn't tell you."

"You were our captive once," Athelstan said. "And the head of the interrogation team reported you had suicide devices installed in your mind against forcible questioning and against any psychotropic drugs we have access to. I assume she was correct."

"I'd be a fool not to say yes," Joshua said.

"How do we seek the Overlord Stone?" Athelstan said. "My security coordinator will obey your orders."

"I await instructions," Kur said, showing no resentment.

"First, here's what I know," Joshua said. "The Al'ar placed the Overlord Stone in a ship, actually a satellite. It was set in space in a certain place of importance to the Al'ar. Sometime after the war, three Federation scout-ships found it. I assume this discovery was not an accident."

Kur looked uncomfortable. Athelstan nodded for her to speak.

"Some Federation investigations on Al'ar homeworlds suggested the existence of the ur-Lumina," she said reluctantly. "The Federation issued orders for a naval patrol to visit the area of interest. We learned of this patrol shortly before it transshipped, and were able to insert one of our agents aboard one of the ships. The agent was equipped with an N-space blurt-transmitter, and was able to report the discovery to us. We had ships standing by capable of capturing the scout-ships, and dispatched them immediately. But when they arrived, they found—"

"Eleven corpses, two ships, and no Lumina," Wolfe said. "Your boy changed his mind while he was sitting around twiddling his thumbs, and decided to render unto Caesar instead of the Chitet. And he wanted to be Caesar."

"So we assumed," Kur said. "We went in search of the individual."

"Who is she?"

"How did you know it's a woman?" Kur demanded.

"Because of the care you've taken not to mention her sex," Wolfe said.

Kur eyed him, then went on. "Her name is Token Aubyn. She was a lieutenant in the regular Federation Navy. All E's on her quarterly reports. An officer with a great career in front of her. She'd been secretly raised as a member of our culture, and chosen to infiltrate the Federation military."

"Home system?"

"Vidaury III, although she spent time on VI as well before she enlisted."

"I assume you've toothcombed that system without results or leads?"

Kur nodded.

"Token Aubyn," Wolfe mused. "Pretty name for somebody that cold-blooded. You have a full dossier on her?"

"We do."

"I want it. All of it," Wolfe said. "No dandy little crossouts for Chitet snitches and sources."

"But—"

"Be silent, Coordinator Kur. We must give Wolfe every possible aid," Athelstan said.

"After all," Joshua said, "it's not as if you plan on letting me escape with anything I learn here, now is it?"

Athelstan didn't answer, but his cold eyes held Wolfe's.

*

Joshua went through the fiche on Token Aubyn quickly, letting his senses, his training, reach for what might be in the data. Then he read, viewed everything very slowly, twice.

Security Coordinator Kur and his alternating guardians waited stolidly.

There weren't many holos or vids. Kur told Joshua that Aubyn reportedly hadn't liked having herself recorded.

The best holo Joshua could find was a head-and-shoulders cameo of Aubyn in full-dress Federation uniform.

"That was her graduation picture from the Academy of Flight on Mars, taken at her parents' insistence," Kur said.

"Where are they now?"

"Dead. In an accident two years ago."

"Convenient."

Wolfe examined the portrait. Aubyn wasn't pretty, but striking. Dark hair, worn very short. She was the gamin type, with hooded eyes just turned away from the lens.

Other documents said she was slender, a bit over average height.

"What about her love life?"

"Nothing known."

"Come on, Kur. Everybody plays pinch-and-tickle sometimes."

"Not necessarily," the woman protested. "Especially in Aubyn's case. Her parents were deep-cover types, so she grew up in a house full of secrets, on two planets. Then, when we gave her our long-range plans for her, she would have been a fool to endanger everything by listening to her glands."

"How romantic you Chitet are."

Wolfe ran the fiche forward.

"Now here's something interesting," he mused. "The final competition for the Academy of Flight broke down to her and one other person. He died just before the final oral examinations. In another accident."

"We checked into that thoroughly," Kur said. "It *was*

an accident. Aubyn was half a planet away when this boy died."

"I say again: convenient."

He returned to the fiche.

"You either did a good job of programming Aubyn, or else she already had her calling. No zigs, no changes of major. Chosen field of study at the Academy . . . sociology. And her thesis was on 'The Dynamism of a One-Party State.' "

"I fail to see any significance in that," Kur said. "When we have convinced the people of the Federation of the benefit of our ways, of course there won't be any necessity for dissenters."

"Thus spake Savanarola," Wolfe murmured. "Did you ever consider that Aubyn was doing research for her own idea of a one-party state? One with Token Aubyn as dictat?"

"Oh," Kur said. "That's insane—and of course we didn't allow ourselves to consider any options that didn't make sense. Our error."

"Do you have data on the eleven men and women she murdered who were in her minifleet?" Wolfe asked.

"We do."

"Then let's start looking for a hole for me to go down," Wolfe said.

"I don't follow."

"Isn't it logical that Token Aubyn, once she decided to steal the Lumina and desert both the Federation and your—social circle to boot, had brains enough to know better than to go home, especially with something that would give her the powers it would?"

"Of course. We've spent a great deal of time trying to find her throughout the Federation and even the Outlaw Worlds. Do you think you can provide a lead?"

"I do."

"Since you're experienced with the Lumina," Athelstan put in, "what powers will she have?"

"I'm not sure," Wolfe lied. "But that's for later, anyway.

"So she went somewhere. If we're lucky, maybe she didn't just pick someplace out of an interstellar gazetteer. Maybe she got an idea from her shipmates. There isn't much to do on those little spitkits but talk, and since Aubyn was a newbie, everybody would've been eager to tell her all the war stories everyone else had heard until their eyes turned green. Maybe somebody talked about his or her homeworld, and maybe that sounded like just the place for a woman with big ambition, no scruples, and God in her pocket. Maybe somebody talking about that place was what gave Aubyn the idea in the first place."

*

Wolfe lay in near-total darkness. He'd been moved into a larger chamber, but it was as sterile as the one he'd been revived in.

Across the room Guide Kristin sat in a low chair. A reading light pooled around her head and shoulders, and she appeared intent on her reading matter, *A Consideration of Logic As It Should Be Applied in Daily Circumstances,* written by one Matteos Athelstan.

Wolfe, momentarily exhausted, turned his mind away from his search and considered her. Her blond hair was sensibly close-cropped. He'd seen the thrust of her breasts under her sensible garment, but had no idea about what the rest of her body looked like, other than it was slender.

He found her face somewhat attractive, a curving vee. It reminded him a bit of an Earth-Siamese cat. *At least,* he thought, *she doesn't have the screeching voice of a Siamese.* He smiled.

The woman looked up, saw Joshua's eyes on her, and quickly looked down at her book.

Interesting, he thought. He blanked her, let himself reach out, *feel* through the ship.

A faint direction came to him, as if he were shouting in a wilderness and heard a tiny echo from a hidden grotto. He let "himself" float in that direction.

There the Lumina is. Of course Athelstan would keep it close. In his office safe. Not original. But secure, at least. For the moment. But perhaps . . .

Now I shall try something.

Reach toward it . . . touch it without touching . . . fumbling . . .

Joshua Wolfe was outside the ship, hanging, floating in N-space.

Find ku, find the Void again. Let the Lumina take you beyond. Warmth, feeling warmth back toward the Federation. Out there . . .

He jerked back, feeling the chill hatred of the invader, the "virus."

No, not there. Not yet.

Look elsewhere. Let the small find the large. Confusion. There are others. But they're small. Feel . . .

Ah! There!

*

"Why did you pick Rogan's World?" Kur said.

"Because," Wolfe said, "I'm guessing she heard about Rogan's World from Dietrich, who grew up there. Nice that he happened to be the motor mate on the scout she commanded as well. Looking at his service record— three court-martials, two nonjudicial punishments—I'd guess he was an excellent representative of the planet."

"You've been there?"

"Nope. Always wanted to, though."

"Why?"

22

"Because of the delicate aroma of corruption," Wolfe said. "And money."

Kur eyed him skeptically.

*

Wolfe sat up in bed, yawning, as if he'd just awakened. Kristin was instantly alert. Wolfe took the robe from the chair beside the bed, pulled it on as he stood.

"Ship air dehydrates me," he said, walking toward the fresher. "Can I get you some water?"

"No," the Chitet said.

Wolfe went into the fresher, took a metal glass from its clip, filled it, and drank. He grimaced at the cold, completely flat taste, then clipped the glass back in its holder.

"I'm grateful," he said when he came out, "you don't insist on watching me *everywhere*."

"Even an animal in a zoo is allowed a private area," Kristin said. "And there is nothing in that fresher that can be used as a weapon."

Joshua went back to the bed, sat down.

"I'm curious," he said. "Why do you insist on taking the midnight–eight watch?"

"Because I am in charge of my team," Kristin said. "Security training dictates an escape attempt is most likely going to be made in the early hours of the morning."

"I'm not planning to escape."

"Good," Kristin said. "Then you shall continue to live."

"Another question," Wolfe persisted. "Does your camera, or pickup, or whatever it is, transmit sound to whoever's sitting on my personal doomsday switch?"

Kristin looked at him, slowly shook her head from side to side.

"Just curious," Wolfe said, pulling the robe off and lying down again.

No. I am not trying to escape. Not yet.

THE DARKNESS OF GOD

*

"I understand most of these requests, and agree with them," Master Speaker Athelstan said. "They certainly fit what I would romantically expect a master rogue and gambler to have. But we may not be able to acquire the exact model of ship you've specified, since the operation must be mounted immediately."

"A yacht's a yacht," Wolfe said. "Something big, impressive, ultra nouveau, that's all we want. Oh yeah, something I forgot— Pick some kind of uniform for the crew to wear. With gold braid."

Athelstan considered, decided Wolfe wasn't making a joke, nodded. "One question," he said, "and this is to satisfy personal curiosity. You specify the ship's library must contain an edition of the complete works of this Earth-poet Eliot. Why?"

"Eliot does more than Hume can," Wolfe said, "to justify God's ways to Man."

"I still don't understand. But then," Athelstan said, "I've never been much of a one for poetry. Utterly illogical."

"It's interesting you should say that," Joshua said. "Most poets think they're more logical than the rest of us."

Athelstan smiled tightly. "Amusing conceit. Do you agree with them?"

Wolfe shrugged. "Depends on how bad my hangover is."

Athelstan frowned.

"By the way," Joshua said. "We'll need some kind of linkup with an expensive comp-catalog. I'll take care of outfitting the rest of the crew myself. You might be too— logical."

*

"That one," Wolfe decided. "And that one, and—not that one. Too virginal. Not that one either. Makes you look too available. For too low a price."

He touched sensors, and the next set of catalog holo-

24

graphs swam into life. He kept his eyes away from Guide Kristin, whose face was red with embarrassment.

"You find this quite amusing, don't you," Kur said, her voice showing a trace of anger.

"Lady," Wolfe said in exasperation, "you're the one who says I've got to go looking for Token Aubyn with gun-guards *and* these three mad bombers. So I'm going to be standing out a little. That's fine, because that's the quickest way to get Aubyn to notice us. But don't tell me how to dress the set, goddammit. I could've used Lucian or Max for my main companion, but I don't think I can fake being a manlover for long. And I'll be suiting them up as soon as I finish with Kristin anyway. You want all of us to mouse in like good brown Chitet? Won't that make Aubyn wonder why her fellow bow-and-scrapers happen to be on Rogan's World? Wouldn't she maybe send a couple dozen goons to check matters out?"

"If she's even there," Kur said skeptically. "I find it hard to accept that one man can put a pin on the map after hundreds of our best minds have analyzed the situation over the years. And I find your continual insults of our culture rather distasteful."

"Funny. I find your continual attempts to kill me the same," Wolfe said. "You're bitching about wearing an expensive gown, and I've got a bomb up my ass. Now shut up and let me keep on with my frills and bows. One other thing. What about the ship?"

"You'll have it in time," Kur said. "It offplaneted Batan this E-day."

"Good," Wolfe said. He looked at Kristin and decided to take pity. "You pick the next two outfits."

"No," the woman said. "I have no experience being a—a . . ."

"Popsy is one of the old words," Wolfe said helpfully. "But give in to your worst impulses, woman, and go

25

crazy. Even Chitet have been known to smile and dance in the moonlight. I know. I saw a couple of them."

He thought for an instant her face flickered, but decided he'd been wrong.

* CHAPTER THREE *

Dear Scholar Frazier:

I'm sending this brief note via a completely trustworthy graduate student of mine, with instructions to hand-deliver it to you, and no one else, for I fear to trust it to conventional means, even if it were coded.

I would strongly recommend against your continuing to seek funding for the expedition to the Al'ar homeworld of Sauros we spoke of at the last seminar. I know this must surprise you, because of my initial enthusiasm, and I'm fully aware of your need to reestablish your credentials, particularly in the field you first became well known in.

However, very unofficial word has reached me that all contact with the team from Halcyon III's Universidad de Descubrimiento has been lost. As you know, they were investigating A887-3, another of the Al'ar homeworlds, and were partially funded by the Federation.

These are unsettled times, so this might not be as worrisome as I find it, but there are two rumors I've heard involving the expedition that need passing along, and two very definite facts:

The first rumor is that the Halcyon III team 'cast some extraordinarily strange messages prior to their disappearance, messages that make it appear as if they'd gone mad. The messages supposedly mention a "red death," a "walking between the stars," among other hysteria.

THE DARKNESS OF GOD

The second rumor is that two other expeditions, also projected toward one or another of the worlds formerly held by the Al'ar, have been cancelled. Supposedly these two expeditions would have gone into the "center" of the Al'ar fringe worlds—the same sector that A887-3 is in.

I'd discount these stories, except for my two facts:

The first and most disturbing is that the heirs and beneficiaries of the scientists on the Universidad expedition have had their death benefits paid in full, even though no official notice of death has been made. This suggests to me that someone at a very high level knows what happened, but no one is willing to admit to it.

The second fact is that I've been advised by my department head to ignore any stories about Halcyon III, and to pass along to her the name of anyone spreading such tales, for transmission to what she called the "proper authorities."

I protested, of course, reminding her of our long tradition of free speech, but she scowled at me and asked if I remembered the necessary restrictions on speech back during the war. I said I certainly did, and considered most of them imbecilic. She told me that if I wished my annual review to go as smoothly as it should, I'd take heed of her warning and stop being silly.

I don't know what to make of all this, Juan.

But I certainly think you should be warned. Something seems to be going wrong out there in the former Al'ar worlds, and I'd suggest you stay well clear until there's further data.

Best,

'Liz

Scholar Eliz Shulbert
L'Ecole de Science
Janzoon IX

* CHAPTER FOUR *

Wolfe's chill eyes swept the hotel lobby. "This'll do," he said.

The manager fawned slightly. "You mentioned you have quite precise requirements?"

"I do. We'll take the penthouse suite in the tower for myself and my personal assistant, and the entire floor below it for my staff and the crew of my yacht. I'll also need the next floor to be vacant. I despise noise when I'm trying to sleep."

The manager realized his eyes were bulging and corrected the situation. "But—there're already guests on some of . . ."

"Inform them that their charges to date are on my bill, and you'll assist in finding them acceptable rooms elsewhere in the hotel—or else help them relocate to another, equally prestigious hotel." A large bill changed hands. "If they insist on staying . . ." Wolfe shrugged.

The manager managed to look as if he were bowing without moving. "I'm sure with such generosity—I'm sure there'll be no problem."

"Good. Also, I'll need one of your private dining rooms on constant standby, a conference room, and three of my men added to your staff to ensure proper security."

"As you wish, Mister Taylor." The manager spun. "Front!"

THE DARKNESS OF GOD

A platoon of bellboys scurried forward and began sorting the mountain of luggage, including the fourteen matched bags in pink reptile hide.

Kristin stepped close to Wolfe. She no longer wore the drab simplicity of a Chitet. Her blond hair, starting to grow out, had a slightly iridescent streak curving along the hairline above her left ear. She was wearing tight red silk shantung pants, sandals, and a bare-midriff blouse in white.

"I feel like everyone is watching us," she murmured.

"Not us," Wolfe corrected. "Mostly you."

A bit of a smile appeared.

Lucian and Max were also dressed for their roles, one wearing a black-white checked silk shirt, the other a green-patterned shirt, with the currently popular white false-leather tight jackets. They wore dark trousers, short boots. Neither man bothered to conceal the bulge of a holster on his right hip.

Wolfe was all in black, a silk turtleneck, finely woven wool pants, and a black jacket.

"You'll see," he told the manager, "that my ship-crew is taken care of when they finish porting arrangements?"

"But of course."

This time the bow was real.

*

Kristin wandered through the huge, multilevel suite in a completely un-Chitet-like manner. Everything was stained wood, old paintings, and antiques, and the aroma of money hung close. Wolfe followed, saying little. Part of him was remembering another woman, named Lil, in another hotel on another world; the rest of him was concentrating on—something else.

"You know," she said, "I almost think you're trying to seduce—I mean, convert me away from what I believe

30

in. There is no rationale for this luxury . . . but it certainly feels nice."

Wolfe didn't answer. He had his eyes closed, facing one of the enormous windows that looked out over the smoky industrial city of Prendergast, Rogan's World's capital, toward the hills that ringed the port.

"Is something the matter?" she asked.

Wolfe's eyes opened.

"No. I was just trying to see if anybody's watching or listening."

"Lucian, Max, and I all checked for bugs," she said. "We're *all* very well trained."

"In another life," Joshua said, "I wore both belt and suspenders."

"What are suspenders?"

"Something to keep the chicken from crossing the road. Never mind. We're clean as far as I can tell."

Kristin turned away and appeared intent on the view.

"Master Speaker Athelstan told us that everything depends on finding this person," she said carefully. "I took that to mean our charade must be as perfect as possible."

Wolfe waited.

"So if I'm supposed to be your—your popsy, then, or whatever you call it, well, then, we should . . ." She broke off, furiously coloring.

"You blush too easily," Wolfe said gently, not letting himself smile. "But don't worry about it. You sleep anywhere you want to. If anybody happens to insert a spybeam without me noticing, well, we had a fight and you're miffed. All right?"

Kristin nodded, still not looking at Joshua.

"Which brings up a question," Wolfe said. "How come the twenty-four-hour-a-day watch isn't being kept? Did somebody decide I'm telling the truth and I'm not going to cut and run from you?"

"I can't answer that," Kristin said. "But there have been additional measures taken that aren't quite so obvious. And don't think they're trusting you any more than before."

"They, eh? Not us."

"What?"

"Never mind. So we're down, we made a big splash, yacht and all, and we're in place as fools with money."

*

"Rogan's World," mused Joshua. He lifted a snifter to his lips, sipped. "Where honesty's a word in the dictionary between *hogwash* and *horseshit*. And everything's for sale and they have everything you want." He considered the snifter. "I never thought I'd find Hubert Dayton again. I've got one bottle hidden . . . somewhere, against the Day of Reckoning."

Kristin wore a thin blue robe, with a satin and lace gown under it in the same color. The remains of a lavish room service meal littered the linen tablecloth on the mahogany table.

"To success," Wolfe toasted.

Kristin lifted her waterglass in return.

"That's a sinful practice," he said.

"Why? I've never liked alcohol," Kristin said. "It distorts your judgment and makes it easier for you to do stupid things."

"Precisely why I'm quite fond of it." He spun his chair and looked out over Prendergast. "I wonder why all commercial ports get so crooked so easy," he said.

"Maybe because when everything's got a price tag on it, you start believing everything does have a price tag on it."

"Not bad," Joshua said.

"Thank you. And when everything's just passing by," Kristin went on, "maybe it's easy to think you can do whatever you want, and pass on with the current, or else whatever you did'll be washed away in the morning."

Joshua nodded. "I'll buy into that one, tentatively, my little epigrammatist.

"So, here we have a spaceport—shipyard—heavy manufacturing—and by the way, Rogan's World produced half a dozen Federation politicians whose reputations, shall we say, spread a stain far beyond their reach. And at least as many artists in various mediums. Wonder if corruption is a spore-bed for creators?

"Interesting, change, though. According to the 'pedia I scanned, nothing and nobody interesting's come out of Rogan's World for quite a while. Since just after the war, to be precise."

"What does that mean?" Kristin asked.

"Probably nothing. But it could be somebody doesn't want Rogan's World to draw any attention at all."

Kristin looked frightened. "Could the Overlord Stone give somebody *that* kind of power?"

Wolfe nodded.

"So how do we find Token—that woman."

"Good," Wolfe approved. "The less we use her name, the safer it is. For I don't truly know what the Great Lumina could give, especially to someone who's been using it for as long as she has."

"How do we find her?" Kristin asked.

"We don't. We let her find us." Wolfe smiled. "Apropos of absolutely nothing, I like your perfume."

"Oh. Oh. I thought the name in the catalog sounded— interesting. Thank you." Kristin looked somewhat confused.

*

"How long have you been bell captain?" Joshua asked.

"Oh, seven, eight years," the woman said. Her name tag read HAGERSMARK. "Long enough to be able to help our guests in whatever ways they want." She pocketed the bill Wolfe handed her.

"Supposing that I—or one of my crew—wanted company?"

"Easiest thing in the world," Hagersmark said, looking bored. "Any variation you want."

"What about—inducements that don't happen to be legal?"

"I don't know that word."

"Things to smoke, inject, whatever."

"Like you said, whatever."

"Just curious," Wolfe said. "But what I'm really interested in is action. This hotel seems a little—quiet."

"The management likes to keep it that way," Hagersmark said. "They figure guests can find their own joyspots. Or bring 'em back here. As long as you pay, you can do whatever you want. But you want action. I assume . . ." She rolled fingers as if manipulating a set of dice.

"You assume," Wolfe said.

"How big?"

He handed her a bill.

"That suggest anything?"

The woman eyed it, reacted.

"You *do* mean action," she said. "Best bet's a private game. But you'll need to meet some people to set that sorta thing up. Be around in the right places. Best bet's either Nakamura's or the Oasis. The Oasis generally attracts a little looser crowd."

"Thank you," Wolfe said.

Hagersmark started toward the door, then stopped. "So that's your game, eh? Everybody in the hotel was wondering."

"I'm just someone who mostly lives the quiet life," Wolfe said. "But every year or so I like to vary things."

"Of course, sir," she said piously. "Have a nice, quiet time."

*

A day later, Wolfe was waiting for Kristin to finish dressing when the discreet tap came at the door.

Max was sitting across from him, watching.

He *felt* out, uncurled from the chair he was in. "Kristin. Stay out of sight."

"What's wrong?"

"We've got visitors. And the desk was supposed to buzz us before anyone came up."

The knock came once more.

"I'm ready," she said. "Shall I call for backup?"

"Not yet. Max, you get out of here, too. But be ready for life to get interesting. Don't do anything unless I start screaming."

The Chitet hesitated, then hurried into one of the bedrooms and half closed the door.

Wolfe went to the door and opened it. Two men stood outside. Both were young, wore full evening dress, and had cold eyes above careful smiles.

"Mister Taylor?"

Wolfe nodded.

"We're sorry to intrude, but perhaps a moment of your time might be beneficial to us both."

"So Hagersmark didn't stay bought," he murmured and beckoned them in.

"A drink?" he offered.

"No, thank you. We don't want to take up any more of your time than necessary. My name's Henders, this is Mister Naismith."

"I'm at your service," Joshua said courteously.

"My associate and myself understand that you're a man who's interested in the sporting life."

"At times."

35

"Perhaps you weren't aware that the two clubs that you might find most congenial—I refer to the Oasis and Mister Nakamura's establishment—are, in fact, private."

"No. The person who told me about them didn't mention that."

"That's why we thought we might pay a visit, and arrange for you to become a member of both casinos."

"How convenient," Wolfe said. "I assume 'membership' also carries other benefits?"

The younger of the two men scowled, but Henders kept his smile.

"In fact, it does. There are other establishments in Prendergast and across Rogan's World that welcome members. But the real advantage for a man such as yourself is the availability of exchange currency at any hour of the night or day. Also, since there's an unfortunately high crime rate on Rogan's World, in the event of your having significant winnings, our organization can arrange an escort to wherever you wish, or even for a bank to open at any hour for a deposit."

"And, of course, should I decline membership, it's not unlikely that I might get mugged, should I happen to be a winner," Wolfe said wryly.

"Such things have happened."

"I further assume that the cost of such a membership is high."

"We predicate the cost on a member's evident assets," Henders said, looking pointedly about the suite. "In your case, especially considering the rather impressive display you've made since you've been here, it might indeed be expensive. But well worth the cost, I can assure you."

"And the levy is . . . ?"

"That would depend on how long you plan on staying," the man said. "Generally, we like to have our members current on a weekly basis. However, for longer stays, or for permanent residents, other, more equitable arrangements can be made."

Wolfe strolled to the bar, poured a small pool of Armagnac into a snifter.

"I must say, I admire Rogan's World," he said. "Generally, the first gunsel who tries a shakedown is a featherweight."

"What the hell are you talking about?" snarled Naismith. "This is a perfectly legit offer."

"Of course it is. I'm merely making light conversation. My response, in most cases, to such a hit is quite rapid. I find the second level of goonery, after they've recovered from finding their junior in an alley, is markedly superior."

"I know you have your own security element, Mister Taylor," Henders said. "But I don't think you're aware of the organization you may be challenging."

"Oh, but I think I am," Wolfe said. "That's why I was complimentary about Rogan's World. I've noted you gentlemen aren't the usual bluff-and-bluster back-alley types with alligator mouths and jaybird asses, but actually have links to significant people. I don't object to payoffs," he went on. "It's an accepted part of my operating cost. But I'll be triple-damned if I'll play the fool and slip any punk who taps my shoulder and breaks bad the dropsy."

"I see," Henders said. Naismith couldn't decide whether to get angry or just stay puzzled. "You certainly have analyzed the situation quickly and, I must say, correctly. I think, Mister Taylor, you might become a valued addition to a certain group here. You appear to have a great deal of wisdom."

"Not wisdom," Wolfe said. "Common sense. How much?"

"We would consider—ten thousand credits appropriate. At least for a starter. If circumstances indicate otherwise, that amount can be lowered."

"Or raised, if I'm sufficiently lucky."

Henders inclined his head.

Wolfe went into another room. The two gangsters looked at each other. The younger man licked his lips nervously.

Wolfe came back in with a leather envelope, thick with bills.

"Here," he said. "The credits are clean, good, and out of sequence, and it's a pleasure to be part of your—organization.

"Now, if you'll excuse me, we have plans to dine tonight. Perhaps at Mister Nakamura's."

The two men left.

Max came out of the bedroom. A gun was in his hand.

"Why'd you pay them? I completely fail to understand your reasoning in allowing us to be victimized."

"Which is why you're a Chitet and I'm a gambler," Wolfe said. "Kristin! I'm starving to death!"

*

"I see why you're the ranker of the trio," Wolfe said. "I don't think Max had a clue."

"He's a good man," Kristin said defensively. "Maybe I realized the nature of the situation a little faster than he did because I've been around you more."

"Probably," Wolfe said. "Crookedness can be contagious."

Kristin smiled. She wore a clinging gown, muted silver with deep burgundy flowers on it, low-cut, Empire-waisted, and utterly diaphanous. Under it was—perhaps—a sheer bodystocking.

Wolfe wore a white short-waisted formal jacket, matching pants, black silk shirt, and a white throat scarf.

He shifted position and moved the bomb at the base of his spine to a more comfortable position. "I once told somebody that I heard Time's winged chariot at my back, but I never thought it'd end up as a literal expression," he murmured.

Kristin quirked an eyebrow.

"Just a private thought," Joshua said.

Kristin cut a bite, chewed. "This is wonderful. What is it?"

"On a Chitet menu, it'd no doubt appear as muscle tissue from a juvenile steer, wrapped in a shell of dough, with cow secretions, plus various fungi."

"Pish," Kristin said. "That won't affect my appetite. We do that kind of word game as play when we're growing up."

"Play? What you're tucking away if boeuf Wellington. Named after a general who was pretty good at waiting for his enemy to make the first mistake."

"Of course we play—I played—when I was a child. What do you think Chitet do? Just march up and down in formation and drone prime numbers at one another? We're people, like any other," Kristin said, a bit of heat in her voice. "We just happen to have a better way of thinking, of living than anybody else."

Wolfe started to say something but thought better of it. "Okay. I was wrong. You're creatures of the sun, the light, and the dancing waves. Now eat your vegetables or I won't read you any more Charles Peirce before bedtime."

"I know who he was," Kristin said.

"See my point?"

Kristin looked puzzled. "No. I don't."

"Never mind."

THE DARKNESS OF GOD

*

Joshua heard music coming from another part of Nakamura's as they strolled out of the restaurant.

"Care to dance before we go to work?"

"No," Kristin said. "I never learned how. My creche didn't see the point of doing anything when music played, anyway. It's enough to simply appreciate it intellectually."

"Take that, Dionysus," Wolfe said.

"Precisely," Kristin said. "The Apollonian side must control events, or everything is chaos."

"Sometimes chaos can be fun."

"And who is whose prisoner?" Kristin retorted.

"Point and match to Guide Kristin," Wolfe said.

They continued into the casino.

Joshua considered the half-full room as a formally clad man glided to him.

"Mister Taylor? Welcome to Nakamura's. Might I inquire as to your pleasure?"

"Nothing right now," Wolfe said. "But I do have a question. Is Mister Nakamura present?"

"Mister Nakamura passed on over a year ago," the pit boss said. "The club is currently held by a consortium of businessmen."

"I see," Wolfe said. "Perhaps another time I might be interested in your tables. But not at the moment. Come on, Kristin. The Oasis calls."

*

"This," Wolfe said, "might become my home away from home."

"Why?" Kristin asked. "It looks just like Nakamura's. Why this one instead of the other?"

"Because this one looks a bit—closer to the bone, shall we say? Observe the bar, and the half-dozen young women who gave both of us the scan when we walked

40

through. Expensive companions for the evening—or the hour. Or consider the gamblers."

"I don't see anything unusual."

"See how many have friends standing behind them. Friends who just happen to have bulges in their hip pockets or under their arms. Friends with blank faces and eyes that never stop moving."

"Oh. You mean you wanted a crooked place to gamble?"

"Sssh, my love. Don't disparage the jam pot. And we might be able to find an honest game here. Or turn it into one."

"Now I don't understand what you're thinking any more than Max does," Kristin said.

"You don't have to." Wolfe took a wad of credits from his pocket. "Here. Go spend these. Come back when you need more."

"I really don't understand gambling games," she protested, "although of course I've studied probability theory."

"Good. Think popsy. Lose in a spectacular manner."

*

Wolfe noted a heavy, short man strolling through the gaming room, his eyes comfortably assessing the night. His expensive clothes wrapped him like a toad in a turban. Three blank-faced men flanked him; a fourth walked unobtrusively in front.

"That is—?" Wolfe asked the croupier, indicating with his chin.

"Mister Igraine. The owner."

"Ah. Is he a plunger?"

"I assume you mean does he play? Frequently. And well," the croupier said. "If you'd be interested in one of his private games, it might be arranged."

Wolfe looked back at the dice layout, then saw Kristin hurrying toward him.

"Look!" Kristin said excitedly. She was holding up a thick sheaf of bills.

Wolfe spun a chip to the croupier and picked up his dwindled stake. "I'll go sit and sulk for a while," he said. "Try to remember where my luck went. And I'll think about what you said about Mister Igraine."

He led Kristin to a quiet corner. "Obviously you're doing better than I am," he noted.

"These people don't know anything about the odds," she said. "I've never gambled before, but it seems pretty simple. I know you told me to lose, but am I supposed to look like a complete fool?"

Wolfe laughed.

"Once a Chitet . . . Very good, Kristin. You'll start a new legend as the bimbo who never loses."

"So do I gamble some more?"

Wolfe considered. "I don't think so. I've set the scene, and dropped maybe fifteen thousand. That ought to be enough. Tomorrow night we'll reap what I hope we sowed."

*

A chill wind blew across the city, clouds swirling past overhead, but the penthouse's balcony had three braziers, with what looked like real wood burning in them.

Kristin looked across the city's lights at the hills in the distance.

"Maybe she's over there . . ."

"Maybe."

She moved closer to him. "It's late," she said.

"It is," he agreed. "But gamblers and raiders work best by moonlight."

"Among others," Kristin said, her voice low.

Wolfe looked surprised.

"Yes," he said, almost in a whisper, "among others."

He stepped closer, until his hip touched her buttocks, waited for her to step away. Kristin didn't move. He slid his arms around her waist, nuzzled her hair.

Joshua felt her breathing come more quickly.

He slowly turned her to him. Kristin lifted her cat face, eyes closed, lips parted.

He kissed her, felt her tongue come to meet his. He slid the straps of her dress off her shoulders, and her bare breasts were firm against him.

The kiss went on, and her lips moved under his, tongue darting.

He picked her up in his arms, carried her through the suite's living room into a bedroom, started to lay her on the bed.

"No," she said. "My shoes . . ."

"Don't worry about it. We have maids."

She lay back, naked to the waist, legs curled, her eyes half-open, watching as he undressed.

He touched the light sensor, and the room was dark except for a stream of light from the doorway.

Joshua went to the bed and knelt over Kristin, one arm around her, the other sliding her dress up, cupping her buttocks, kneading them. She was not wearing a bodystocking, but had shaved her body smooth.

She moaned, lifted her leg across the back of his thighs.

"Yes," she whispered. "Oh yes, my Dionysus."

*

Kristin stifled a scream, writhed against him, then collapsed, her legs sagging back to the bed. Joshua stayed on his knees, lifted her legs about his waist, caressed her breasts slowly.

"I'm back," she said after a time.

Joshua moved inside her, and she gasped.

"Not yet," she whispered. "Give me a moment."

"One and only one."

"Maybe," she said, "there is *some* merit to chaos."

"In its place," he agreed. "Logic doesn't belong in the bedroom."

"I should be able to argue with you," she said. "But I don't think my brain is working right now."

Joshua lifted her buttocks, pulled her close against him. "Never interfere with success," he said.

"No . . . I mean yes," she managed as he began moving slowly inside her. She rolled her head from side to side, wrapped her legs more tightly about him. "Oh yes. Send me away again."

*

Joshua came out of the bedroom, robe wrapped around him. Lucian was scanning some papers.

"I'll have instructions for you in an hour," Wolfe said. "Then nothing. We won't go back out until tonight."

Lucian looked at Joshua with disapproval, said nothing, picked up a com and touched buttons.

It was an hour after dawn.

Joshua picked up the tray room service had just brought and took it back into the bedroom.

Kristin was at the window, naked, leaning on the railing.

Joshua put the tray down, dropped his robe, walked up behind her, and kissed her back.

"Do you think anybody down there can see us?" she asked.

"Probably," he said cheerily. "And they're getting ready to record every single lascivious move."

Kristin giggled.

"That's a nice sound," he said.

Kristin didn't reply for a while, then:

"This doesn't change things."

"Sure it does," Wolfe said. "It means you don't have to sleep on the couch unless you want to. And you already said you had permission from Athelstan to be flouncing around like you are."

"You know what I meant."

"I know what you meant," he agreed, hands sliding around her body, cupping her breasts, pulling her against him.

"Joshua, I don't think I can do it anymore. I'm sore."

"Umm-hmm."

"You're not stopping."

"Ummm-umm."

"Oh. Oh. Oh GOD!"

*

"It's time for work, people," Wolfe said. "Here's the order. Kristin, Max, I want you with me. Pick the best two of the gun-guards as backup. Get them into formals. Ten, no, fifteen more in the heavy lifter we've rented. If Kristin or I call for backup, bring the gunnies in ready for shooting. Lucian, I want you standing by our flit, pretending you're the chauffeur. We may need to leave in a hurry and we want our back guarded."

"Negative, Wolfe," the bearded man said. "My orders are to stay with you."

"For the love of—does it do any good for me to swear on—on *Critique of Pure Reason* that I don't have any intention of double-crossing you? And there's already two of the team on me like white on rice?"

"Negative," Lucian said firmly. "You may have subverted one of us," and he gave a pointed look at Kristin, "but some of us know where our duty lies."

"That's enough," the woman snapped. "I still command, and I still speak for this gathering. You, Lucian. In the other room. Now!"

The Chitet looked sullen, but he obeyed. Kristin followed, slamming the door hard behind her, and Wolfe heard loud voices.

Passing from grandeur to grandeur to final illusion, Wolfe thought hopefully. He and Max avoided looking at each other.

Kristin and Lucian came back out and sat down.

"As long as we're all getting along so well," Wolfe said. "What's the possibility of my being permitted one lousy little gun? There's no—" He broke off. Both Kristin and Lucian were shaking their heads.

"Oh well," he said. "I'm glad to get you two to agree on something. So I'm going in naked, then. But if anybody even twitches, I want somebody to put a bolt through him. We still aren't even in sight of the target."

*

"You've done quite well for yourself this evening," Igraine said. His voice was as smooth and oily as his hair.

"Compared to last night," Wolfe agreed. "You would think I'd have learned to stay away from dice by now."

"So roulette is your game," Igraine said. "Mine, too."

Wolfe had carefully noted the attention the casino's owner paid the wheel in his inspection tour the night before.

"I like it," Wolfe said. "Especially when it's straight, with only a single zero."

"I have no need to be greedy," Igraine said.

"Faites vos jeux, m'sieurs," the *tourneur* intoned. There were eight others around the wheel.

Wolfe put on the cloth a stack of chips from the considerable pile he'd already won.

"Manque," he said.

Igraine reached out, tapped the enameled letters of *passe*. The *tourneur* nodded, and other bets were made.

"Rien ne va plus," he announced, spun the cross-handles with his fingers, and flipped the ivory ball against the wheel's rotation.

The wheel slowed, and the ball bounced, bounced again, stopped in a compartment.

"Quatre," the *tourneur* said.

"Congratulations," Igraine said. "Again?"

Wolfe nodded.

*

It was either very late or very early.

But no one appeared sleepy.

There were about forty people around the table now, and the only sound was the *tourneur*'s voice, the whisper of the spinning wheel, the clatter of the ivory ball, and the low murmur after the clatter stopped.

The wheel had only two bettors, Igraine and Wolfe. Chips were stacked high beside Wolfe, and credits piled next to his untouched drink. Igraine had nothing in front of him.

Lucian stood across from Wolfe, Max was next to him, and Kristin on Joshua's other side.

Igraine's shirt was sweat-soaked, and his hair hung in disarray over his forehead.

The *tourneur* had closed the table twice, and guards had brought first chips, later credits.

"Rouge," he announced.

"Non," Wolfe said, stepping back, and the *tourneur* spun once again.

The ball dropped into the zero compartment.

"You have a sixth sense about things," Igraine complained.

"It felt like about time for zero to hit," Joshua said. He pushed chips forward.

"Rouge."

"Noir," Igraine said.

He glanced at the *tourneur*, nodded imperceptibly.

Wolfe *felt* out, *felt* the man's foot shift to the right, *reached* out. The *tourneur*'s body twitched a little, again. The man looked worried.

"M'sieur?" Wolfe inquired.

The *tourneur* licked his lips, spun the wheel.

"Deux. Rouge."

Wolfe collected his winnings.

"All right," Igraine said. "That's enough."

"For you," Wolfe said. "But I'm still playing."

"By yourself, then."

"You can't afford the game?"

Igraine started to say something then clamped his mouth shut.

"You still have something to bet," Wolfe said. He looked around at the club. "One roll. All of this," he indicated the money in front of him, "against the club. You play black, I'll stay with red."

Someone behind Wolfe said something, and a woman gasped. He didn't turn.

Kristin's hand slid closer to the gun in her tiny breakaway purse.

Igraine gnawed at his lip, suddenly smiled.

"Very well. Spin the wheel!"

The *tourneur*'s foot moved, tapped the hidden switch under the carpet. The wheel spun, the ball bounced wildly about.

Red/black/red/black flicker, slowing, the ball rattling from compartment to compartment, rolling, dropping into a red compartment . . .

Wolfe *reached* out, *felt* white smoothness, *pushed* . . .

The ivory ball clicked to rest.

"Vingt-quatre," the *tourneur* said. *"Rouge."*

*

"Did you do that?" Kristin demanded.

"I'm not sure," Wolfe lied. "I sure wanted that ball to jump a little bit."

"Without a Lumina."

"I was probably just lucky."

"Joshua," Kristin said. "I'm not a fool. I know probabilities, and there's no way you could have won that many times with so few losses."

"Sure there is," Wolfe said. "Igraine had to win that many times to get the club, didn't he?"

"Not proven and an example of illogical thinking," Kristin said. "So now we own a gambling club. That'll be the trap for Aubyn?"

"No," Wolfe said. "It's just the beginning."

Kristin yawned. "Tell me about it in the—oh my. It *is* morning."

"Gamblers, raiders, and lovers keep late hours, remember?"

"Not this raider. I'm beat."

"Are you sure?" Joshua asked, running a tongue in and out of her navel.

"I am. Go to sleep. You've got too much nervous energy."

*

Wolfe woke suddenly. His sheets were sweat-soaked. He blinked around, then remembered where he was.

It was past midday, and the suite was silent. Kristin lay next to him, breathing steadily, regularly.

Red . . . creeping from star to star, fingers, tentacles reaching toward him . . .

Wolfe shuddered.

Can it sense me?

Impossible.

THE DARKNESS OF GOD

He lay back, tried to blank his mind, but *felt* the invader, pulsing like a bloody tumor, out there in the blackness.

Quite suddenly something else came.

It was almost as foreign, almost as alien.

But it comforted.

Light-years away, beyond the Federation, he *felt* them.

The Guardians, truly the last of the Al'ar, hidden in the depths of the nameless world they'd tunneled deep into. Waiting. Waiting for Wolfe, waiting for him to return with the Lumina.

Waiting for the "virus."

Waiting for death. Hoping it would be welcome.

*

He was awakened a second time by soft warmth around him, moving, caressing.

Joshua looked down, and Kristin lifted her head.

"I didn't want you to think I don't like doing it with you," she said.

"Never crossed my mind," Joshua said.

"Good," she said, sitting up, bestriding him, her hands guiding, then she gasped as she sank down, enveloped him. "Oh good."

*

"Preposterous," the well-dressed man said.

"Not at all," Wolfe said calmly. He walked to the end of the conference table, looking at each of the ten men in the room, trying to feel their response. "I've owned the Oasis for two weeks now and have managed to almost double my receipts. I think it would be logical for you gentlemen to allow me to take a minority position in Nakamura's. Both clubs attract much the same clientele, and it's senseless to compete.

"You'd not only see improved profits, but you wouldn't

have any of the problems of running a casino—which none of you, I've observed, had any experience doing prior to Mister Nakamura's death."

"Why should we let you muscle in?" a fat, mean-faced man said. "We've done very damned well for ourselves in the past year."

"We have indeed," the first man said. "We've learned the peculiarities of the trade, and are familiar with who to—deal with, and who to ignore."

"Matter of fact," the fat man said, "whyn't you let us buy *you* out? Seems more logical."

He laughed.

"That's very amusing," Wolfe said. "And I do admire a logical man."

His smile was thin.

*

Wolfe's fingers crept up the doorframe, found the sensor. Violet light flashed. His hand continued feeling the doorway. He found another alarm, neutralized it.

He was one of two dark spots against the dark stone of the alley. Both he and Kristin wore close-fitting black jumpsuits and balaclavas.

Wolfe's hand dipped into a pouch, then moved swiftly around the door's lock. There was a sharp click.

He picked up a long, thin prybar, slid it into the crack, and lifted, straining. There was a loud clatter from inside; Kristin flinched involuntarily.

"Now, if they don't have a sound pickup . . ."

Wolfe cautiously opened the door, staying well away from the opening. No auto-blaster ravened, no alarm tore the night. Wolfe lifted away the wooden balk he'd jimmied out of its slots.

"Now, milady, if you'll hand me the first of those interesting packets we prepared earlier . . ."

THE DARKNESS OF GOD

Fire Ravages Nite Spot
Popular Club Destroyed
In Mysterious Inferno

Press for More

PRENDERGAST—A series of predawn blasts rocked the capital, totally destroying Nakamura's Nightclub. According to fire and police officials, arson is suspected, since none of the casino's elaborate fire and security alarms went off. The damage is vast, and the well-known club, long a favorite of Prendergast's monied socialites, must be considered totally destroyed, said a spokesman for the consortium that has operated the club since . . .

"What comes afterward?" Kristin asked. She was curled in Wolfe's arms.

"You mean tomorrow? They'll try to make sure I'm a good example of what not to grow up to be."

"I know that," Kristin said. "I've already instructed the guards like you told me to. And I think you're insane. I mean after we get the—after we get what we came for."

"If we get it," Wolfe corrected.

What?

You Chitet try to kill me?

I try to get out from under, with the ur-Lumina?

Kristin lay in silence, waiting.

"There is no after," Wolfe said, his voice unintentionally harsh.

*

They took Wolfe just as he was going toward his lifter, just outside the hotel. Three men came out of the shrubbery, guns leveled, and Naismith slid from a parked lifter holding a big-barreled riotgun steady.

"Anyone moves, everyone dies," Henders said calmly as he came up the driveway.

The doorman saw the artillery and became a red-clad statue.

One of Henders' men moved behind Max and the other two security men with Wolfe, expertly searched them, and took their guns.

"You ought to get yourself some new punks from the repple-depple," Naismith cracked. "If you come back."

"Shut up, Naismith," Henders said. "Mister Taylor, if you'd come with us, please? Someone wants to talk to you quite badly."

*

They have him, the signal went up to the orbiting *Planov.*

"Very well," Master Speaker Athelstan said. "Continue monitoring." He turned to a man sitting at a control board. "I am not completely assured the subject hasn't made an ally of these gang members. Be prepared for instant activation of the device."

"Yes, Master Speaker," the man said, and rechecked the trigger for the bomb on Wolfe's back.

*

They rough-frisked Wolfe before pushing him into the sleek gray lifter that appeared as the thugs hustled him away from the hotel.

Confusion . . . confidence . . . certainty . . .

"He's clean," the searcher reported.

"A man with the overconfidence of his congeries," Henders said.

Wolfe looked mildly impressed. "Not bad," he said. "But how about 'A gun limits the possibilities'?"

"I'd agree," Henders said, "but only for the sap on the far end of the barrel."

Wolfe shrugged.

They put him in the middle of the backseat, with Naismith and another thug on either side of him, guns almost touching his sides. Henders got in beside the pilot, turned in his seat, and kept his pistol pointed at Joshua's head.

"The head of my organization isn't pleased with you," he said. "You'd better have some explanations."

Wolfe yawned. "I generally do," he said.

He closed his eyes and appeared to go to sleep.

Henders looked worried, then held the gun ready.

*

The warehouse was gray, anonymous, on a dingy street close to the spaceport. Henders pressed a button, and a door slid open. The lifter floated in and grounded, and the canopy lifted.

They muscled Wolfe out and took him along a bare concrete corridor, then down steps to a door. A guard stood outside with a heavy blaster.

Without a word, he opened the door, and Henders, Naismith, and the third gunman pushed Joshua inside.

The room was almost big enough to have an echo; dark-paneled wood walls hung with jarringly modern anima-art. There was a door to one side that was closed.

Naismith and the gunman stood to either side of Joshua, guns aimed.

At the far end of the room was an old-fashioned kidney-shaped desk. Leaning against it was a strangely misshapen man. From the waist down, he was tiny, almost small enough to be a jockey. Above that, he had the barrel chest and muscled arms of a stevedore. He wore his thinning hair long, tied into two queues that dangled behind his ears.

He had a strong, determined face, but with the pouty, small mouth of a decadent.

"You can call me Aurus," he said. "That's as good as anything else. It means gold, and gold's what I am."

His voice matched his shoulders: deep, full of authority. Aurus went on, without waiting for Wolfe to respond.

"Taylor, we get a lot of damned fools here on Rogan's World, of a damned big variety. But you're something new."

"Always nice to widen a man's experience," Joshua said.

"Don't crack wise," Aurus advised. "I don't give a rat's ass if you go below with or without your teeth, and it's hard to talk through a mouth full of blood. A fool," he repeated. "Of a unique sort.

"You downplanet with enough pizzazz for a circus, obviously trying to catch somebody's eye. Fine. I'm good-hearted, there's always room for somebody else in my organization, so I send a couple of my best operators out to meet you. No problem. Everything goes well; Henders comes back and tells me here's someone we can do business with.

"Three days later, you clip poor goddamned Igraine out of his joint. I really want to know, before you die, how you counter-rigged his wheel. I'd ask the croupier, but Igraine fed him to the eels last night.

"So you're a fast mover, I now think. Then you go and jump the cits that front Nakamura's place and tell them you're the new mensch on the dock. Did you ever consider they were working for me? Did you ever think maybe you should've talked to me before you started pushing your muscle around?

"Not you. Throw a bomb, get the heat worked up, and think you just pulled some sort of brilliant move. Dickhead. Let me be the first to advise you, Mister Taylor. Your flashing around is going to do nothing but cost me money, and get you dead."

Aurus' face was getting redder. He went behind his desk, lifted the stopper from an elaborately worked decanter, and poured a drink into an equally fancy snifter. Henders walked from behind Wolfe to the side of the desk, holding his gun steady.

"Contrary to what you just said, I *did* think about talking to you," Wolfe said, before Aurus could lift his glass. "But I didn't think it was worth my while."

"You didn't . . ." Aurus shook his head in disbelief. "No. You didn't think. All you did was—"

Wolfe's hand flashed out, palm up, fingers curled. He had Naismith's gunhand at the wrist, twisted once, and bone shattered with a sharp crack. Wolfe, now with Naismith's gun, spun away as the gunman on the other side pulled his trigger.

But Wolfe wasn't there, and the blast seared into Naismith's side, ripping through his stomach wall. Naismith screamed in utter agony and fell sideways as his guts spilled, a stinking pile of pink, gray, red.

Joshua shot the gunman in the head, and blood spattered high to the ceiling.

The man who'd called himself Aurus was scrabbling in a compartment behind the desk for a gun.

Henders fired and missed, and Joshua crouched, aimed, fired.

The blaster seared Henders' arm away, and his gun cartwheeled across the desk.

Joshua shifted his aim and fired. His first bolt took Aurus in the shoulder, smashing him back against the wall. He flopped against it, mouth opening to shout, to scream, and Joshua blew his chest apart.

The door came open, and Joshua shot through the gap without aiming. He heard a shout of pain.

He ran, crouching, for the desk, and went prone behind it, pistol aimed at the doorway. He heard shouts, running feet. The door crashed open, but nobody came in.

He saw the barrel of a heavy blaster and took aim. A head flashed into sight, was gone before he could fire.

"Shit," the shout came. "They got th' boss."

Another voice: "C'mon, Augie. We're gone!"

There were more shouts, running feet, and the sound of lifter drives whining to life. It was quiet then except for Naismith's moans and the whir of the anima-art's motors.

Joshua went to Naismith and shot him in the head. Then he went to the door and looked out. The body of the guard was sprawled just beyond it. Wolfe went up the steps and found the warehouse deserted, its door yawning.

"Thieves *do* fall out," he said to himself.

He went back down into Aurus' office.

Henders was barely conscious, clutching the cauterized remains of his arm.

Wolfe kicked him sharply, and the man screamed, bit if off.

"I'm not getting soft," Joshua said. "But maybe somebody'll be interested in hearing the details from a survivor."

He reached into a jacket pocket, took a card from a case.

The card read only:

John Taylor

Investments

He wrote the com number of his hotel, and

Perhaps we should talk

He dropped the card on Henders' chest, took the magazine from the blaster, tossed the gun into a corner of the room, and left.

Henders tried to sit up, collapsed.

After a time, he started moaning.

*

"You're blood-crazy," Master Speaker Athelstan said firmly.

Joshua looked around the compartment, meeting hostile stares from Kristin, her duo, and Security Coordinator Kur.

"I do not believe this," he said. "Not one of you understands the fine art of making a good impression, do you?"

"Perhaps," Kur said, "we don't have your obviously wide experience in criminal matters."

"Obviously not," Wolfe agreed.

"It does not matter whether we understand or approve," Master Speaker Athelstan said. "A course of action has been determined by you. There is no other choice than to follow it. Joshua Wolfe, what comes next?"

Joshua held out his hands.

"Business as usual."

*

"You had no gun hidden," Kristin asked.

"No."

"Yet you killed five men who *did* have guns."

"Four. Henders should be alive, if a medico showed up in time."

She stared at him.

"Perhaps," she said finally, "we have not been careful enough with you."

*

Eight nights later, a message was waiting when Wolfe returned from the Oasis near dawn.

The screen was blank except for six numbers.

Joshua went out of the hotel, found a public com, dialed the numbers.

A synthed voice said, "Yes?"

"This is John Taylor. I was given this number."

There was a hum for almost thirty seconds, then:

"At 1730 hours today, leave your hotel and walk east

along Fourteenth Boulevard. You will be met. Come alone and unarmed."

The line went dead.

* CHAPTER FIVE *

Joshua spotted them as he left the hotel: two men behind, a man and a woman far ahead, across the boulevard. There'd be other pairs down the side streets. It was a classic box pattern, hard to elude, more likely intended to show Wolfe the opposition's resources than anything else.

All were pros, and none showed the slightest interest in Wolfe.

He was grateful he'd convinced Kristin not to put a shadow backup, and to play it straight, at least at first.

"If they're trying to kill me," he reasoned, "at least that'll bring 'em further into the open. I'm pretty sure I can duck another attempt by thuggery, if they're no better than the late idiot who called himself Aurus."

But he still felt clammy fingers at his back as he walked. He made three blocks before a long, sleek lifter pulled out of a side street. Its window hissed down.

"Mister Taylor?" The driver was young, freckled, friendly looking.

"Yes."

"I'm your transport."

Wolfe got into the luxuriously appointed vehicle. The driver waited for a slight hole in traffic, then sped across the boulevard. He took a left, two rights.

"I didn't bring any backup," Wolfe said.

"Of course," the young man said. "I'm just careful."

Two smaller lifters, with four men in each, came from side streets, fell in behind Joshua's vehicle.

"Yours?"

"Mine," the driver acknowledged.

"You are careful."

*

"Sorry, sir, but I'll have to check you before we go inside," the driver said, trying to sound truly apologetic.

Damn them for untrusting bastards and not taking that damned bomb off. Wolfe caught himself grinning. *How dare these Chitet think I'd ever do anything nefarious or possibly dare to haul ass without giving them the chance to blow me up. I'm shocked. Shocked, do you hear me?*

He got out of the lifter, pretending to be impressed by the looming, colonnaded gray stone building they'd landed in front of, and the forested grounds around it, while he was *reaching* out, *feeling* . . .

The driver took a sweep from the door pocket and moved it across Wolfe, who turned, raising his hands, a bored expression on his face, as the sweep moved up his spine.

The driver's expression blanked, just as the detector's needle pegged and a buzzer sounded. He looked perplexed, then shook his head and paid no notice to the alarm triggered by the bomb. He continued on, moving the sweep under Wolfe's armpits, around his waist.

"You're clear," he said. "So let me take you inside to Advisor Walsh."

"Won't be necessary," a jocular voice came from the mansion's steps. "The mountain has come to Yahweh, or however it goes."

The man appeared as cheery as his voice and his driver. He was small, balding, with twin ruffs of white hair above his ears, and a smile accenting the lines of happy aging on his face. But his eyes were obsidian, and the two men flanking him looked equally dangerous.

"Mister Taylor, you've wreaked some havoc on my organization," he went on. "I'm Edmund Walsh, and I think we should have a talk."

*

"I suppose you expect me to begin with some sort of moral lecture on how I'm so outraged by this new generation of villains like yourself, who lack all respect for tradition, the amenities, and so forth," Walsh said. "I had Sathanas' own time finding Hubert Dayton," he said. "Finally had to buy a bottle from your hotel. I believe this is how you like it, however."

He handed Wolfe a half-full snifter and a glass of ice water.

"It is, sir," Wolfe said. "And no, I wasn't necessarily expecting a lecture about the good old days. Wasn't expecting or not expecting anything, to be precise."

"Good," the old man approved. "What they call no-mind, eh?"

He noted Wolfe's flicker.

"Oh yes, Taylor. I'm hardly an oaf. When I heard the report of the damage you did to Aurus and his goons, I suspected there was a bit more to you than just being quick with a gun. Some say a man properly trained could even control objects. Such as roulette balls?"

Wolfe smiled politely, sipped Armagnac, and made no response.

"Anyway, back to where I started. You'll have to bear with me, Taylor. I'm getting old and have a tendency to ramble. You'll likely find that weakness in yourself, as you age." The black eyes glittered. "That's assuming you plan on getting older."

"It's on my agenda."

"Good. At any rate, one reason I won't talk to you

about how gunnies like me were such noblemen in our youth, when the world was young and every day promised a new fool to hijack, is I got the same lecture from some other old bastard back then. I read me a little history, and found what he'd said to be complete codswallop. Goons is goons, as they say. And I suppose we all end up romanticizing the past."

Walsh dropped ice cubes into a glass, poured from a pitcher. "I'd dearly love to be saltin' it back with you," he said, letting a bit of false sentiment into his voice, "but the stomach won't stand for it. Most of it's synth lining, but still I've got to live the clean life. At least they don't have me on pablum yet."

Walsh walked out of the bar-cubby down a long, high-ceilinged hall, into a drawing room with bookcases and tables holding ship and machine models. On the walls were testimonials to Walsh's virtues. He motioned Wolfe into a large leather chair, sank into one across from him. "Admire my digs?" he asked.

"Imposing," Wolfe allowed.

"Glad you didn't say you liked this pile of rubble," Walsh said. "Damned cold and hard to heat. You know why I choose to live here instead of somewhere comfortable?"

"Because you want to impress the gunsels?"

"That," Walsh admitted. "But there's something else. When I was a boy, my mother used to come here. At the time the place was the home of a shipbuilder. A hard, hard man named Torcelli, who'd cut his way to the top and wasn't about to let anybody get up beside him. My mother was one of his mistresses. She brought me here twice. Torcelli saw me, and got uncomfortable about something. I've wondered if I'm his bastard, but I doubt it. Mother wasn't exactly the choosiest with her attentions, and his seed would've been weak by then.

"But the place took my mind, and I never let it leave

me. I guess that gave me some sort of visible goal, eh? Get on top my own way, then buy this relic and restore it to prove I'm at least as good as Torcelli was. Better, since I've been here longer."

Walsh drank water. "Not that this matters," he said. "But when you retire, or anyway step back from the day-to-day battles, you find yourself thinking back. Wondering what made you do this, do that, and what you gained or lost from it." Walsh looked out a window. "See, over there, by the lake? My elk. There's six of them. Had them brought in from Earth. Ungainly bastards they are, and they're hell on my roses. I guess I'll have a roast one of these years, eh?" He put his glass down, leveled his eyes on Wolfe. "Even though he didn't bother to clear it with me, I can't say I disagreed with Aurus' wanting to kill you. You *did* put a dent in his immediate plans."

"A man who can't hang on to what he has doesn't deserve it," Wolfe said.

"I'll agree with those sentiments. Ruthlessness is an imperative in my organization—and, I truly believe, in any other thriving organism. However, some feel that you've gone a bit far, a bit fast."

"I didn't see much of anything in my way," Wolfe said.

"At the level you began at, that probably is true. Even Aurus had begun to slacken off lately. However, that doesn't mean you can make that assumption about anyone and everyone."

"Such as you."

"Such as me. I may be old, but I'm still a far bigger shark than you, sonny. Don't ever forget that an old tough is merely a tough that's gotten old."

"I try not to underestimate my opponents," Wolfe said. "Or to judge everyone as an opponent without reason."

Walsh waited a moment, then nodded. "You aren't stupid," he said. "Take a look at the walls, and tell me what you see."

Wolfe obeyed, walking slowly through the drawing room, examining a holo here, an old-fashioned photograph or framed tab story there. He lingered at one, which showed Walsh, not many years younger than he was now, at the podium at a banquet. Smiling faces, men, women, looked up at him, hands caught in the moment of applause. Wolfe noted the unknown symbol on the podium, moved on.

Walsh waited patiently until Wolfe returned to his seat, drinking Armagnac. "Well?"

"Like you said, I'm not stupid," Wolfe said. "I got two impressions from all those plaudits. First, and least important, is that you've had a helluva long run here on Rogan's World, and it doesn't look like there's many who don't owe you."

Walsh nodded once.

"But that wasn't, I think, what you wanted me to get," Wolfe continued. "I'd guess it was a suggestion that all things come to him who waits, and seeing pictures of Edmund Walsh over the years might make me think about developing patience. Or else."

"No," Walsh said, nodding, "you aren't stupid."

Wolfe waited for something else, but Walsh seemed content to remain silent. He drained his snifter. "So what do you want me to do?" he asked.

"Just what you're doing," Walsh said. "Gambling is one of the areas I've never been happy with. A little too unorganized for my tastes. I need a good man in place. You've got two clubs now—and you can have whatever of Aurus' goodies you fancy. But no more fancy grabs, eh? Nothing that makes headlines. You'll get more, in good time. And it won't be a long time, either. But don't get greedy for a while. Stick around, and you, too, can end up with people throwing banquets for you as an elder philanthropist with a colorful past. Even giving you government titles that don't pay shit, but get you a lot of respect. Get antsy now, though, and . . ."

Walsh didn't finish.

Wolfe stood. "Thank you for the wisdom, Advisor Walsh."

His voice was nearly devoid of irony.

*

"I don't like it at all," Wolfe repeated. "That was Aubyn in the picture, sitting beside Walsh. So we're close. But if Aubyn—or Walsh—had been interested in making any kind of a deal, he would've said something, instead of playing 'tomorrow's another day.' He knows good and well gangsters don't listen to promises. So the only reason I could figure for the meeting is Aubyn wanted to take a look at me. She got it, and now she's trying to figure out her next move. Think about it, Athelstan! She's thinking about tactics, and we're picking our noses and looking at pictures on a wall! That means she's ahead of us."

Onscreen, both Athelstan and Kur started to speak, stopped. Kur inclined her head in deference.

"Thank you," Athelstan said. "First, I'll voice my obvious suspicion—that you're trying some subterfuge to derail our plan."

"Why should I?"

"Perhaps," Athelstan said, "because you've sensed the ur-Lumina, feel that you can seize it on your own at a later time, and realize once we have possession it's absolutely lost to you."

"Utterly illogical," Wolfe said. "You've no reason to think that except your own suspicions. Or paranoia."

Athelstan's lips pursed, then he recovered. "Admitted. I withhold the canard for the moment."

"Another possibility," Kur put in. "You're frightened."

"Hell yes I'm frightened," Wolfe said. "This Aubyn has had the biggest goddamned brass lantern as a toy for five years, rubbed it all she wanted, and has a whole goddamned battalion of genies lined up for all I know. She's clever, she's mad, and she's a sociopath. I'm ground zero for her while you sit up there in your spaceship thinking lofty thoughts."

"Be careful," Kur warned.

"Why? You'll kill me? What do you think Aubyn wants? To get in my pants?" Wolfe turned to the other three in the room—Kristin, Max, and Lucian. "What do you think? Are we just running scared?"

Max made no reply.

"Insufficient data for me to make a judgment," Lucian said.

"Negative," Kristin said. "Wolfe's analyses have been correct thus far."

"Joshua Wolfe," Kur put in, "calm down. You've run agents, you know how easy it is for one to panic when he's one step short of his target. Haven't you ever had to order anybody to hold fast?"

"I have," Wolfe said grimly. "Three times, no more. I lost my ferret twice, barely made the hit the third time. Then I started paying attention to the man on the ground."

"This is not a democracy," Athelstan said firmly. "There is generally but one logical way, and since I've been chosen to speak for the Chitet, I have decided we should stay the course. We are getting close to our target. To withdraw now would be to abandon all our accomplishments."

Wolfe stared at the screen. "I've won a lot of money

from people like you," he said quietly. "People who think what they've thrown in the pot gives them some kind of rights on the showdown."

"You're not assessing the situation with proper logic," Athelstan said. "Continue the mission."

*

Walsh waited while the woman with hooded eyes paced back and forth, thinking.

"No," she decided. "there's nothing more to be gained by waiting and observing. Proceed as we discussed."

*

"I don't feel like making love tonight," Kristin announced.

"Nor I," Joshua agreed, leaning across her and turning off the light. "I wish that your fearless leaders had heard the old Earth-Chinese proverb that of the thirty-four possible responses to a problem, running away is best."

"Master Speaker Athelstan knows what is right."

"Yeah," Joshua agreed. "For Master Speaker Athelstan. Never mind. Go to sleep. It's liable to get noisy pretty quick."

Joshua lay back, trying to quiet the jangle. After a time, he felt Kristin relax into sleep. Then he took tension, fear, anger from his toes, moved it upward, pushing it as a broom sweeps water, up his body, through his arms, through his chest and into his brain. He found a color for these things, deep blue, coiled the tensions, the fears into a ball, forced it out of his body, and made it float precisely three inches above his head, between his eyes. He ordered his mind to obey him, that all would be doomed if that blue ball sank into his body once more.

Joshua was almost asleep when he *felt* something. Far out, across the city—although when he reached for it, nothing was there.

Then it returned, brooding, dark.

Wolfe slid out of bed, dressed in dark shirt, pants, and a pair of zip boots. He returned to the bed, and lay on his back.

Waiting.

*

The door to the bedroom crashed open, and Wolfe was crouched in a defense stance as Kristin half shrieked and sat up.

Lucian was in the doorway, gun in his hand, eyes wide. "They killed him!" he cried. "They've killed him!"

Suddenly he burst into racking sobs, and the gun fell onto the carpet.

Wolfe heard the blare of the vid in the room outside and ran into the living room.

Onscreen was dark space, lit by the flaring ruin of a starship. For an instant Wolfe was thrown back years, to other screens and other ship-deaths.

Then the smooth commentator's voice registered:

". . . still unknown registry and origin, although sources within Planetary Guard advise the ship had been in a geosynchronous orbit over Prendergast for at least two months.

"I repeat the flash: An unknown starship, orbiting just off Rogan's World exploded minutes ago. Initial reports suggest the ship was attacked by unknown assailants. We have no word as to the ship's name or registry, nor any information about passengers or crew.

"We have a news crew en route, and another on its way to Planetary Guard headquarters. These images are coming to you courtesy of the Guard, from one of the navsats offworld.

"Please stand by for further details."

The screen blanked, but Max continued staring at it.

"Master Speaker Athelstan," he said in a whisper. "The bitch got him. She killed him." He exploded onto his feet, shouting. "Goddammit, she killed him! She killed Kur . . . all of them!"

Kristin, naked, was in the bedroom door. Her face was blank in shock and horror.

"Come on," Wolfe shouted. "She hit first! We're next!" He ran back into the bedroom, scooping up Lucian's gun on the way. Lucian was crouched on the floor, head in his hands, sobbing, repeating over and over: "It's ended . . . The dream is gone . . . It's ended . . ."

"Come on, man! Or die with your frigging dream!"

Lucian didn't move.

Wolfe hurried into the gun-guards' quarters and found them as shattered as Lucian. He found the team's cash-box, smashed it open, and shoved wads of credits into his pockets.

"What are you doing?" Max demanded. His gun was wavering, but still aimed at Wolfe.

"We're getting out of here," Wolfe said. "Or else we'll be as dead as Athelstan."

"No," Max decided. "No, we can't leave. No, we can't—"

Wolfe was on him, gun crossblocked out of the way as it went off, blasting a three-inch-wide hole in a painting of a shepherd and his flock and the wall behind it. Joshua struck Max once on the forehead with the heel of his hand and let him fall.

One of the gun-guards had his pistol half drawn, and Wolfe kicked him back against the wall. He had Lucian's gun in his hand, and the other guards froze.

"Get your things and get out," he ordered. "Move! We'll try for our ship at the yard!" He didn't wait for a reply, but darted into the main room.

Kristin had found a pair of blue pants and a red pullover; she sat on the floor of the bedroom, sorting through boots very methodically and slowly.

Wolfe yanked her to her feet. "Out! Now!"

Kristin started to protest, nodded dumbly.

"Come on, Lucian!"

"Lost . . . All lost . . ."

Wolfe could spare no more time. He grabbed Kristin's hand and pulled her out of the suite toward the private lift.

The glass-fronted lift's door slid closed, and Wolfe punched 2.

"Where's your gun?"

Kristin's hand felt her waistband, then she shook her head.

"Good," Wolfe said sarcastically. "One gun against— Jesus God!"

Two tactical strike ships with the insignia of the Planetary Guard broke through the cloud cover and dropped down toward the hotel. They banked, then hovered about one hundred feet above the hotel's roof. Flame spat from one, then the second. Wolfe slammed the lift's emergency buttons. It obediently stopped, and the door slid open.

Wolfe pitched Kristin out onto thick pile carpet as the missiles smashed into the hotel, and exploded.

The tower rocked under the impact, and alarms howled.

Kristin was crying, whimpering. Wolfe lifted her face, slapped her hard, twice. "Come on, soldier! Or die right here!"

Kristin shook her head violently, then her eyes came back to normal. "Where . . . What . . ."

"Find the emergency exit. There's got to be one somewhere."

There was, at the end of the long corridor. Doors were opening, and bewildered men and women were stumbling out. Wolfe pushed through them, found the stairs, clattered down their long, cement-gray steps, hearing siren screams clamoring everywhere.

THE DARKNESS OF GOD

A man with a gun stood at the door leading into the lobby. Wolfe shot him without asking questions, took his gun, and they went on down, into the underground parking structure.

There was no one in the attendant's booth, and Wolfe went to a wooden cabinet, yanked it open, and found a rack with ignition keys dangling from it.

"Good. Organized," he muttered. He scanned the gravlifters parked nearby. "A-27—here it is." He pulled a set of keys from a numbered hook, pulled Kristin toward a nearly new sleek luxury lifter. He pointed the ignition sensor at the vehicle, and the door slid up.

"Inside," he ordered, and Kristin managed to fumble her way into a seat.

Wolfe slid in, pushed the sensor into the ignition slot, let the drive whine to life. He lifted the craft and steered it up the ramps, toward the exit.

A bright red heavy gravlifter was just grounding, blocking the exit, red and blue lights flashing. Firemen wearing exposure suits piled out, heavy-laden.

Wolfe slid the drive-pot to full thrust, brought the stick up, and sent the lifter careening across the wide sidewalk onto the boulevard. A fireman saw him and barely dove out of the way.

There were other firecraft grounding on the boulevard, and he saw someone waving. Someone aimed a gun, fired, and the bolt went somewhere Wolfe couldn't see.

At full power, he sent the lifter down the street, made one turn, another, then banked the craft up into the darkness and smoke as the hotel gouted fire like a torch.

* CHAPTER SIX *

Wolfe held his breath and sliced through the bomb strap. Nothing happened. He pulled it away, feeling it tear at his skin like a bandage long in place. He let the bomb thump to the lifter's floor.

Kristin watched dully, making no attempt to stop him.

He started to say something, rethought his words. "You'll get over it," he said gently. "Everybody's Christ gets killed sooner or later."

"You don't understand," Kristin said. "It wasn't just Athelstan—it was a whole dynasty that woman murdered. Kur—Athelstan's aides—his best logicians—Aubyn may have destroyed us."

Again Wolfe held back his words.

"That's as may be," he said. "A little martyrdom never hurt a good cause. But later is for mourning. Right now, we've got to think about our own young asses."

"It doesn't matter," Kristin said. "You can go your own way—go wherever you want. I'll try to get off Rogan's World somehow. Perhaps—when—if we recover, we'll mount another operation against Aubyn for the ur-Lumina."

"You want to get slapped again? Knock off the defeatism. You ain't dead till you're dead, as the eminent grammarian said. I dragged you out of that hotel; I can drag you a few feet further. Besides, I might need somebody at my back."

"How do you know I won't kill you?" Kristin asked. "I guess that's what Athelstan and Kur would have wanted me to do."

"Lady, a piece of advice: stop second-guessing corpses." Wolfe's voice sharpened. "Now pull it together, dammit!"

The image of that universe-encompassing "red virus" filled his mind.

"I can't—won't—say why," he went on. "But there's no time for you to wander back to Batan and debate, oh so goddamned logically, whether you're coming back for the Mother Stone and what color your little pink dresses ought to be."

Kristin took several deep breaths. "All right. What do we do? Take your thirty-fourth easiest option and run?"

"No. Aubyn'll be expecting that. We do what any good—if maybe suicidal—gravel-cruncher's supposed to."

*

"A little obfuscation here," Wolfe said, as he grounded the lifter in an alley behind a business loudly proclaiming itself to be HJALMAR'S LIFTERS—ONLY THE BEST IN PREVIOUSLY OWNED ANTIGRAVITY DEVICES. He opened the lifter's engine lid, located the tool compartment, and muttered under his breath when all he found was a bent screwdriver and a crescent wrench whose jaws barely met. "How are you at deactivating proximity detectors?"

"I never learned how," Kristin said.

"And what *are* they teaching the young these days?" Joshua said. "Tsk."

He unscrewed the registration plates of his lifter and changed them for one of Hjalmar's finest. "In case somebody happens to be alert," he said, "I'd rather not get stopped."

He considered the night. The whole planet seemed focused on the still-roaring inferno seven miles distant. "Now watch and learn something," he told Kristin. "Normally any lifter's proximity detectors are up front. Here, just below the driving lights on the traffic side. Pop the little panel, like so. All that you have to do then is yank this wire—here—and the same one on the backup unit. The drive won't pick up any closing signal. Handy thing to know, if you plan on, say, ramming a baby carriage or something scummy like that."

He realized he was babbling a little, from fear of what was to come as much as relief at having the bomb gone.

"And now we go marching through Georgia," he said.

*

Wolfe shot the two guards outside Walsh's mansion and steered the gravsled through the gates. There were lights on in the mansion's east wing.

"Out!"

Kristin obediently tumbled onto the grass. An alarm clanged from the gates, but Wolfe paid no mind.

He turned the lifter toward the west wing, set the height designator at five feet above the ground, and slid the drive-pot to full power.

As the lifter accelerated toward the mansion, Wolfe jumped out and went flat.

Someone heard the turbine whine, ran out of the main entrance, saw the speeding lifter, and shot at it twice. Going about sixty miles an hour, the lifter smashed into the stone building, flipped, and crashed through the great bay windows. A moment later it exploded. All the lights in the mansion died.

"That's our calling card," Wolfe said. "Let's go introduce ourselves."

There were shouts, screams, and another alarm went

off. Wolfe ignored them and trotted across the dark lawn and up the steps.

A man—perhaps the shooter—was gaping at the flames starting to flicker in the far wing. Wolfe shot him neatly in the neck.

"Where . . . ?" Kristin started.

"Shut up." Wolfe reached out, *felt,* and went through the door into the house.

*

"Breathe gently," Wolfe advised.

Edmund Walsh, half-dressed, obeyed. His face was white, silhouetted in the glow from a pocket flash on the bureau in front of him.

"Move away from the dresser," Wolfe ordered.

Walsh did, moving very slowly, hands lifting to shoulder height as if they belonged to a marionette.

Wolfe pocketed the gun beside the light. Walsh started to protest. Wolfe reached out and stroked the old man along the neck with three fingers. Walsh dropped bonelessly. Joshua shouldered him. "One little memory trot, and we can be on our way." He turned off the flash and dropped it into a pocket.

*

Joshua went unhurriedly across the drawing room to the wall lined with testimonials, holographs, and photos behind the glare of the flash. He pulled one holo free and tossed it to Kristin. "Don't lose this. We'll need it."

Emergency power went on, flickered, went out.

Wolfe listened to the shouting from the other wing and heard the screams of firelifters approaching. "Out the back," he decided. "Look for something to steal."

*

The windowless delivery vehicle sat behind the mansion's kitchen. The ignition key was in place, the lifter's driver probably having reasoned that no one but a desperate fool would dare steal from Edmund Walsh.

Joshua slid Walsh into the back, started the drive, lifted the craft silently, and sent the lifter across the grounds, away from the flames and excitement. He found an unguarded rear gate and floated down the long avenue toward the city.

"What we need," Wolfe said, "is something nice, quiet, and dark. Like—like this."

The sign read FLORIET REGIONAL PARK, and the entrance was blocked by two barrels. Wolfe shut off the lifter's lights, grounded the craft, rolled a barrel out of the way, moved the lifter through, and replaced the barrel.

He lifted the 'sled without turning the lights back on and went slowly along a curving, narrow drive. He passed slides, swings, and climbs, then grounded the lifter in the playground's center.

Wolfe propped Walsh against a wooden clown with peeling paint. He started slapping Walsh on the cheeks with two extended fingers, not hard, not gently. "Stop faking," he said. "The nerve block wore off a couple of minutes ago."

Walsh's eyes came open. "You're better'n I thought, Taylor. I didn't think you'd live through our little demonstration—let alone come back this fast."

"I *am* better. A lot better. But I don't have time for compliments. I need some information."

"Fresh out."

"I don't think so," Wolfe said. "I'm in a hurry, so it's going to hurt. Show him the picture."

Kristin handed him the holo of Edmund Walsh being feted at a banquet, standing behind a podium with an unusual symbol on it.

"What's the emblem mean?"

Walsh compressed his lips.

Wolfe set the gun on the sand and took Walsh's left hand. Walsh tried to pull away but wasn't able to. Wolfe slid two fingers down to Walsh's little finger, twisted.

Walsh yelped.

"Ring finger." Joshua broke that one as well.

"Middle . . ."

"Stop!" It was Kristin.

Wolfe turned, stared at her. She shuddered, turned away.

"Middle finger . . ."

"I'll tell you!"

The bone snapped with a crack, and Walsh stifled a scream.

"I *said* I'd tell you!"

"Talk."

"It's the logo of the Fiscus-MacRae Fund."

"What's that?"

"A big—really big—research firm," Walsh said, biting his lip against the pain. "They do political research, sociological studies—that kind of thing."

"Yeah," Joshua said. "That kind of thing. Nice cover—you can do anything you want to with something that vague. Nobody's going to ask who's coming, who's going, or why, whether they're gangster or pol. And research justifies a ton of electronics, doesn't it? Enough for a whole world's command center. Not stupid at all."

He pointed to a woman sitting at the podium table, a mildly striking woman with short, dark hair. Her face was in silhouette, and it was hard to say what she was looking at. "Who's she?"

He *felt* Walsh stiffen.

"I don't know."

"You'll run out of bone joints before I run out of patience," Wolfe said.

"Oh, I'm talking, I'm talking. I was just trying to remember—"

Wolfe broke his index finger.

"I'm telling you the truth!"

"You're more afraid of her than you are of me?"

Walsh stared into Wolfe's eyes. His head moved up, down, a bare inch.

"We'll have to rectify that," Joshua said. "Kristin, you might want to go back to the lifter. This is going to get messy."

"No," she said. "I'll stay."

"Then stay quiet. Listen closely, Edmund. I'm going to hit you once, just above the cheekbone. Your eye is going to come out of its socket. I'm going to pull it out by the ganglion then pull until the ganglion snaps. After that—who knows? We'll concentrate on your face, first, because that'll be pretty damned gory, and second, because it doesn't do any lasting damage. But I'll leave you your tongue, hearing, and one eye. You want fear—we'll deal on that level. If you still aren't talking, I'll get something sharp from the lifter, and we'll start down from your navel. Look at me! Do you think I'm bluffing?" Wolfe turned the flash on his own face and waited.

"No," Walsh muttered after a moment. "You're not bluffing. You'll do it. But she'll do worse."

"I agree," Wolfe said. "She's had more practice than I have. But there's a difference. I'm now. She's later."

"How much of a start will you give me?" Walsh said.

"When you talk, I leave."

Walsh slumped back against the statue. "I don't have any choice. She's the deputy director of Fiscus-MacRae. She uses the name of Alicia Comer. I don't know much about her," he said. "She's not from Rogan's World. I heard she's a helluva fund-raiser, which is why Fiscus-MacRae uses her. She was one of the founding partners, come to think."

"Walsh, you're still lying. But that doesn't matter. Where does Comer live?"

Walsh hesitated, then told him.

"Where's the fund located at?"

That, too, came out.

"All right," Wolfe said. He rose.

"You're a bastard, Taylor," Walsh managed.

"I know," Wolfe said. The gun slid into his hand, and Wolfe touched the trigger. Kristin half screamed as the bolt sliced through the old man's head and blood sprayed across the clown.

"You told him you wouldn't . . ." Kristin managed.

"Yeah," Wolfe said, his voice flat. "I lied. I do things like that."

*

Low-power lasers made lines in the near-dawn darkness in an irregular figure, sealing off an area around the spacecraft. Ten bodies still littered the tarmac. Seven were variously dressed; three wore the livery chosen for Wolfe's pilots. Morgue 'sleds to one side of the ship-park waited for the scattering of police to finish their work. Three noisy 'cast teams waited, held back by an angry cop. No one paid much attention to the rangy man wearing a coverall that said SPACEPORT GROUND HANDLER as he walked up to the cop.

"Are your officers out of the ship?" he asked.

"Uh—yes. I think so."

"Good. Mister McCartle wants the ship moved down-row, into one of the hangars."

"Nobody said anything to me about that."

"He told me you'd know," Wolfe said. "Said the police wanted it out of the way to keep off souvenir hounds and like."

The policeman hesitated, looked into Wolfe's eyes, then smiled. "Oh. Yeah. That makes sense. Which hangar?"

Wolfe looked pointedly at one of the reporters, who'd edged closer. The cop leaned closer, listening.

"Eight-Six-Alpha," Wolfe said. "All the way down to the end, in A row."

"You need any help?"

"Not unless there's still bodies inside."

"Nope. Taylor's crew must've come out shooting, not that that did them much good. Regular Kilkenny cats here. Doesn't seem to be any damage to the ship, but maybe you want to not do any VTOing."

Wolfe half saluted and went through the line of light, through the ship's hatch. The lock closed behind him.

Joshua slid into the pilot's seat, unlocked and activated the controls. Eyes closed, he touched sensors. "I do not like the feel of this beast," he muttered, touching the secondary drive sensor.

The drive hissed into life.

Wolfe picked up a com button, stuck it to his larynx. "Rogan Prime Control, this is the *Eryx*."

"*Eryx,* this is Prime. Be advised your ship has been seized by proper authorities. I can't allow you to lift without authorization."

"Prime, this is the *Eryx*. Police Captain McCartle in command. I've been ordered to relocate this ship to the police field for a complete analysis. Plus we don't want the ship sitting around for gawkers. This whole mess is too loud anyway."

"Hell," the voice swore. "I'm always the last to get the word." There was silence, as Wolfe *felt* out for the woman. "All right. How do you want to lift it?"

"Don't put me in the regular pattern, Prime. I'll be holding 1,000 feet, course 284 magnetic, on visual."

"That was 1,000 feet, course 284, *Eryx*. You're cleared to take off."

"Thanks, Prime. *Eryx* out."

THE DARKNESS OF GOD

*

The yacht settled down on an almost-deserted open stretch of road, where a gravlifter waited. It grounded, skidded, lazily turned on an axis, and settled, blocking the road. The gravlifter's canopy lifted and Kristin ran toward the ship. The lock opened, and she went up the gangway and through the open lock door into the control room.

Wolfe nodded as she sat down in the copilot's seat, and took the *Eryx* off again.

"That wasn't the best landing I've seen," Kristin said.

"Not my fault," Joshua said. "I'm the original hot-dog danny normally. This pig you found in a boneyard and decided would make a good yacht's got more slop than a hophead's legs."

"We had to move quickly."

"So you did," Joshua grunted. "Let's hope it'll hold together long enough to get us offworld and somewhere."

"What's your plan?"

"It's changed," Wolfe said. "I was hoping to find the Lumina and go straight after it."

"What about Aubyn?"

"I don't give a damn about her," Wolfe said. "No Lumina, no power. Nor do I give a shit about how Rogan's World is run anyway. But she's with the Lumina now, so it's going to be a two-for-the-price-of-one goat rope."

"How do you know where she is?"

"I *know*."

"Can you take her?" Kristin said.

"That's what we're going to find out. Grab the controls, and keep it level. I'm going to be busy for the next few seconds."

*

Reaching out . . .
Feeling . . .

Wolfe jumped in his seat, feeling the death-sweep rush toward him.

Shit. The bitch is waiting for me. I wonder if she's got enough power—if she's used the Lumina enough—to kill me with just her mind.

Unknown.

Breathe . . . breathe . . .

All right. We'll have to go and have ourselves a look.

"I've got the con," he said, and sent the *Eryx* swooping down toward open farmland below. There were no buildings, vehicles, or workers in sight, and he landed the ship behind a long, high mow of drying grass.

He slid to a com, touched sensors. "Central Library," he requested.

The screen blanked, lit with a rather unimaginative panel of books.

Wolfe touched keys; F,I,S,C,U,S,-,M,A,C,R,A,E#F,U,N,D

FILE FOUND

V,I,S,U,A,L,#H,E,A,D,Q,U,A,R,T,E,R,S

SEARCHING . . .

The screen showed a sprawling series of ultramodern buildings, centering around a glass pyramid that might've been a cathedral.

"Son of a bitch," Wolfe swore. "Old Edgar Allan's got a *lot* to answer for."

"What does that mean?"

"Nothing." Wolfe thought. "Since we don't happen to have a battalion or two of marines in our back pockets, I guess I'll just wander in and see what's going on."

"Joshua?"

"What?"

"Why doesn't Aubyn have troops surrounding the building, if she controls Rogan's World? I surely would if I were her."

A bit of a smile came to Wolfe's mouth. He leaned

over and kissed her on the cheek. "And I'm very glad you're not. Why no soldiery? I don't know. Maybe Aubyn thinks the most important thing is for nobody to know who's the puppet master here. Hell, for all I know, she's aware of her enormous crimes and doesn't think she morally deserves the army."

He didn't voice his real thought: that Token Aubyn didn't think she needed any backup.

"That doesn't make any sense," Kristin complained.

"Since when does *anybody* make any sense? All right. I'm betting I'll find Aubyn—and that other thing—in the main building. I'm bringing this hog down on the other side of that rise. That should give you cover against direct fire."

He picked up a bonemike from the control board, fitted it around his neck. "If you don't hear anything—or you hear a lot of male screaming in my general tone of voice, get away from the ship, back into the city, and go to ground. Here. Take the credits we took from the hotel. That'll get you a good running start in case Aubyn's the vindictive sort. And good luck."

"Aren't you the one who's going to need the luck?"

"I am. Wish I still believed in it."

*

Not far from Fiscus-MacRae's central building were two monolithic abstract sculptures, set by themselves in the rolling lawn.

Inside one, two men crouched behind a semiportable blaster, peering through a vision slit just above ground level. One lifted a microphone. "This is Two-Seven. One man, approaching from the east. I think he came from that ship that grounded about fifteen minutes ago. Shall we drop him?"

Inside the building a balding man with the muscles of a weightlifter spoke into his com. "This is Kilkhampton.

Stand by." He looked at the woman once known as Token Aubyn.

Her eyes were closed. They opened. "No," she ordered. "We'll let him get closer. Is he armed?"

The bald man looked at another screen. "I see some sort of ferrous material mass at his waist. Probably a pistol."

"Let him come. He's outgunned."

The bald man eyed Aubyn, then opened his com.

*

Joshua Wolfe walked slowly, steadily, toward the building. His hands were at his sides, well away from the holstered sidearm. His breathing was slow, deep. In through the nose, out through the mouth, sixteen breaths a minute.

He stopped, held his hands out level, and his breathing slowed, four deep inhalations per minute. He *felt* out, beyond.

Inside the building, he *felt* the Great Lumina, a deep hum beyond hearing, a glow beyond vision. It swirled in his mind like a maelstrom, pulling him forward, pulling him toward death. He tried to take its power, failed. Another was blocking him, someone closer, more familiar with the Lumina's power.

Aubyn.

He *felt* her waiting for him, an ant lion deep in her pit, a spider waiting for the web twitch.

She was *reaching* for him, for his mind.

He refused contact. Forced himself away.

He noted the men hidden in the statue/gun emplacement, and other armed men equally well camouflaged around the seemingly deserted institution. There were other guards inside the building. They, too, were recognized.

He *reached* beyond them, beyond Rogan's World, into space. He felt the shrieking of the "red virus" in space as it clawed toward Man's worlds.

He *reached* beyond that, beyond Man, toward a nameless world deep in the void.

He *felt* the touch of the last of the Al'ar, the Guardians, waiting for him, waiting for the Lumina.

He took strength, brought it back.

Again he *reached*, this time into memory.

The one he'd thought was the last of the Al'ar, Taen, lifted his head, and a Chitet bolt took him. Taen fell, dying, dead, across Joshua.

Wolfe remembered that moment, brought it forward. His breathing changed once more, quickening, almost panting, but far too regular, coming from his diaphragm.

Joshua felt the roar of life, of death, blood pouring through his veins. As he had once before, he took Taen's death and cast it forth, like a net. He let it sweep out, around, over the towering glass building.

*

"What the hell's he doing, just standing there—"

Kilkhampton gagged suddenly, as if struck in the throat, grabbed for his chest, half rose, and toppled across the control board.

Aubyn was on her feet. She grabbed for his com.

"Any station—all stations—report immediately!"

There was no response.

Aubyn started to key the sensor again, tossed it away. She left the room and walked quickly but calmly for the lift.

*

Wolfe entered the huge circular room and looked around. There were two mezzanine balconies above, then the diffused crystalline light from the faceted-glass roof. To one side was a large reception desk of exotic woods, with an elaborate com. No one was behind the desk.

There was a body sprawled near one wall, a gun lying not far away.

The marble floor formed a swirl of black and white, leading the eye to the lift at the far end. The air smelled as if lightning had struck nearby not long ago. Wolfe's breathing was slow, regular, deep.

A woman waited in the center of the room. She was about ten years younger than he was, not pretty, but striking. She wore a hand-tailored deep blue business suit. Her dark hair was cut close and looked a little like a cap.

She appeared unarmed.

Joshua drew his pistol with two fingers and spun it clattering across the marble to the side. Aubyn jumped in surprise, then recovered. Her eyes, hooded, sought Wolfe's.

"I am Token Aubyn," she said. Her voice was low, musical.

"You do not need my name," Joshua said.

"You are not a Chitet," she said.

"No."

"But you were helping them."

"For my own purposes."

"Which are?"

Wolfe looked up at the glass ceiling. "Congratulations," he said. "One crystal makes another invisible. Nice way to hide something in plain sight."

"I am trying to *reach* you," Aubyn said calmly, not responding to what Wolfe had said. "What I call mind-seizing. But you're different from others—from other minds I've chosen to use for my purposes. Your thoughts are different. Alien. I almost feel like I did when I first saw the crystal, and thought into it and knew I had to have it for my own."

Again, Wolfe made no reply.

"The crystal," Aubyn said, "what I've heard is called a Lumina, is mine. I found it. I killed for it. And I'll kill again. This is my world, and soon I'll be ready to reach out for more.

"You—or those Chitet fools I once believed knew something—cannot, must not stop me."

Wolfe *felt* discordance, as if someone had rubbed a finger along a wet glass, a glass with a hidden flaw in it, and the growing tone that could not be heard *felt* wrong, *was* wrong.

"I am not a fool," Aubyn went on. "I know the Lumina, and what it can give. So even though you're strong, stronger than I thought at first, I must deal with the situation immediately. You must die now."

There was nothing to see, but Wolfe *felt* energy sear, *saw* it as a flashing ball. He took it, welcomed it, and it was gone.

Aubyn looked startled.

Joshua felt force, coming down, crushing force, coming from all directions. He fought, tried to stand, but it was too strong. He slipped sideways and fell heavily, half-curled, one hand resting on his ankle.

Aubyn walked toward him.

Wolfe lay motionless.

Aubyn's footfalls were very loud on the marble.

Wolfe's right hand flickered to his boot top, and a tiny, six-pointed, razor bit of steel flashed.

Aubyn jerked as the shiriken scarred her face and blood spurted.

Joshua *felt* the Lumina then.

Zai . . . I welcome this . . . I accept this . . . ku . . . reach . . . reaching . . .

The room was filled with a great luminescence, hard, cold, all the colors that could be imagined, and he took its power, sending, receiving as it rebounded, building.

He dimly heard shattering glass, then the grating, rending of alloy beams as they cracked, smashed.

There was something floating in the middle of the room, a great gem of many facets, each facet flashing.

The Lumina.

Wolfe came to his feet.

All the universe held was Token Aubyn's eyes, boring into his. Aubyn's eyes, and somewhere beyond, the Lumina.

Joshua *reached*, welcomed the Lumina's energy, welcomed the thin Al'ar force from far beyond in interstellar space, shaped the power, focused it, and the room flared with intolerable light.

Wolfe shouted—fear? rage?—as Aubyn's body exploded into a sheet of flame for a bare instant. Then it was gone, and her unscathed body collapsed to the floor. Not far from her body was a gray, indistinct stone, about the size of Wolfe's head.

The Lumina.

Wolfe stumbled toward her and made sure she was dead. He spoke into the bonemike. "Bring the ship in. We've got a cargo to load."

He let himself sink back to the floor, felt the chill of marble against his cheek, and welcomed nothingness for a time.

* CHAPTER SEVEN *

"For a renegade," the comfortable-looking man named Fordyce said, "your Joshua Wolfe has been doing very, very well by Federation Intelligence. Are you sure you aren't running a *very* deep private operation here?"

Cisco shook his head. "No, sir. I've been with FI too long not to remember my pension whenever I start getting too creative."

"Of course," Fordyce drawled blandly. "Certainly *I* never thought of such subterfuge, but was content to soldier my way up through the ranks, knowing my innate ability would be recognized in the fullness of time." He roared with laughter.

The title on the entry door to his secured suite read OPERATIONS DIRECTOR.

"You must admit," Fordyce went on, "he has done us a world of good. Athelstan dead along with almost all of his advisors and security people, which puts a big crimp in the Chitet's ambitions for a few dozen years. Admirable, simply admirable. If he were still on the payroll, we'd have to promote and gong him a couple of times. And I won't even consider the seven rather senior officials in FI who decided, after the debacle on Rogan's World, to either take early retirement or transfer to less, shall we say, active sections of the government. Rather a good job of smoking the moles out, I'd say."

"Yes, sir," Cisco said. "So what do you wish done about Wolfe?"

"I'd say nothing. Let him sneak back to his Outlaw Worlds and mind his own business."

"We can't do that, sir."

"Why not?"

"We've picked up some very strange data," Cisco said. "You're aware of those Al'ar objects called Lumina?"

"I am." Fordyce's tone became flat, disapproving. "Manna for oo-ee-oo-ee idiots and mystics."

"The Al'ar didn't think so," Cisco persisted.

"That doesn't mean they have any relevance to us," Fordyce said. He waited for Cisco to withdraw the point, but the gray man just sat, lips drawn into thin lines. Fordyce sighed. "Very well. What new data about these Lumina further complicates the issue of Joshua Wolfe?"

"We've been getting reports of some sort of a super Lumina the Al'ar had at the end of the war. I don't know if it was a secret weapon that didn't quite work out, or what, for it was never deployed as far as I can tell," Cisco said. "Supposedly this is what the Chitet were after, and why they hijacked Wolfe when I had him comfortably zombied and on the way back here for debriefing."

"Of *course* this Great Lumina would give anyone who touched it superpowers," Fordyce said cynically. "Such things always seem to have a reputation like that."

"That's the story," Cisco said reluctantly. "Supposedly this woman who bossed Rogan's World, who was called Alicia Comer, but who was in fact a deserter from the Federation Navy named Token Aubyn, had possession of this Lumina, and used it to carve her way upward." Cisco told Fordyce as much of Aubyn's history as he'd been able to get from Naval and FI records.

"Interesting," Fordyce said, lacing his fingers on his

desk. "I still view the whole matter skeptically. Now let me return your question to you: What do you want to do about Wolfe, assuming that he has possession of this ruddy great chunk of colored glass? Put out an all-Federation hue and cry? That'll certainly attract attention, particularly with the rather strange happenings these days."

"No, sir. But I'd like to let word slip out at a high level that FI's very interested in talking to him. Alive only. Anyone who can provide his services to us will be appropriately, if quietly, rewarded."

"That seems a viable alternative," Fordyce said. "I assume you can do it through the usual conduits—old boys and such?"

"I can." Cisco started to rise. Fordyce held out a hand.

"A few minutes ago, I referred to the current level of excitement. Have you been following events?"

"Not really, sir. Since I got out of the hospital from the gassing, I've been concentrating on Wolfe."

"Things have been a little unusual of late. Quite some time ago, we lost one of our spyships. The *Trinquier*, which was operating under civilian cover as an exploration vessel, vanished. Then an investigative team—straightforward scientific chaps—on one of the Al'ar homeworlds disappeared, after making some very aberrant screams for help. We had to make some threats in the scholarly community to keep that silent. Finally, we sent out a task force—six ships, including the *Styrbjorn*—seven weeks ago, to investigate along the *Trinquier*'s projected mission plan. The entire task force has fallen out of communication. We're presuming all six ships are lost, with no explanation whatever."

Cisco sat down heavily. "The *Styrbjorn*? I used that ship a few times. Sharp crew. Good captain. There's no way they could be surprised—or get into an accident."

"Unusual, isn't it?" Fordyce said. "I'm starting to get a very strange feeling. We may be in for *extremely* interesting times."

* CHAPTER EIGHT *

"So it's just like the old-fashioned romances. Logic—common sense—probability are discarded, and one man defeats an entire kingdom," Kristin said. "You have the Lumina, and we Chitet have nothing." She sighed, got up from the control chair, and went to Wolfe. "I suppose you'd better hold true to the romance and kiss the princess you've won."

"That I can do."

After a while, she pulled back. "Although I'm not much of a princess."

"You're more of one than I'm a prince," Joshua said.

"So you have me to do with what you will. What do you will?"

"Let us see," Joshua said, twirling nonexistent mustachios. "First I shall remove all your clothes except your space boots. Then slather you with freshly made tartar sauce. I'll wake the six furry creatures I have back in cold storage . . ."

Kristin laughed. "I never realized you had a sense of humor before."

"I generally don't, when somebody's got a gun on me."

"No, seriously, what . . ."

The ship jolted, went in and out of N-space. Wolfe's stomach crawled. Kristin slid out of his lap as he came out of the chair. "Not good," he said. "Ships aren't supposed to do that without giving hints. Let's go see the worst." He started for the engine spaces.

Four hours later, they knew the worst.

"Less than sixty drive-hours and this drive'll make a good ship anchor," Wolfe said. "Damn these bargain-basement yachts."

He called up a gazetteer onscreen and opened a voice sensor.

"Nearest inhabited planet," he said.

The screen blinked twice, then an entry scrolled:

```
Ak-Mechat VII. Class 23. Currently ex-
ploited for minerals. Est. pop. 7,000. No
controlled field. No cities. Three popu-
lated sites, little better than mining
camps, are located as shown . . .
```

Figures scrolled.

"Two jumps," Wolfe said. "Not good. Then a goodish chug on secondary. And it's a bit chilly. I'm not considering hollering for help."

"Is there any other choice?" Kristin asked.

"Surely. Press on regardless for real civilization and hope my mechanical diagnostic abilities are pessimistic."

"Could they be?"

"No."

"I just realized I always wanted to visit this Am-Kechat."

"Gesundheit. But it's Ak-Mechat."

*

Kristin quietly slid open the hatch to the small freight compartment. The space was empty, except for the Great Lumina. It hung in midair, fluorescing colors. She heard, over the increasingly shrill hum of the ship's drive, deep, slow breathing, coming from nowhere. She heard the clank of metal; she saw a thin piece of alloy steel lift, stand on end, then bend in an invisible vise. The steel clanged to the deck and Joshua appeared. He was naked, drenched in sweat. For an instant Kristin didn't register. "You did that," she said.

Wolfe took several more breaths before he nodded. "I still don't quite have full control. I wanted the metal to bend, and then fall slowly to the deck."

"When you do—what then?"

Wolfe shook his head. "I can't tell you. And I doubt if you'd believe me, anyway."

"I just read, in one of your books, about a queen who believed as many as six impossible things before breakfast. Try me."

"All right. I want to use the Lumina to close a door, or maybe seal a door. Something that I think's here, with us in this spacetime, has to be either destroyed or put on the other side. And then the door must be sealed."

"I have no idea what you're talking about."

Joshua picked up a towel from the deck, wiped his forehead. "Neither do I, most times. Forget about it. I'm for a shower, anyway."

"Need your back scrubbed?"

"Always."

*

Kristin rolled her head back and screamed as Wolfe drove within her, holding her knees crooked in his elbows, forearms pulling her against him.

She came back to herself, was aware of hot water needling her face, her breasts. Wolfe set her down. She managed a smile. "I was somewhere else," she said.

"So was I," Joshua said. He kissed her, eased her feet to the deck.

"What are you going to do about me?" she asked.

"Not sure," Wolfe said, picking up the soap from the deck. "I guess I'll turn you around and scrub your back. Like this."

"Mmmh. No. Stop for a minute. I meant—you aren't going to let me come with you."

Wolfe's hand stopped for a time, then continued, rubbing in a small circle. "Lady," he said slowly, "I don't think you want to come with me."

"Why not? I'm not going back to the Chitet."

"My turn to ask why not," Wolfe said.

"I'm not sure yet," Kristin said. "But—something died. Changed, anyway, when Master Speaker Athelstan got killed." She was silent for some time. "No," she said softly. "I'm lying. Things changed some time before that. After—after we started making love."

"Sex shouldn't change what you believe," Joshua said. "Or the way you live."

"No," she said softly. "No, it shouldn't."

Again there was a long silence. Joshua leaned close, whispered in her ear.

She giggled, bent forward a little, hands on her upper thighs. "Like this?"

She gasped.

"Like that," Joshua managed.

*

They came out of N-space on the fringes of the Ak-Mechat system. Wolfe went back to the drive chamber, ran a diagnostic program, and returned to the bridge. "That drive is about as defunct as it's possible to get without going bang or maybe even thud," he announced. "I can't chance an in-system jump. So it's a long, hard drive for planetfall. Get out a good book."

*

Kristin slept, her breathing a gentle bubbling.

Joshua lay beside her, *feeling* out. He *felt* the red, the burn, the soundless buzzing insect roar of the life-form that had destroyed the Al'ar's universe and was reaching into his own. He pulled back from the searing pain as it built.

He *felt* the red presence, the "virus" far closer now than before.

*

Joshua read in a calm, even voice:
Now you shall see the Temple completed:

After much striving, after many obstacles;
For the work of creation is never without travail;
The formed stone, the visible crucifix,
The dressed altar, the lifting light,
Light

Light

The visible reminder of Invisible Light.

He paused.

"I'm not sure I follow," Kristin said slowly. "I assume this Eliot of yours wasn't writing about the Lumina."

"Not by some more than a thousand years."

"Go ahead."

"Stanza Ten," Joshua continued.

You have seen the house built, you have seen it adorned . . .

Wolfe took the ship in slowly, making two transpolar orbits of Ak-Mechat VII as he killed speed and altitude. "They weren't being funny about the field being unmanned," he said. "All I'm getting from down there is a navbeeper. Guess if anybody's got any incoming cargo they make private arrangements. We'll land next time around."

But the *Eryx* didn't make it. Minutes short of the field, holding at about three hundred miles per hour, fire spurted out the drive tubes and the secondary drive went silent. Wolfe looked at Kristin, who was double-strapped into a control chair. "This one might be tough. I'm gonna try to porpoise it in."

He brought the ship down, down, until it hurtled barely twenty-five feet above rocky outcroppings. "Last time around I thought I saw moors around about here," he muttered. "Come on, Heathcliff."

He felt the controls getting sloppy, vague in his hands. They were fifteen feet above gray rocky death.

"Gimp one for the winner," he prayed, flaring external foils, and the *Eryx* climbed briefly, shuddered, near stalling. He pushed the nose down, and the rocks were gone. Wolfe saw the many-shaded browns of water and land.

He yanked the main stick hard back. The *Eryx* tried to climb again, reached vertical, then stalled, toppled, and fell, pancaking onto the dark moor of Ak-Mechat VII.

*

Wolfe forced the fuzzing blur from his brain and pushed his eyelids up. The control room was a murky skew of wiring, screens, and instruments that'd popped from their housings. Kristin sagged in her chair, a bit of blood seeping from her nostrils.

The antigrav was gone, and the deck was at a twenty-five-degree angle. Wolfe unsnapped his safety belts and got up. His body was battered, bruised.

He staggered to Kristin and unfastened her. He started feeling for damage; her eyes came open. She coughed, then sat up quickly and vomited.

"I'm all right," she said, wiping her mouth with the back of her sleeve. "That *was* a hard one."

"I think we'd best see about leaving," Joshua said, as the ship rolled back until the deck was almost level. "I don't think we're on any kind of firmness."

He made his way to the lock, where there were three packs made from cut-apart crew coveralls. Two held supplies, the third the Lumina.

Wolfe manually cycled the inner lock, went through the chamber, peered through the tiny bull's-eye, then opened the outer lock door.

The *Eryx* was half-buried in mire that was pulling the ship deeper second by second.

"Come on, lady. All ashore that's going ashore," he shouted, grabbing the packs and muscling them to the lock. He chose a patch of muck that looked a bit more solid than the rest, and tossed one pack onto it. It didn't sink.

"Now you," he said, and half threw Kristin after the pack. She landed half on the solid place, nearly slipped into the mud, but recovered.

Wolfe threw the other pack and the Lumina to her, poised, and jumped. He looked around. Close mountains rose gray against gray overcast, lighter gray clouds that looked like rain. Behind him were the foothills they'd almost crashed in. All around was the moor, stretching empty and brown, with dark waters ribboning through the land.

Beside them the *Eryx* rolled once more, and this time its open lock went under. Air gouted in bubbles, and the *Eryx* sank deeper and vanished. A single muddy bubble broke with a *glop*.

"At least we're not leaving footprints," Wolfe said. He put the tied-together trouser legs of the pack holding the

Lumina over his neck and tied the other, more unwieldy pack behind. He waved toward the mountains.

"Let's go find some civilization. I need a drink."

*

They moved quickly, in spite of bruises and the swampy land. Joshua *felt* ahead, and went surefootedly from solid hummock to matted tuft, slowly heading toward the mountains where the gazetteer had said the mines were. He hoped they'd find the field first, and that it wouldn't be completely unmanned.

They'd made several miles when thunder growled, and they looked for shelter. A hilltop rose ahead, and they made for it. There were two large boulders with a patch of soft mosslike growth between, sloping down to a stretch of black, open water. Wolfe took Kristin's pack, unzipped it, and took out a rolled section of plas. He secured the plas to the boulders with paracord, then spread insul blankets under the shelter.

"A garden of unearthly delights, madam."

Kristin looked about them. "Actually, this *is* beautiful," she said. "Look at the way the moor goes on forever and ever, and the little flowers in the moss here." She eyed the pool of water nearby. "Would there be monsters in that?"

"Damfino," Joshua said. "Whyn't you go play bait? I'll try to rescue you before the horrid beasties get more than a nibble or two."

She kicked moss at him, stripped off her coveralls and boots, and cautiously waded into the water. She kept her gun in one hand for a while, then set it close at hand on the bank and started splashing water about. "Come on, you filthy disbeliever. Clean your vile hide," she called.

Wolfe obeyed, taking soap down. They washed, shivering as it grew colder, and the storm grew closer.

"Look," Kristin pointed into the water. A foot-long brown creature drifted past her foot. "A fish?"

"Maybe."

"Could we eat it?"

"Maybe. Come on, Lady Crusoe. Later for the local fauna. We brought dinner."

*

They'd finished the self-heating ship rations before the storm broke, and rain came down in soft, drifting waves around the shelter, beading on the plas, then pouring down it. Joshua leaned out and let rain drizzle on his tongue, feeling like a boy. Bitter, but drinkable, he thought, and ducked back into the shelter.

Kristin, aided by a small flash propped on a rock, was arranging the blankets. She slid into the improvised bed. "Are you planning to sit up all night?"

Joshua joined her, lying back against the moss. Kristin turned the flash off and put her head on his shoulder. After a while, she sighed. "This is nice. It's like this is the only world there is."

"Maybe it'd be nice if it were."

"Why couldn't it be? We could eat fish, and—and maybe the moss is edible. We could live on love for our desserts. These shipsuits won't ever wear out. And maybe you'd look good in a long beard, my little hermit of Ak-Mechat."

Wolfe laughed, realizing the sound was almost a stranger.

Kristin ran her fingers over his lips. "I do *like* this," she said again. "All alone on what feels like an island."

"Thus proving John Donne a liar," Wolfe said, yawning.

"I know who he was, you overeducated name-dropper," Kristin said. "I had to analyze the illogic of some Christian thinkers when I was in creche, and he was one of them."

"Damned odd training the Chitet have for their warriors," Wolfe said.

"But I didn't think John Donne was always wrong. We all *are* part of the main, aren't we?"

"Hasn't been my experience," Wolfe said, voice chilling, remembering a teenage boy in an alien prison camp, alone, staring down at rough graves.

"Or have you just chosen not to be a player?" Kristin asked. "I read the fiche Chitet Intelligence had, Joshua. It was pretty scanty, but it said you were a prisoner of the Al'ar when you were a boy, and then you escaped and were a soldier until the Al'ar vanished. Perhaps if I'd gone through something like that, I wouldn't feel connected to the main very securely either."

"Sometimes," Joshua said, "it's the least painful way."

"Which is why you've gone through so much for the Lumina. Just for your own benefit. Of course."

Wolfe was quiet for a very long time.

"You Chitet sharpen your razors way too damned much," he said. "Goodnight."

*

The field was as advertised—nothing more than a square mile of hardpack, with reflectors at the perimeter. There was no sign of life. Two stripped wrecks lay drunkenly nearby, not far from a long shed, with the navbeacon in a square cupola atop it.

The shed was unlocked, and had a sign, stamped in duralumin:

Welcome to Ak-Mechat VII.
Feel free to use any of the mokes inside. There are three destination settings: Graveyard, Lucky Cuss, and Grand Central. If you break one of them, fix it or leave some credits so we can. It could be a long hike for the next sourdough.

THE DARKNESS OF GOD

*

"I was hoping," Wolfe said, "there might be at least a watchman with a com we could rent to call offworld. Let alone something like a freelancer with a ship for hire. Ah, for the rough freedom of a pioneer world." He scanned the sign again. "Naturally, according to the gazetteer, Graveyard's the biggest mining town. Wonder who the cheery bastard was that named it?"

"Why didn't they build the field near the mines?" Kristin asked. "Or relocate it, once they found whatever they're digging out."

"A lot of people like to see visitors coming from a long way off," Joshua said. "Or maybe none of them could agree about where the new field ought to go. The less I try to figure out why people do things, if I don't have to, the better I sleep at night."

"Joshua, do we have enough credits to get someone to pick us up?"

"Probably," Wolfe said. "But we're not looking for simple transport. At least not for long. Eventually, I need a ship of my own. I'm pretty sure they don't run passenger lines where I'm headed. But there's all kinds of ways to pay for things. Mount up, and let's see if we can make Graveyard before dusk."

*

The moke was as simple as engineering could make it: a nearly rectangular craft with a bench seat behind an open windscreen, a small cargo department, controls for starting/stopping the drive, a joystick, an altitude control, and the three buttons for the programmed destinations, with a small satellite-positioning screen that gave nav instructions.

Wolfe and Kristin loaded aboard the least-battered moke, lifted it out of the shed, and followed the screen's directions. The moke beeped if they tried to make any deviation from the preset course.

It grew colder the closer they got to the mountains, and clouds lowered. A wind spat flurries of snow into the cockpit. They were moving uphill, following a track that had been leveled some time ago by earth-moving machinery, curving between trees, storm-twisted evergreens with hand-size leaves.

"We're not going to make it before nightfall," Wolfe said. "Let's start looking for the least dismal place to camp."

A creek crashed over rocks not far from the trail, near a downed tree and a cluster of rocks that would serve for a windbreak. They grounded the moke and lifted out their packs. Wolfe used the plas to form another tent with the downed tree as a back, and Kristin spread the blankets. He found dead branches for a fire, piled them high, and sparked them into smoky life with his blaster on low.

"What do you want to eat?" he asked. "Stew, featuring the ever-popular mystery meat, or seven-bean cassoulet?"

"Let's go with the stew," Kristin said. "The tent's too small to chance the cassoulet."

Wolfe set out two mealpaks, then opened the improvised pack that held the Lumina. "I'd like to try something," he said, "and I need a lab rat."

"Charming way to put it," Kristin said, sitting cross-legged on the blanket. "And I can't say I care for doing anything with *that*."

"Why not? It's just a tool that was built by some weird-looking folks."

"There's too much blood—too much strangeness about it," Kristin said. "But go ahead. What are you going to try to do?"

"I won't tell you—I don't want to suggest anything. But whatever you feel like doing—try not to do it."

Joshua knelt, set the Lumina in front of him, and breathed deeply, slowly, for several minutes. Then his breathing came quickly, and his hands came out, palms up.

The gray, nondescript stone flamed to life.

Wolfe's fingers curled, and the heels of his hands touched. Kristin started to get up, then sank back. She moved once more, returning to her cross-legged position as Wolfe's breath exploded out.

"No," he said. "It didn't work."

"You wanted me to get up, and go out to the lifter, right?"

"I did."

"Why didn't the Lumina make me do it? You've used it to kill people. Why did it fail on something simple?"

"I don't know." Wolfe thought about it. "Maybe because you're close to me—maybe because you're strong-willed. Or maybe I didn't have a gut-drive to make you do something."

"So you're not an Al'ar," Kristin said.

"No."

The thought flashed:

Not yet. Wolfe thought—hoped—he felt relief. "All right," he said. "Once more. Think of something. Anything."

Kristin closed her eyes and was silent. Wolfe began breathing rhythmically once more.

His breath pattern stopped.

"A black tube," he said. "With something white, reflecting at the top. Some sort of industrial tool?"

"I'd give that one a close, but lousy on the interpretation. I was thinking about that formal you bought for me, back on Rogan's World, that I never had a chance to wear. With pearls."

Wolfe looked at her for a long time. "When—if—we

get a chance, I'll get you some more pearls. And take you somewhere you can wear them."

The dusk shattered in a scream, and Wolfe and Kristin rolled out of the shelter, guns ready.

A creature slashed madly at the ground, three yards on the other side of the moke. It was about twelve feet long, moved on four legs, and was almost Wolfe's height at the shoulder. It had long, dark brown hair, with two arms ending in scoop-shaped claws. It had no neck, and its skull was set close into its shoulders, with red, glaring eyes and dark incisors lining a circular mouth.

Kristin was kneeling, aiming, pistol butt cradled in her left palm, elbow on her knee as the monster screamed again, stumbled toward them, reared, claws stretching.

"Wait," Wolfe said, his voice calm.

Reach . . . *nothing is here . . . calm . . . peace . . . not-prey . . . not enemy . . . soft wind . . . not harm . . .*

The beast roared again, but this time not as loudly.

Calm . . . not-prey . . . not enemy . . . wind . . . full belly . . . not-thirst . . . not-hunger . . .

The creature stood still for an instant, then turned, and, unhurriedly, shambled away.

Kristin let out her breath, lowered her gun. "Now why did *that* work?"

"Let's add another guess," Wolfe said. "Fear is an excellent motivator."

"Let's see if you're still at peak drive," Kristin said. "Read my mind now."

Wolfe began to breathe, then a smile came. "I got the signal perfectly." He came toward her, lifted her in his arms, and carried her back into the tent. "It didn't hurt that you were playing with the slider on your shipsuit," he said.

"I'm still transmitting," Kristin said throatily. "Do you know how I want to love you?"

THE DARKNESS OF GOD

Her hands reached for his suit fastener and pulled it down; her head came forward and she took him in her mouth.

*

Early the next morning, they reached Graveyard.

* CHAPTER NINE *

EMERGENCY BULLETIN
LANCET, EDINBURGH, SCOTLAND, EARTH

A new, **highly infectious**, almost **invariably fatal** disease has been reported on several worlds at the fringes of the Federation and appears to be spreading rapidly with no discovered means of transmission.

SYMPTOMS AND SIGNS

The incubation period is unknown. The onset is very rapid, beginning with **intense pain** and a **high fever**, spiking as high as 106–109 degrees Fahrenheit. The pulse is rapid and thready and hypotension occurs. Almost immediate **inflammation** of the entire skin occurs, accompanied by **delirium**, **confusion**, and **incoordination**. The secondary stage of the disease produces what appear similar to **deep burns**, with destruction of the epidermis and dermis over the entire body. Unusually, the common loss of feeling accompanying deep burns never occurs, and **pain** continues to grow to an intolerable pitch. Patient will enter advanced shock almost immediately, while disease continues to destroy tissue. Death generally follows within one to two hours after the first symptoms are noted.

THE DARKNESS OF GOD

DIAGNOSIS

No recoveries known from full onset of disease. The few survivors evinced only beginning signs of the disease which then disappeared without any treatment. Current fatality estimates: Over 99%.

ETIOLOGY

Unknown.

EPIDEMIOLOGY

Unknown.

TRANSMISSION

Unknown. Disease seems to strike at random. Two reports, which cannot be taken as believable, suggest those who had contact with the Al'ar or who have "psychic abilities" (phrase not admitted as meaningful) are most at risk.

TREATMENT

None reported as effective. Patient should be treated for extreme shock and given standard third-degree burn treatments. Beyond that, treatment is symptomatic.

WARNING WARNING WARNING WARNING

This disease is highly contagious, with no known cure, and few reported recoveries. Patients should be isolated, as should medical teams involved with their treatment. Any information suggesting effective diagnosis or treatment should be immediately communicated with this station. To prevent possible panic, this information should be regarded as **highly secret** and should not be given to the general public or media.

* CHAPTER TEN *

The canyon was a deep vee-notch, with bluffs towering overhead. There were half a dozen mine entrances cut into the walls, high rectangles. Around each were scattered outbuildings.

There was a mine not far distant from the track, and as the moke slid past, a long line of ore cars slid out, controlled by a miner in a tiny overhead gravsled.

Kristin waved, but the man had no response until he realized what he was looking at. Then he waved back frantically, almost tipping over the 'sled.

"It appears," Joshua said, "that Graveyard's male-female ratio's about normal for the outback. What a place to settle down, Kristin. Total adulation until somebody gets drunk or jealous and grabs for a gun."

They rounded a corner, and Graveyard spread below them. There was one central street, with a dozen dirt ruts radiating off it. Buildings, mostly prefab, dotted the canyon's floor and walls; rocky outcroppings covered with dirty snow lay between them. Above the town were large, two-story buildings.

"Superintendents' quarters," Joshua said. "Looks like things have gotten prosperous enough to have absentee owners."

"How do you know?"

"If they were palaces, the owners'd be here. Hired help never gets mansions."

"You've been on worlds like this."

"I've been on worlds like this," Wolfe agreed.

There was a hand-lettered sign:

GRAVEYARD
POP. 400

Someone had crossed out the population, and scrawled in:

500 and still booming!!

A man sat against the sign. One hand was propped up with a stake, and there was an ace of spades pinned to his open palm.

There was a fist-sized hole in his chest.

Joshua lifted an eyebrow but didn't say anything. He drove the moke down the central street at quarter speed, eyeing the buildings. Some appeared to be residences, others had signs: HARDWARE, EXPLOSIVES, COMPUTERS, GROCERIES, DRY GOODS, ASSAYERS, GALACTIC COMMUNICATIONS. There were other, larger signs: THE BIG STRIKE, HAMMAH'S HANGOUT, THE DEW DROP INN. Others were operated by those with less imagination or a more direct approach: GIRLS. ALK. GAMBLING.

They passed a small building with a very neat sign on it:

First Church of Christ, Lutheran

Pastor Tony Stoutenburg

"First Find Peace in Your Heart, Then Give It to Others."

"Now there," Joshua said, "is the loneliest man in Graveyard." Kristin smiled briefly.

There was one ornate building on the street. It had started life as several modular shelters stacked and butted end-to-end, then workers had laboriously planed the twisted wood of Ak-Mechat into siding and fastened it into place. Others had cast and painted dragon heads from plas, and fastened them to the upper cornices.

There was a neat sign:

THE SARATOGA

Proprietor: Richard Canfield

On its porch, seemingly oblivious to the cold, was a tall, slender man with immaculate shoulder-length blond hair. He wore brown, formal-looking clothes, tucked into knee-high boots. Gems glittered at his cuffs, fingers, and one earlobe.

Wolfe raised a hand.

The man eyed Wolfe, nodded in return, and went back into the Saratoga.

"You know him?"

"I know who he is. And what he is. I was rendering professional courtesy."

"Canfield? And a gambler?"

"Sharp, lady. Very sharp."

Wolfe hesitated, then swung the controls of the moke around and grounded the machine in front of the Saratoga. "This'll likely be the center of things," he said. "Maybe a little bit safer than renting a hovel on some backstreet. You go register, and I'll find out where to get rid of this beast."

"Which brings up a question," Kristin said. "What name do I register under?"

"Our own, of course," Wolfe said. "Honest folk like us have nothing to hide."

*

The room was fairly large, with a big bed, furniture that'd been antiqued with a blowtorch, and fake wood paneling. There were photographs on the walls, not holos, of ancient Earth scenes.

"You won't believe what this room costs," Kristin said.

"Sure I would," Joshua said. "When you're the only game in town you set your own prices. Plus it's warm, dry, and better than a cribhouse. Just what a horny miner who's got more credits than sense wants when he gets paid. Or, since there's still some freelancers working the hills, when he thinks he's found something out there in the rocks."

Kristin looked skeptical, bounced on the bed. "At least it doesn't squeak," she agreed.

"Fine. I don't believe in advertising," Joshua said.

"Now what?"

"Now we start whining for help."

*

"An open com line to where?" the small man with the large beak asked.

"I'll make the connection," Wolfe said.

"I can't allow that."

Wolfe dropped another bill on the counter. Then a second.

"All right," the man said. "Go in that booth there. I'll cut the controls through to you."

"No," Wolfe said. "I want you to take a walk with my friend here. Show her some of the sights of Graveyard."

"That's against corporate regulations!"

"I know you wouldn't dream of eavesdropping, but I'm a *very* private man," Wolfe said. Three more bills fluttered down. The man put out a finger, touched them.

"For how long?"

"Not long," Wolfe said. "I'll go looking for you when I'm finished."

*

"You've been out of touch for a while," the distorted voice said from half a galaxy distant.

"Been busy."

"So I gather," the voice said. "Don't know if I should be talking to you."

"Oh?"

There was nothing but star-hum for a bit.

"All right," the voice said reluctantly. "I didn't get where I am by picking sides. FI would like to talk to you, real bad. And I don't mean with you as a free agent."

"That's a known."

"Did you know they've put the word out that anybody who grabs you and delivers you to Cisco or one of his bottom-feeders will get absolution? Alive only, which I suppose is a blessing."

"I didn't. Am I hot publicly?"

"Not yet. But sooner or later some bravo'll open his mouth to the law."

"Of course. You thinking about collecting?"

There was a blurt of static.

"Come on, Wolfe. I've seen what happens when somebody decides to pin your hide to the wall. I'm not an operator anymore, either. I just sit here and put people in touch with people they'd like to do business with."

"Good," Wolfe said. "I don't like dealing with ambitious folks."

"What do you need?" the voice asked. "And what's in it for me?"

"I need a ship. Clean, fast, armed if possible."

"How much you willing to pay?"

"Once I've got the ship—whatever the price tag is."

"Once you've got the ship—come *on,* Wolfe. Once I've won the Federation lottery I can afford to buy a ticket. Ships are expensive."

"They didn't used to be."

"You didn't use to be Federation Intelligence's poster boy, either."

"All right," Wolfe said grudgingly. "I'll hunt elsewhere."

"No," the voice said. "I didn't say I couldn't get you one. But since it doesn't sound like you're sitting on barrels of credits right now, we'll have to find another way of payment."

"That's what I told somebody not too long ago," Wolfe said. "So what's the tag?"

"Now we're doing business," the voice said. "Let me consider a couple offers I've got lying around."

The voice went away. After a while it came back.

"There's this official on a certain world who seems to think he's a minor deity. Some people I know would like him to discover the joys of disembodiment and see what he's like in a new incarnation."

Wolfe took a deep breath. "I don't have much choice."

"Good. This one won't be . . . Wait a second. Cancel the above, my friend. I've got something a whole lot better. And it won't mess with any morals you have left. The bodies shouldn't start bouncing until you're well out of town."

"What is it?"

"Very simple. I've got a package—or rather some people I know have a package. They want it delivered to some people on another world."

"What's the catch? Seems there's always enough hotrods around for courier runs," Wolfe said.

"The package itself is hot—in both old-fashioned

senses of the word. And the ship-driver I'm going to use I have—some small questions about. He may or may not have done me wrong a couple of years ago, so I want somebody I can trust with him." The voice paused. "Oh yeah. The people it's going to are also warmish."

"Break it down, man."

"Fine. I've got twenty-five pounds of fissionable material somebody on World A wants taken back to his, her, or their Old Sentimental Home, so a group of people who call themselves Fighters for Victory can build a little bitty bomb."

Star-hum.

"You interested?"

"I'll do it."

"Good man. I assume you'll have some specifications about being picked up, wherever you are, since you never were a trusting soul."

"I will."

"Nice to be partners again, Joshua."

*

Wolfe let the little man have his office back. He seemed grateful, scurrying about like a chipmunk making sure his grain hadn't been discovered. Joshua looked for Kristin, found her down the street, talking to a medium-size cheerful man with a neatly trimmed beard.

"Joshua, this is Pastor—it is Pastor, right?—Stoutenburg. Joshua Wolfe."

"Honored," Wolfe said. "Not sure I've met many ministers in my life."

"We seem to be a declining breed," Stoutenburg admitted. "Christianity's a little old-fashioned and slow these days. But at least I'm not as extinct as priests."

Wolfe inclined his head and didn't open the argument.

"Pastor Stoutenburg—Tony—has been giving me the history of Graveyard."

"Such as it is," Stoutenburg said. "It can be summed up pretty briefly: Find minerals, dig minerals, use credits to look for new sins."

"Has anybody had any success?" Joshua asked. "With the sins, I mean."

"Not that I'm aware of," the preacher said. "But they seem fairly content recycling the old ones."

"Are you making any headway?"

Stoutenburg shrugged. "I'm not looking for rice Christians, but I think I'm getting a few more folks at my services every week." He grinned. "Since we're on an Earth seven-day week, twenty-two-hour day here, I refuse to believe the reason is I'm the only place where you can come down on a Sunday morning without having to pay for quiet."

"What's the town like?" Kristin asked.

"Really? Seven hundred to a thousand people, everyone dependent on the mines. There are, so far, half a dozen major veins of stellite. Most everyone except for me spends good weather wandering the hills looking for more, and the possibilities of success are good. It appears most people think riches are either here or right around the corner, so why not spend it like they already have it. I won't grant Graveyard the honor of calling it Satan's favorite resort—we're not big enough or decadent enough for that yet—but there's a sufficiency of people building its reputation." Stoutenburg nodded with his chin. "Here's one of our finest boosters."

Wolfe turned and saw Canfield strolling toward them. Ten feet behind him were a very large man with a shaven head and an angry expression and a medium-size man clad in all gray. Both openly wore holstered pistols. Wolfe noted with interest the guns were heavy current-issue Federation military blasters.

"Morning, Father," Canfield said. "Who're your friends?"

Joshua introduced himself and Kristin.

"I don't suppose," Stoutenburg said, "that it makes any difference to remind you I'm not a priest, Canfield. Father doesn't apply."

"Sorry . . . Father. It's easy to forget." Canfield eyed Wolfe. "So you're a guest at my establishment—and talking to the representative of the other half. Trying to copper your bets, Mister Wolfe?"

"No," Joshua said. "It was figured out a long time ago which way I'm intended."

"Which is?"

Joshua smiled blandly. Canfield looked puzzled, then smiled in return.

"Are you planning on settling here in Graveyard?" he asked.

"We're just passing through."

"Ah," Canfield said. "Well, may your stay be a successful one." He inclined his head to Kristin, then moved on.

"I wonder if he'll ever figure out that we're all just passing through," Stoutenburg said gently.

"Probably not," Joshua said. "His kind take their markers far too seriously."

*

They were just finishing dinner when the shouting started in the nearby gaming rooms: "Cheat . . . Bastard double-counter . . . Goddamned rayfield scummek . . ." Kristin swiveled; Joshua managed to watch out of the corner of his eye, still appearing disinterested.

Three men dragged a fourth out the casino entrance. One wore the green eyeshade of a croupier; the other two were the gray man and the shaven-headed behemoth who'd accompanied Canfield. The fourth wore the high plas boots of a miner and a clean, patched shirt and pants.

The miner broke free at the door and swung at the croupier. The man in gray struck him down from behind with an edged hand, and the big man kicked him hard six times. Now he had a broad smile on his face.

"Joshua! Do something," Kristin hissed.

"No. Wrong time to play Samaritan."

The big man stopped, walked around the miner, aimed carefully, and sent his boot crashing into the side of the man's head. The impact sounded mushy, as if bone had already been broken.

The other two picked up the motionless miner, pushed the outer door open, and threw him out into the street.

The big man swaggered back through the dining room, looking at each table, each diner. No one held his gaze for more than a moment. He stopped at Joshua and Kristin's table, and glowered at them. Joshua felt Kristin's hand slide to her waist, where her gun was hidden. Wolfe stared back at the big man, his face calm.

The man blinked, jerked his gaze away, and went back into the casino, the other two behind him.

"Poor planning," Wolfe said as he picked up the dessert menu.

"Why? What?"

"A good gambling hell always has a back door," he said.

*

Kristin said her appetite was ruined, so Wolfe called for the check and signed it. They started out.

"Wait," Wolfe said. "Let's look in the other room."

Kristin started to object, then closed her mouth, followed him.

There were dice tables, a line of gambling machines, several green-topped tables where men with false smiles and quick hands waited. Canfield leaned against the bar in the back. He saw Wolfe and came to him.

"I'm surprised you haven't come in looking for action before," he said.

"I'm afraid you misjudge me," Joshua said. "I'm not a gambling man."

Canfield looked surprised, then recovered. "Perhaps your lady?"

"She tried it once, but got bored with always winning," Wolfe said.

Canfield smiled coldly, nodded, and returned to the bar.

"I'm afraid I misspoke," Wolfe murmured. "Playing at his tables would hardly be considered gambling."

*

"I'm a little angry with you," Kristin said.

"I know," Joshua said. "But we've got enough problems without taking on somebody else's. Besides, the Canfields are self-eliminating."

Kristin climbed into bed, shut off her lamp, and rolled over with her back to Joshua.

*

Joshua was already dressed when Kristin woke.

"Joshua," she said softly. "I was wrong last night. We *do* have enough troubles of our own. Don't be mad at me."

Wolfe came over, sat down on the bed. "Funny, *I* was just going to apologize for last night. And I'm never mad at you." He kissed her. "I've just got some people I want to talk to. I've decided we need something to keep our minds busy until the ship gets here. So I'll meet you for lunch."

He kissed her again, and she pulled the covers away. "Now, don't do that," he said. "Or I'll never get out of here."

"Would that be a bad thing?" she asked, her voice silky.

"As I said before, I refuse to get involved in theological disputes."

*

Wolfe buzzed their room and asked Kristin if she wanted to meet him in the dining room.

As she crossed the lobby, Canfield approached her. "Mrs. Wolfe . . ."

"The name is just Kristin," she said.

"Kristin, then. I wanted to make sure I—or anyone else at the Saratoga—haven't done anything to upset either of you."

"What makes you think we're angry?" Kristin asked, realizing with amusement she was echoing Wolfe's words.

"Well, I thought I recognized your friend as being one who's of the sporting sort. I was wondering why he refused my invitation to join us at the tables, and wanted to make sure nothing was amiss."

"Nothing's wrong, Mister Canfield. Perhaps Mister Wolfe just isn't sure you can cover the size of his bets."

Canfield flushed, stammered. Kristin bowed and went on into the dining room.

Joshua rose, kissed her as he held a chair out. "I saw you chatting with Canfield."

"I was. He wanted to know if we were miffed at him."

"Miffed? No, we're not miffed," Joshua said. "He's upset because we didn't stumble into his thimbleriggery?"

"I assume that means a fixed game?"

"It does."

"Well, then . . ."

Joshua laughed when Kristin told him what she'd said to Canfield. "That must have tweaked him a little. By the way, some of the people I talked to said Canfield's not only got the Saratoga, but runs the games in three other places. Your friend Tony was right—he's hell-bent, pun possibly intended, on running this town. He also seems to have an interest in a couple of the bordellos, and owns a lot of the open property around Graveyard. And he buys any high-grade stellite that happens to come his way. For about thirty-five percent of the market value. The assay office pays sixty percent. But Canfield doesn't ask where you got it."

"What's stellite?" Kristin asked.

"Interesting metal," Wolfe said. "Kind of pretty. Light purple in its natural state. High heat application can change the color to a dozen or more different shades. Corrosion-, wear-, stress-, and heat-resistant, very light-weight, so it's used for internal stardrive controls and other delicate, high-stress applications. Or machined, worked, and polished, it can be jewelry. Ultra-expensive. As I said, you've led a sheltered life, m'dear. If you'd seen the holos of the rich and insipid, you surely would've seen examples of it dangling hither and yon."

"I've never been interested in yons," Kristin said. "Especially on the rich. So Canfield is the boss of this town?"

"Not quite yet," Wolfe said. "He'll need to own a mine or two before he can rename Graveyard. But he's working on it. Now, let's eat, for I've got to meet a man after lunch."

"I want to come with you."

"Sorry. I love you enormously. But this one's way too dirty for you. In the literal sense.

"What's the matter?"

Kristin was staring at him. "You never used the word 'love' before."

Joshua met her eyes, then looked down at the menu. "That's right," he said after a while. "I haven't, have I."

THE DARKNESS OF GOD

*

Wolfe left the main street, hiking up a rutted sidetrack toward one of the mines. He appeared not to notice a medium-size man in gray following him from a distance.

There was no fence, no guard around the mine. He sauntered toward the yawning high-roofed horizontal main shaft. A man wearing a white safety helmet spotted him. "Hey!"

Wolfe walked to him.

"What's your business?"

"Looking for a man named Nectan."

"He's down th' hole. I'm Redruth, th' super. You ain't workin' for me, you ain't here. And you sure ain't goin' down. Too damned dangerous."

"What happens when the owner comes to visit?"

"Huh?"

"Doesn't he have friends? Don't they get to see what's making him rich?"

"That's different!"

Wolfe extended a bill. "Think of me as a friend."

Redruth considered it, shook his head. "Naw. Too damned dangerous."

Another bill joined the first, then a third.

"You get killed, it's your ass."

"I get killed, shove me up a drift, drop the ceiling, and swear you never saw me," Joshua said.

Redruth grinned. "Get a helmet an' ear protection from the toolman over in that shed. There'll be a lift goin' down in twenty minutes or so."

Joshua nodded his thanks.

The man in gray watched from a distance.

*

The lift floated close to the high ceiling. The driver leaned back.

"You ever been in a workin' mine afore?"

"Not stellite. And not this big."

" 'Kay. Thisun's a good 'un," the driver said. "No wood on th' planet t' speak of, so they pitpropped with metal, so it's safer'n your house." A chain of ore cars rumbled past below, a man in a sled controlling it from above, and the two sleds slid past, almost bumping.

"Now's th' fun part," the man shouted, and Wolfe's stomach moaned as the sled suddenly fell, straight down an absolutely vertical shaft.

"We bet on who c'n go down th' fastest," the miner bellowed at Wolfe, apparently paying no attention to his controls.

"Let's lose this one," Joshua shouted back.

"What?"

"Never mind!"

The miner pushed a stick forward, and the lift slammed to a stop. Joshua's guts didn't.

Breathe . . . breathe . . .

"That was interesting," he shouted as a new noise grew around them.

"Yer all right, Mister. Most tourists puke f'r half an hour, I pull that on 'em."

"I used to run a roller coaster in another life," Wolfe said.

"What?"

"Never mind."

The sled floated down another passageway as deep as the one far above them. Machines growled and groaned around them, seemingly without human control. Joshua spotted a few men here and there, keyboardlike control panels hung around their necks. Then the lift driver grounded the sled near a passage that led sharply upward.

"G'wan up th' slope to the face," the miner shouted. "Nectan's up there, likely. I'll wait here. Don't want t' get too close. I'm what they call claustrophobic."

THE DARKNESS OF GOD

*

A long conveyor belt almost filled the shaft, and chunks of rock bounced along it toward the main passage. The air was hot and smelled of machine oil and ozone. In spite of the earmuffs, the grinding scream tore at Wolfe's hearing. At the end of the belt was a square machine with a metal-framed clear operator's cage on the side. The screeching stopped for an instant, the machine moved forward an inch or two on wide tracks, and the worm began tearing at the rock again. Wolfe climbed onto the machine's body, carefully made his way to the back of the cage, waited until the grinding stopped, then crashed his fist against the back of the cab.

A dirty face turned, eyes gaped in surprise, and the machine's howl lowered. The operator opened the door, motioned Wolfe inside.

There was a tiny seat beside the operator's station, and Wolfe sat. The man closed the door, and there was almost complete silence.

He grinned at Wolfe's expression. "Like night 'n' day, don't it be? An' there's real air t' suck on."

Wolfe nodded.

"So who th' hells're thou?"

"Joshua Wolfe."

"I assume thou has business."

"I do, Mister Nectan. I want to talk about the time you let a man named Canfield bankroll your prospecting."

Nectan shook his head.

"Nay, nay. I learned m' lesson well. No need t' repeat it."

"Left arm," Joshua said. "Broken in two places. Lost most of your teeth on one side. Four broken ribs."

"An' still don't sleep right of a night," Nectan said. "So thou can be well outta here, an' tell Canfield I said I'd naught speak, an' I'm a man of m' word."

Wolfe looked at him, and Nectan started to get angry. He glared at Wolfe, then the anger faded from his face.

Wolfe was breathing slowly, regularly.

"Who're you—I mean, who're you with?"

"I'm with me," Wolfe said. "I collect all sorts of interesting facts. Sometimes I put them to use."

"M' da always said I was born a fool an' I'd likely die one, t' boot," Nectan grumbled. "All right. You ask. I'll answer. An' th' only reason I'm doin' it is 'cause I hope one day Canfield reaches for something that's way beyond him."

*

The man in gray watched Joshua Wolfe walk away from the mine, back toward Graveyard, and went after him.

The road wound down, through huge boulders, high piles of spoil. The wind was cold this high above the canyon floor, and the man pulled his coat tighter about his shoulders as he hurried downward. He came around a bend, saw the empty track in front of him, and swore. Wolfe must've started running.

He broke into a trot, then heard a metallic *snick* behind him. The man skidded to a stop, almost falling. He lifted his arms away from his body very slowly.

"Good," Joshua approved. "Thought you'd recognize a safety going off."

He walked forward, fished the man's pistol from its holster. "Nice choice of iron," he said. "Anderson Variport. Just like the Federation big boys carry. Now let's step over here where it's peaceful, and have a chat."

*

"How did you spend your day?" Joshua asked jovially.

"I went for a walk after you left," Kristin said. "And I ran into Tony—Pastor Stoutenburg."

"Uh-oh," Joshua said. "You've got to watch those men of the cloth. First you're praying together, then—then they come up with strange ideas like marriage. Be careful."

"I'm careful, you loon," Kristin said. "He was going out looking for funds—"

"Begging."

"All right, begging. I asked if I could go with him. He said he'd rather I didn't, that he was going into the bars, and I might be misunderstood. I said I could handle things, and he said I could go."

"How did you do?"

Kristin flushed. "All right."

"What's all right?"

She looked away, cheeks red. "Seven hundred and ninety-seven credits, and two IOUs."

"Good heavens."

"Plus six proposals of marriage, seven miners who wanted something else, and a woman in one of the girl-houses who wondered if I was looking for a job."

"Twice good heavens. What a productive morning. It looks like you've found a real home here in Graveyard."

"Tony said he would've thought he was lucky if he'd made fifty credits," Kristin said.

"There's nothing like good works," Joshua said.

Kristin noticed Joshua was wearing a gun. Not the small pistol she knew he had tucked out of sight in his belt, but a large, heavy military blaster worn on an equally military-looking weapons belt. "What's that for? Are we expecting trouble?"

"I *always* expect trouble. I decided I needed to be a little more open in my habits. And somebody I met this afternoon decided to give this to me."

"Where did you go?"

"To chat with a miner. Fascinating line of work. I may take it up as soon as hell gets a nice ice-frosting."

"About Canfield?"

"About Canfield. And then I had another little talk with one of his men—that charmer in gray who helped Canfield's main bully the other night, who used the name Saratov. The bald goon's chosen name in these parts, by the way, is Brakbone. Delightful folks around here, I must say."

"Joshua, what are you doing? Why are you doing this?"

"I got bored," Wolfe said. "And Mister Canfield irritates me."

"How did you get the man in gray to talk to you?"

"I exerted charm and lovability."

"What's he going to tell Canfield?"

"I seriously doubt," Wolfe said, "if he'll be communicating anything of import within our lifetimes. Now, is there anything on the wine list that's dated in years instead of days of the week?"

*

Kristin woke to the soft thump of Wolfe's bare feet hitting the floor, then saw him silhouetted against the open window, naked, with his pistol ready. Her own reflexes cut in, and she was crouched beside the bed, pistol ready.

"I heard shots," Wolfe said. "Two of them." He cautiously peered through the window. "Lights, about a block down," he said. "Other people heard them as well."

The bedside lamp flickered on, and Wolfe started dressing.

"What're you doing?"

"Involving myself in other people's business."

"Why?"

"To redeem myself in your eyes and esteem."

Before she could decide whether to laugh or worry, Wolfe had his boots and coat on, and was at the door. He buckled his gun belt on.

"Join me if you want. I think this is going to be interesting. The pot may have boiled before I put it on the fire."

*

Ten minutes later Kristin was dressed and in the street. So was half the population of Graveyard. They were crowded around a small semicircular hut just off the central street. The door stood open, and, as she approached, two men dragged out a third, whose head was lolling.

Kristin heard him muttering: "Di'n't do it . . . di'n't do nothin' . . . jus' wan'ed sleep . . . had a li'l too much t' drink . . . mad at Raff, wan'd t' sleep it off . . . woke up an' he was dead . . ."

Somebody shouted, "Lock him up in the assayer's vault."

Someone else bellowed, "Why waste th' time? He blew off Raff . . . do th' same with him! Right here, right now!"

There were yells of agreement, but the two men bulled through the crowd without yielding.

Canfield stood near the door to the hut.

"Come on, boys," he shouted. "Settle down! Killing Steadman won't bring del Valle back, now will it? Come on, now. Drinks are on me! Let's give old Raff a proper sendoff!"

The crowd clamored approval, streamed toward the Saratoga.

Kristin saw Wolfe walk up to Canfield and ask him something. Canfield frowned, snapped a retort. Wolfe stood there, waiting. Canfield grimaced, then nodded his head. Wolfe went into the hut.

Canfield hurried after the crowd, but Kristin followed Wolfe.

There was a body sprawled on the floor to the right of the entrance. A man with a medical hardcase was bent over the corpse, and there were three kibitzers. He stood. "One shot. Took del Valle just below the sternum. Death would have been almost instantaneous." He clucked. "Amazing Steadman could shoot that straight, as inebriated as he appears."

"A minute of your time, Doctor?"

The man surveyed Joshua.

"And who're you?"

"Someone who's curious."

"Go on to the bar with the others. I'd as soon not go through the gore more'n half a dozen times. And I need a drink."

"As a favor, Doctor."

The man looked angry, then, as Wolfe held his eyes, his face softened. "You're new," he said. "Anything to do with any kind of law?"

"Not for a while," Wolfe said.

"That's a pity. We could use some around here. All right. Hell, I probably need to rehearse what I'll tell those drunk yahoos anyway. The dead man's Raff del Valle. Exploratory geologist and miner. Highly respected. Which means he found two mines, made a mint, and let everybody help him drink it away. Didn't bother him—he said he liked looking for it as much as finding it. Maybe more, because he was sober then, and he had a temper when he set to drinking.

"The guy who shot him's Lef Steadman. He picked Raff up out of the gutter, moved him into his hooch here, bankrolled him for his last *Wanderjahr* looking for traces, and was his partner. Fifty-fifty split, I heard, expenses off the top. Del Valle came back three days ago happier'n a pig in shit, which meant he'd found something.

"Or thought he had. Anyway, he started drinking, and he and Steadman had a series of arguments. They didn't get loud, so nobody knew what they were about. Probably one of 'em wanted to change the split, assuming del Valle got lucky for a third time. Anyway, things finally broke down to a shouting match at the Big Strike, and Steadman stomped out, swearing he was going to hammer Raff the next time he saw him.

"Pretty obvious what happened. Del Valle must've not thought Steadman was serious and come back here with a skinful. Came in the door, and saw Steadman laying for him. He had time to get a shot off—which drilled a hole over by that window—then Steadman put him in his meat locker. Simple enough. Now all we've got to do is figure what to do about Steadman."

"What're the choices?" Wolfe asked.

"Either he gets lynched, which is the odds-on favorite, 'cause Raff was a popular lush, as I said. Or else somebody takes pity and busts Steadman out and he makes tracks for Lucky Cuss or Grand Central, and tries to get offplanet before somebody with a grudge happens to run into him."

The man shrugged.

"I'd go seventy-thirty. Against."

Wolfe's lips quirked. "I'll take a hundred of that."

The man looked surprised. "Why?"

"Let's say—I like the long shots."

The doctor smiled. "Why not? Give me a chance to even up what I owe Canfield. Jung—Nyere—you heard him. You're . . ."

"Wolfe. Joshua Wolfe. You can find me at the Saratoga."

The other two men nodded understanding.

"Good," the doctor said. "Now, if you two'll give me a hand with the body, I'll lock up here."

"If it's no bother," Wolfe said, "I'll take care of that for you, and turn the key over to Canfield."

"You playing detective?" The doctor didn't wait for a response. "Surely. Why not. Give Steadman a chance. A man ought to go down with all his colors flying. Come on, boys. Let's get the stiff on ice. I'm real thirsty."

Kristin waited until the three had left, half dragging the corpse. "So you don't think it happened that way?"

"Don't think. Know."

"How? Through the Lumina?"

"No. Pure common sense. Look around."

Kristin calmed herself and tried to breathe the way she remembered Wolfe doing, tried to blank her mind and turn it into a receptor.

The building was about ten by forty feet. The main room took up most of that. To the rear on the right was a closed door Kristin assumed hid the fresher, and on the left a divider that marked off the cooking area.

There was one door, and three windows, one larger one on the side where del Valle's body had lain, two smaller ones on the other side. There wasn't much furniture—two chests, one open wardrobe crudely made from shipping crates, two beds, two improvised desks. There were two boxes holding books and fiches by each bed, and a larger box with a lid at the foot of each bed.

Kristin looked at the titles. One held *Elements of Geology*, *Mineral Analysis*, *Field Guide to Ak-Mechat*, other geological titles and, incongruously, Burton's multivolume *A Thousand Nights and One Night*. The other bookcase contained books with titles such as *Million-Credit Thinking*, *Turn Yourself into a Money Machine*, and *Self-Improvement Through Riches*.

"Just from their reading matter," she said, "he's guilty as blazes."

Wolfe chuckled from where he was quickly rummaging through del Valle's box of papers. "Did you find anything that looks official? Like maybe a land claim?"

"No. Do you want me to go through this box? It'll probably have his papers."

Wolfe crossed to it, quickly sifted through the few papers and fiches that defined Steadman's life. "Nothing here, either," he said. "And we're running short of time, I think. I can smell a lynch mob in the building. Look at this." He held out a pistol. "This is Steadman's gun. It was lying on the floor. I picked it up in the confusion."

"Pretty standard," Kristin said. "A 12-mill-bell Remington-Colt."

"Take a sniff of the barrel."

Kristin obeyed. "Nothing."

"Like it maybe hasn't been fired for a while? Can't tell by the magazine, which is only half-charged. Now look at the setting."

"It's on wide aperture."

"Try to reset it."

Kristin pushed at the inset lever below the blaster's bell mouth. She grimaced. "Stuck. Evidently Steadman didn't trust his ability at snap-shooting—and didn't clean his gun very often."

"Interesting observation," Wolfe said. "The way the story goes is del Valle came into the hut. He saw Steadman sitting behind his desk—there. Steadman had his pistol aimed, but he was drunk. Del Valle had time to draw, and shoot. He put a nice neat—notice, he *was* a marksman—hole over here by this window. Before he could correct his aim, Steadman dropped him. Then Steadman passed out until the crowd got here. Nice neat murder for profit, blown because the idiot had to get drunk before he had courage enough to kill Raff del Valle, and got himself too drunk."

"So they say," Kristin said.

"Uh-huh. And there's something else interesting about this window we really don't have time for. Come on. We've got to wake up the land office clerk."

*

Fortunately the clerk slept in a small apartment above his office. Wolfe bullied him into full consciousness, asked two questions and got sleepy, grumbled answers, and told the man to go back to sleep.

"Now, let's see what's going on at the Saratoga."

*

A slattern was draped over a bench outside the hotel, muttering, "Hangin's too good . . . hangin's too good . . ."

"I see the elite have already assessed the situation," Wolfe said. "Keep your gun ready."

They went inside.

The dining room and bar were full, and the harried barkeeps were simply giving bottles to anyone who asked. Two women who took their hair color and personality from a bottle were behind the beer taps, and the room was a shout of judgment.

A miner stood on top of the bar, shouting, "Dunno why we're all jus' talkin' . . . We know who done it, an' likely why, t' screw poor Raff outta his new claim . . . why wait?"

There was a roar of approval.

"We ain't got no courts anyhow," he finished in a surprisingly reasonable tone.

Canfield's bodyguard, Brakbone, leaped onto the bar. "He's right! Let's get this thing over with right now!"

"No!" someone cried out behind Joshua. "He's wrong!"

Wolfe—and the crowd—turned, and saw Stoutenburg at the entrance.

"Oh shit," somebody said in the silence. "Now we gotta get preached at."

There was laughter.

Stoutenburg ignored the comment, pushed his way through to the bar. "I know a lot of you—most of you— think I'm no more than some sort of nag. But the book I believe in says 'Judge not, lest you be judged.' Think about it for a minute, and don't pay any heed to whether Somebody greater than you said it that you maybe haven't learned to believe in it yet. Think about what would happen if you made a mistake—had too much to drink or smoke or 'ject, and you did something terrible. Would you want somebody deciding what to do with your life right then, in the heat of passion? Especially if they'd been drinking, smoking, or whatever? Shouldn't a man's life be considered in calmness, sobriety?"

"Naw," somebody shouted. "Di'n't somebody say you get a jury of your peers? Ol' Lef, he got messed up an' kilt Raff, so we got messed up an' now we're gonna kill him. Ain't that justice?"

The mob, enjoying itself, roared with laughter.

Stoutenburg flushed, held his anger back.

"Come on, Tony," Canfield said, coming out from behind the bar. "Father. We respect you for being honest, but nobody believes that old-fashioned stuff."

"Don't they?" Stoutenburg shouted.

Canfield pretended to survey the crowd.

"Doesn't look like it from here. Looks to me like everyone's pretty happy with the decision that's been reached. Except for maybe Steadman."

He waited until the laughter died.

"What do you want, Father? A trial?" His voice turned mocking. "The preacher wants a trial."

"That sounds very good," Canfield went on. "But just for openers, who'll defend Steadman? We've all got to live with each other come tomorrow morning."

"I don't," Wolfe said.

Silence grew, except for a drunk giggling in a corner. Wolfe walked to the bar, the sound of his bootheels very loud. "I don't," he said once more. "Let's have a trial. I'll defend Steadman."

"And who the blazes are you?" somebody shouted.

"Get the hell outta here," Brakbone snarled. "God-damned outsiders got no right to be talkin' anyway."

"Who made you an insider?" Wolfe asked. "Canfield imported you two months ago, and all of a sudden you're an original settler?"

Brakbone stepped back, suddenly unsure.

"All right," Canfield said loudly. "Let's have a trial. That'll make everything acceptable, won't it? I'll be the prosecutor. Joshua Wolfe here'll try to fake us out. But we know what the verdict'll be, don't we?"

There were shouts of agreement.

"Somebody fetch Steadman," someone yelled. "Man oughta get a fair hearing to his face before we kill him."

*

Lef Steadman was trembling like he had a fever, partially fear, partially the wake-up pill that he'd been fed that sobered him but also produced a hangover like the unoiled hinges of hell.

"Why're you doin' this?" he whispered to Wolfe.

"I'm a good citizen and your new best friend," Joshua said. "Now keep your damned mouth shut, no matter what, or I'll rip your windpipe out."

Canfield paced back and forth, clearly enjoying the situation. Kristin stood next to Stoutenburg. Wolfe noted with approval she had one hand inside her jacket, on her gun butt.

"We don't need to worry about oathing," Canfield said. "We can tell who's lying and who's not. Prosecution goes first. Get Doctor Nonhoff up here."

The doctor wasn't much soberer than the rest of the crowd by then, but he made his way through what he'd found, and what he thought had happened.

"Your witness," Canfield said.

"No questions."

"All right," Canfield said. "I guess the only other testimony we need is from Lef Steadman."

Steadman stood up, and somebody threw a bottle at him. It missed and smashed against the back of the bar.

"Hold it down," Canfield shouted. "Anything else like that and I'll close the bar!"

Steadman told his story. Yes, he was Raff del Valle's partner. Maybe former, after the argument last night. Yes, he'd put up the credits for him to go out on an exploratory survey looking for a new stellite vein on a fifty-fifty split if del Valle found something. He'd even let him live with him when he came back into Graveyard from the mountains.

Del Valle had come back boasting that he'd found something big, bigger than either of his other two strikes. Steadman had suggested they register the claim right away, but del Valle had said there was no hurry. He'd filled out the form papers, and they would take them to the land agent in the morning.

In the meantime, he was thirsty. So they started from bar to bar. Steadman kept arguing with the older man, begging him to get the registration filed, that he might get drunk and blab the location, and somebody would steal their claim.

"I was drinkin', but not as heavy as Raff, an' he lost his temper, like he does—did—when he's sweet as a peach.

He finally said he was goin' for me, an' I best clear out. I got out of whatever place we was drinkin' at, an' thought I'd best go back to th' hooch, an' get some sleep. I made it, an' remember losin' my guts outside. Thought I'd best sit up, try'n sober up some, so I wouldn't go an' puke in my blankets. I must'a passed out like that."

He stopped. There was silence.

"Then shoutin' sorta brought me to," he said, "an' there were all those people around, an' Raff was dead on the floor."

"Very nice," Canfield said. "I don't think diminished capability is much of a defense. If we even believe it. I think he was pretending to be as drunk as he was, setting up an alibi. Your witness, Wolfe."

"One question," Wolfe said. He took the Remington-Colt from his belt. "Is this yours?"

"I dunno," Steadman said. "Lemme have a look at it."

Wolfe gave it to Steadman, and a gun jumped into Brakbone's hand. Steadman yelped in panic.

"Don't worry," Joshua said. "It's defanged. Nice piece, by the way."

Brakbone growled, reholstered his pistol.

"Yeah. It's mine," Steadman said. "Had it around for a couple of years, only started carrying it a month or so ago. Sorry I had to look at it, but I ain't much of a pistoleer." He handed the weapon back to Joshua.

"No further questions," Wolfe said.

Steadman lifted his head, and there was black fear in his eyes.

"What kinda defense are you? You gonna let them just kill me?"

"Go sit down," Wolfe said. "And remember what I told you." Deliberately, he let his hand brush his gun butt. Steadman flinched and stumbled back to his chair.

"I think we've got enough," Wolfe said, and voices in the crowd echoed him: "Yeah. Kill the bastard!" "Shoot 'im!"

"Not quite yet," Wolfe said calmly. "Let's consider a couple of things. Start with the sequence of events. According to Doctor Nonhoff, Steadman was sitting at his desk when del Valle came in. He was drunker than a lord, so he would've had to have the pistol in his hand, waiting to assassinate his partner. But somehow he didn't shoot first. Del Valle hauled iron and, at about seven feet, put his bolt three feet away from Steadman, and punched a hole in the wall next to the window. Maybe he was drunker than Steadman by then. But that's still pretty crappy shooting.

"At that point Steadman came to enough to shoot del Valle quite accurately in midchest. A nice neat hole, according to Doctor Nonhoff. Anyone want to see Steadman's pistol? Here," Wolfe said, handing it to a burly miner. "You've been hollering for a lynching loud enough. Take a look at the gun."

The miner fumbled it in his hands. "It's a gun."

"Brilliant, sir," Wolfe said. "Notice it's set on wide aperture. To make the hole Doctor Nonhoff said it did, it should've been set on narrow. If Steadman had shot del Valle the way it's set now, it would've made a big wide messy crater, right? So reset it for me."

The man pushed the small lever, then pushed harder, his teeth set. "There! Damn thing felt like it was rusted solid!"

"Indeed," Wolfe said. "Does anyone but me think it's interesting that when I picked the gun up in Steadman's shack, it was on wide aperture? And remember he just said he wasn't much of what he called a pistoleer, so as a gunfighter he would've wanted a wide shotgun blast to have any hope of hitting anything. So what must've happened was he reset the aperture, shot del Valle, then reset it before he passed out."

There were mutters. Somebody said, "That's not enough."

"Another little thing," Wolfe said. "Pity that Remington-Colt's not a powder-burner, so this isn't that indicative either. But the pistol doesn't smell like it's been fired anytime since the Al'ar War to me."

"Like the man told you," Canfield said. "That *isn't* enough. If Brown here could've moved it once, someone could've moved it earlier."

"Yeah," Brakbone said. "Like him." He pointed to Joshua. "You're the on'y one said it was set on wide."

The crowd agreed, but not as loudly as before.

"Sure I could've changed it," Wolfe said. "But let's assume for the moment I didn't. Let's try another explanation for what happened. Del Valle made an ass of himself when he was drunk. Steadman got out of there, threw up, staggered into his hut, and passed out sitting at the desk. His gun ended up on the floor. Who knows how it got there. Maybe it got in his way and he yanked it out of his belt and dumped it on the floor; maybe it fell out when he was being dragged out after the shooting. He's passed out, so we can forget about him for the moment.

"Then del Valle shows up. He's drunk, too. But he's not so drunk he doesn't see somebody laying for him, somebody with a gun pointing through the side window. Somebody with a heavy Federation pistol that holds a nice, hot beam. Maybe something like this Anderson Vari-port." Wolfe slid the weapon he'd taken from Saratov out of its holster, then replaced it. "Nice piece. I've only seen one other like it since I've been in Graveyard. Del Valle draws, snaps a shot, misses. The man in the window doesn't."

"Bullcrap!" That came from one of the bartenders.

"If someone wants to go take a look at the shack from the outside," Wolfe went on, "he'll find there's jimmy marks on the window, enough to snap the lockbar and get the window open, so the iso-glass wouldn't mess up the shot. And there's a nice scrape on the left-hand side of the window, where someone might've braced a blaster to make sure he didn't need but one shot. That would've made the shooter right-handed."

Wolfe looked at Brakbone. "You're right-handed, aren't you? And you carry an Anderson."

"What the hell are you talking about?"

"Just making an observation." Wolfe paused. "This lawyering is thirsty stuff. Somebody pass me a beer."

There were a few laughs. One of the blowsy women drew a mug and leaned it across the bar. Wolfe drank heartily.

"Thanks," he said. "Here's something else. The paperwork. Steadman said del Valle wrote up the claim form. I just checked with the land office clerk, and del Valle hasn't filed anything in two years."

Canfield's expression flickered for an instant.

"I went through both their gear," Wolfe said. "I didn't find any claim."

"Steadman must be lying," Canfield said.

"Possibly. Murderers do things like that. Now here's something else. I've noticed a lot of people around here have a hobby of going out on the land every chance they get, and trying to see if they can strike it rich like del Valle did."

"Sure," a woman said. "On'y way you'll stop bein' a comp'ny fool or a wage slave."

"No question," Wolfe agreed. "And today I talked to a man who had another kind of hobby that was even more interesting. Seems he and his partner used to help any-body interested in prospecting. In the old days it used to be called grubstaking. These two loaned prospectors the credits, and all they wanted back was ten percent interest per week, plus five percent of the principal. If you didn't, or couldn't, pay, it could get somewhat painful, I was told."

Wolfe deliberately stopped, looked around the crowd. "I see some people out there who're looking away from me," he said. "I guess you know what I'm talking about."

"I assume you're going to make some kind of point out of all this," Canfield said.

"I think so. I talked to another man who found some-thing, or anyway he thought he did. It looked to him like a very promising claim. His two 'partners' decided they wanted the mine to be in their names. He argued with them. He went to the hospital, and the claim was filed in their names. But that mine didn't pan out, because the two went back to their old ways. One of the grubstakers was named Saratov."

He heard a low growl from the crowd, like a tiger awakening.

"That's one of my employees," Canfield said. "And I haven't seen him since this afternoon."

"Maybe he's busy," Wolfe said. "Since this isn't a court of law," he went on, "I've got a suggestion. Sara-tov's partner, like most of you know, is Mister Brakbone here. What say, before we go and do something rash like kill Lef Steadman, we send somebody to inspect Brak-bone's quarters, looking for interesting pieces of paper? I think a man's life might be worth that, don't you?"

"The hell you will!" Brakbone shouted, and dove at Wolfe.

Wolfe heard Canfield shout, "You stupid shithead!" as

Brakbone was on him, reaching for a stranglehold. Wolfe's hands went up under his and took both arms by the muscles, pinching sharply. The two tottered back and forth, struggling. Brakbone shouted something, harsh alk fumes stale in Wolfe's face.

Joshua suddenly bent both knees, stepped forward, pushed up on Brakbone's left arm, and turned, pulling and ducking under the man's left as he stumbled forward, off-balance. Wolfe turned sideways and snapped a knife-hand strike into Brakbone's lower ribs. The man grunted in pain, flailing for balance as Joshua pivoted around him and struck for his groin. The strike missed. Brakbone kicked, catching Joshua in the chest, and Joshua stumbled back. Brakbone came in, and Joshua snap-kicked for Brakbone's head. Brakbone's hands blocked; Joshua crouched, let the momentum of his kick spin him, and whipped his leg as he fell, sending Brakbone tumbling.

Brakbone's pistol dropped out of its holster. As he fumbled for it, somebody kicked the gun into the crowd, and Brakbone came to his feet.

The two men circled. Joshua aimed a knife strike toward Brakbone's throat; Brakbone ducked aside, whirled and swept a kick into Joshua's gut. Wolfe doubled over, pulling for air, let himself fall sideways, away from Brakbone's follow-through, and rolled back to his feet.

Brakbone had a fixed, tight smile on his face. People were shouting, Wolfe paid no mind. Circling . . .

Brakbone sent two punches at Joshua's head. He ducked them, threw a sword-hand hooking punch at Brakbone's temple. It missed the death-spot but smashed into his cheekbone.

Brakbone yelled in pain, tried another kick. Joshua ducked it, struck, missed.

Breathe . . . breathe . . . all the time is yours . . . let the wave take you . . .

Brakbone attacked again, and Joshua stepped sideways, toward the big man, his forearm snapping up in a block. Brakbone's arm was flung away, and Wolfe smashed his knuckles into Brakbone's chest, kept moving into him, striking, striking, and Brakbone fell hard on his back.

Brakbone rolled away from Wolfe's foot stamp, backsnapped to his feet, and struck. Wolfe blocked one strike, then another, came in hard to smash Brakbone's lower side with his palm.

Ribs snapped, and Brakbone howled. He stood, swaying.

No sorrow, no joy, as I take what is not mine to take . . .

Wolfe's right hand came up, curled, and he struck down, barely a touch, near Brakbone's collarbone. Brakbone's hands reflexively grasped his throat, then fell away as his eyes rolled up and he fell bonelessly forward.

Wolfe stepped aside, let the corpse crash to the floor.

There was complete silence.

Suddenly Canfield had a gun in his hand.

"This is utter goddamned nonsense," he snarled. "Next you'll be accusing *me* . . ."

Breathe . . . breathe . . .

"Put the gun down, Mister Canfield." It was Stoutenburg.

"No. I'm leaving—let all of this bullshit settle down. When you've come to your senses, then—then we'll see what happens next."

"That's a good idea," Stoutenburg said, taking a step forward. "But I don't think you should leave. I do think we deserve some explanations. Now, or in the morning."

"Not a chance, preacher. Don't make me shoot you."

"You're not a depraved man, Mister Canfield. You won't shoot an unarmed man."

Canfield was panting as if he'd run a hard mile.

Stoutenburg took another step.

Kristin's gun was out, aiming. But the minister blocked her aim.

"Just give me the gun," Stoutenburg said. "There's been more than enough killing."

He was only two feet from Canfield, reaching out.

Wolfe saw, as if his eyes were inches away, Canfield's finger touch the trigger stud, exert pressure . . .

All is still, all is solid, all is stone, there can be no motion, all is ice . . .

Canfield's finger whitened, but the gun didn't fire. Tony Stoutenburg took the gun by the receiver, twisted gently, and had it in his hand.

"I think that's all," he said mildly.

*

"Now what?" Wolfe said, stretched in a steaming bath, feeling his bruises, letting the water outside, the blood within, wash the pain away.

"Now what about what?" Kristin said. She was still dressed, sitting on the bed.

"Since you stuck around after I left, did anybody have any ideas about what to do about Canfield? Or will the lynching bee reconvene tomorrow night, after the hangovers subside? I assume nobody's going to let him out of the assayer's vault anytime soon and let him make a run for it."

"Tony said he'd get some of Graveyard's reputable citizens together, and set up some sort of council. I guess they'll have a court or something."

"So law, order, morality, and straight poker games come to Graveyard." Wolfe yawned. "And all the players take the fun to Lucky Cuss or Grand Central. Hardly seems worthwhile."

"You sound like you're sorry you got involved."

"Not sorry at all. Canfield was a reek in the nostrils of

the Lord. But why the hell does one yutz mean that we've got to have parking regulations and dress codes all of a sudden?"

"What do you want? Anarchy?"

Wolfe started to say something, stopped. When he spoke again, the levity was gone from his voice.

"I don't know. Sometimes I wish I did."

*

The little man who acted like a chipmunk woke Wolfe early the next morning and gave him a slip of paper with a message. It was a simple code Wolfe remembered from the war.

IN-SYSTEM. ETA YOURS THREE E-DAYS. BE READY.

There was no name on the slip.

*

"You could stay on," Stoutenburg said. "Kristin hasn't told me anything about either of you, but I have the idea neither of you has any kind of a home."

"That's true enough, Tony," Wolfe said. "But there's something I've got to take care of. It's maybe a little bit bigger, maybe a little more important than Graveyard."

Stoutenburg inclined his head. "If you say so. You know, at one time, I dreamed of having a big parish. Maybe being a bishop, even. But things happened to me, like I think they've happened to you two. And now I think what I see around me is more than enough."

"Very nice," Wolfe said, without irony. "I wish I had your clarity of sight."

*

"Joshua," Kristin said, as they were loading the moke, "I've got something to tell you."

Wolfe turned, leaned back against the moke's body. "You're not going with me."

"How did you know?"

He shrugged. "I knew."

"They need law around here," Kristin said. "You won't—can't do it. I told Tony I would."

Wolfe nodded. "He's a good man," he said obliquely. "And you'll make a good cop."

"You know," she said, "when Tony took the gun away from Canfield . . . That proved something to me. You don't have to use violence. There's always another way."

Wolfe glanced at her, thought of saying something, changed his mind. "Nice if you're right," he said, voice neutral.

"And didn't you once tell me that there isn't any after?"

"I did."

"Did you mean for us when you said it?"

"Yes," Wolfe said honestly. "For everything."

"I still don't understand."

"Again . . . I can't tell you."

"You see?" Kristin's eyes were pleading, hopeless.

Wolfe stared down into them and took a deep breath. He took Kristin in his arms, kissed her, chastely. "Thanks, angel," he said. "Like I said, Tony's a very good man."

*

A ship lay in the center of the empty port. It was sleek, angled, dull black. Two gunports were open, chaingun barrels in battery.

One tracked Joshua's 'sled as it floated across the field. He drove the moke to the shed and put it inside. He came out, carrying the two packs Kristin had bought for him.

The port slid open, and a bearded, big man came out. He held a gun pointed down at the ground, carefully not aiming at Joshua. "You're Wolfe," he said. "I recognize you from the holos back during the war. I'm Merrett Chesney."

"I've heard of you."

"You're a little late."

"Some unexpected business came up."

"We better bust ass. The client's in a hurry."

"So am I," Wolfe said. He started for the port, stopped, and stared off at the gray mountains in the distance for a long time.

Then he boarded the ship, and the lock slid closed behind him.

* CHAPTER ELEVEN *

EYES ONLY

TO: All Concerned Federation Administrators &
Executives, Grade 54 and Above

FROM: Department of Information

1. Due to certain out-of-the-ordinary events, it has become necessary to impose immediate screening on all interstellar transmissions, particularly those intended for or emanating from any media source.

2. Screening must be made on ALL transmissions involving references to rumors of a "red death," a "burning death," or "interstellar disease."

3. Also to be screened is any mention of Federation ships disappearing mysteriously or encountering any unusual phenomena.

4. Media heads on your respective worlds or areas of responsibility should be notified of these conditions immediately.

5. It is also suggested that this is in no way a restriction of either the Federation-guaranteed freedom of speech or freedom of communication, but rather it is an attempt to help concerned parties avoid either causing panic or

making errors of judgment that might prove
hard to correct at a later date.

> Joseph Breen
> Minister of Procedures
> Department of Information
> Federation Headquarters
> Earth

* CHAPTER TWELVE *

"You travel light," Chesney said. "A virtue in these times."

"It didn't start out that way," Joshua said, then forced his mind away from Ak-Mechat VII.

"When does it ever?" Chesney laughed harshly. He checked the control panel, nodded satisfaction, and swiveled in his chair. "I think the closest I ever came to actually meeting you was off some beastly Al'ar planet. A1122-3 it was. Horrid tropical world. I was beating up the oppos to give one of your teams cover on an insert."

Wolfe thought back.

"You were trying a prisoner recovery," Chesney said.

Wolfe remembered.

"It got a little ugly," Chesney went on. "I had seven old *Albemarle*-class spitkits, and we were zooming and shooting and dancing all over the heavens and then two Al'ar frigates came out of nowhere. We lost three, and were very damned grateful that was the worst it got."

"It wasn't any prettier on the ground," Wolfe said.

"I never heard what happened, actually," Chesney went on. "Never had the proper clearance. No one around to be rescued, then?"

"No," Wolfe said slowly. "No, there were almost seventy civilians down there." He remembered the stumbling, nearly brain-dead men and women who'd been through Al'ar interrogation.

Chesney waited for more details, eyes gleaming a little. After a while, he realized that was all Wolfe proposed to say. "Ah well, ah well," he said. "A long time ago, wasn't it? But back then we were most alive, at our finest. Pity those days aren't still around, isn't it?"

"I don't think so," Wolfe said. "We're still paying, and I don't think the debt'll be settled by the time I die."

Chesney shrugged. "War debts, deficits—those are for governments to worry about, not warriors like you and me."

"I wasn't talking about the money," Joshua said shortly.

Chesney looked at him cautiously. "Well, that's as may be." He paused, then changed the subject: "I s'pose one thing we should settle is the pecking order, then. It's my ship, so I'm in command normally. However, I'm hardly a fool. When we insert and extract your areas of expertise, I'm demoted to first mate. Agreed?"

"That sounds reasonable."

"Good," Chesney said. "Very good indeed. I happen to have a small bottle of a good, perhaps excellent if my shipper is telling the truth, Earth-Bordeaux. Shall we seal our partnership?"

*

Chesney was as experienced as Joshua in long, dull N-space passages, and so the two stayed out of each other's way as much as possible. The ship was small, a converted eight-crew long-range scout of the *Chambers*-class, which Chesney had named the *Resolute*. The engine spaces had been roboticized, as Wolfe had done with his own ship, the *Grayle*. The crew spaces were still anodized in the soft pastels the Federation thought lessened tension, and Wolfe supposed Chesney preferred them that way; they must remind him of his service days.

Something nagged at Wolfe, something about Chesney. But it didn't surface, and so he let his back brain worry at it. He spent the long hours working with the Lumina in his carefully locked compartment, reading from the ship's extensive library, or sleeping. He took over the cooking, since Chesney's idea of a good meal was to reconstitute a steak, fry it gray, and cover it with freeze-dried mushrooms and whatever soup came to hand.

Chesney had hidden a bug inside the wardrobe catch, which Wolfe found and deactivated within an hour after jumping from Ak-Mechat VII. Neither man brought it up.

Wolfe discovered Chesney had more than one good, perhaps excellent, bottle of wine aboard. He nipped constantly, on the sly, an experienced secret toper. Joshua wondered if he was as sly about his alcoholism when alone. Since they were far from action, and a *Chambers*-class ship in transit could be piloted by a drug-hazed gibbon, Wolfe said nothing.

Four ship-days out, Chesney told Wolfe the destination and the clients. They were to pick up the bomb materials on Bulnes IV, then make a short jump to deliver it to the rebels on Osirio, barely twelve light-years distant. "Seems straightforward enough," he said. "Don't suppose, Joshua, you'd be willing to dig through the library, see what the piddling match is all about, though? Not that it matters, but it might be interesting. Even valuable, if the slok comes down."

Wolfe obeyed, also curious, and reported some success.

"I suppose it's some government-take-all planet with a colony, dissidents dissidenting from the official policy, helping rebels and that, then?" Chesney said. He'd been quick to inform Wolfe that not only did he despise politics, but he utterly hated any government that did more than maintain a military and police force.

"Not exactly. The whole situation's interestingly backward. Better listen closely," Joshua said, "because I don't think I'll get it right more than once. Osirio, where we're to deliver the package, was the mother planet. Evidently their best and brightest went out to Bulnes, where we're supposed to make the pickup, and colonized the system. Osirio was brain-drained and is currently in a state of what the 'pedia called decadent autocracy. Aristocratic thugs who run things badly, much like Earth's czars, so there's an active little rebellion bubbling. Assassinations, no-go districts, the stray conventional bombing here and there. The rebels, as far as I could tell, don't have any particular program other than blasting the rascals out. The real dynamism is on Bulnes IV, but the government of Bulnes owes its legitimacy to the mother planet."

"Good Lord," Chesney said.

"Yeah. They're afraid if Osirio falls, they'll tumble right after it."

"Who's right?"

Wolfe shrugged. "The people out of power aren't killing as many people as those in power. Yet. Maybe they'd do better, or maybe they'd start their own pogroms if they won."

"Thank heaven it's not for us to say," Chesney said. "But with a mess like that, it's certainly tempting to make the easy profit."

"I don't follow," Wolfe said.

"The way that wonderful voice we contract our services through set the deal, we get 250K when we pick up the plutonium, or whatever it is, 750 on delivery."

"I know."

"We could do a little personal renegotiation, arrange to get the 750 from the rebels first, then write off the 250 and go about our merry way, then, couldn't we?" Chesney saw the expression on Wolfe's face. "No, I s'pose not. Probably be too messy to arrange, not to mention dangerous while we loop around their silly world, bickering. We'll play the cards as they lay, I suppose."

*

Chesney was fond of talking about the war, particularly about the atrocities of the Al'ar. Wolfe listened and made little comment. Chesney seemed less interested in conversation than in his own monologue.

One time, after third-meal, Chesney asked Joshua, "What made the bastards so cruel? Why'd they kill so many women, children, and civilians who weren't even Federation officials?"

"That wasn't cruel to them," Wolfe said. "Women breed warriors, children—what they called **hatchlings**," he said in Al'ar, "—grow up to be warriors. As somebody back on Earth once said, 'kill 'em all. Nits grow up to be lice, don't they?' The Al'ar think—thought anyone who does things the hard way is a complete fool."

Chesney looked away for an instant, as if some very private thought had surfaced, then back at Joshua. "You were their prisoner, when you were a child, or so the fiches had it, which was why the Federation made you into a supercommando," he said. "So you dealt with them face-to-face."

"Sometimes."

Chesney shuddered. "That would've been horrifying. Like walking into a spider's web. But at least you got to see them when you killed them. That must've been a pleasure."

Joshua said nothing.

"Thank heavens," Chesney said, "they're dead, or at any rate gone from this spacetime. We don't need any more nightmares like them, right?"

Wolfe thought of the "virus" that had driven the Al'ar from their own universe and was now invading Man's. Again he kept silent.

*

They came out of N-space on the fringes of the Bulnes system and wormed their way toward the fourth planet. There were three planetary fortresses orbiting the planet and patrol ships crisscrossing the world.

"Piffle," Chesney said. "Their security chatters like a band of langurs, never keeping silent to see what's going on around it. This should be as easy as stealing coins from a dead man's eyes. Their search patterns are lattices like your grandmother's pie."

"I don't think my grandmother made pies," Wolfe said. "I remember her being quite busy representing her district."

"All right, then your first popsy's see-everything blouse."

"I wasn't that lucky," Wolfe said amiably. "My first love was the daughter of the Federation's secretary of state. She wore tunics that fastened at the neck, hung loosely, and never gave me anything to dream about, plus the baggy knee-trousers that were the style then."

"Ah, but once you got the tunic off," Chesney said, deliberately lascivious, "then you beheld a garden of delights?"

"Nope," Joshua answered. "I never even kissed her, and I'm not sure she knew I did more than exist. In any event, it was more pouting than passion on my part."

"Ah," Chesney said. "Unlucky you. As for me, my first was the tutor my father brought in to teach my brothers some language or other. A definite tart. But when my father caught us doing the naughty, that was the last we saw of her. I've often wondered . . ." Chesney shook his head.

"What happened to your great first love?" he went on, changing the subject, making conversation while his fingers touched sensors and the *Resolute* closed on Bulnes IV.

"She went away to school and married the graduating valedictorian when she was a freshman. Perhaps a successful marriage was what she intended for a career. They both were killed in the Al'ar raid on Mars." Joshua remembered the girl's easy smile, seldom directed at him.

"Just as well—that she married someone else, I mean," Chesney said. "A warrior doesn't need any more anchors than his own mind can provide."

"Yeah," Wolfe said sarcastically. "That's us. Footloose, carefree rebels, leaving a trail of broken hearts as we wander the stars."

*

Wolfe came out of his compartment yawning. Chesney was at the control panel, on the com. He saw Wolfe, said, "Received . . . clear . . ." into the mike, and broke contact.

"You've got contact with our customers?" Wolfe asked.

"Right. First an hour or two ago, then they put out another signal just now," Chesney said quickly. "Damned amateur worrywarts. Babbling like they've never heard of intercepts or locators. Had to cut them off, as you heard."

"The only way conspirators get experience is the hard way," Joshua said, easing into the copilot's seat. "Unfortunately, most get dead in the learning."

"And isn't that the truth," Chesney said heartily. "They even had a password for us. 'Freedom or death.' How terribly jejune. We're about sixteen hours from planetfall, by the way. How about some coffee?"

"Sure," Wolfe said, getting up. "Have it ready in a minute."

"Keep one hand for yourself," Chesney warned. "I might be jinking us around a trifle. There might be a det-bubble or two I've missed."

*

"Interesting place to schedule a pickup for," Wolfe said. "Right in the middle of university grounds. Very clever, unless they're professorial, in which case it's suicidal."

"Which way would you bet?"

"Six to five. Against. On anything."

"That's safe," Chesney said. "Now, if you'll excuse me, I'm about to be somewhat busy."

Chesney brought the *Resolute* screaming in from space, just at dawn. "Hopefully they'll think we're a meteorite for a moment or two, and by then we'll be below their radar horizon and invisible long enough to grab the geetus," he said. "Buckle up."

He flared the ship barely a thousand feet up. Wolfe heard antigrav generators groan and saw red warnings flash on the control panel.

"Shut up," Chesney grunted to the blinking lights. "Stop sniveling, you bitch." His fingers danced across sensors, and Wolfe remembered a pianist he'd seen.

Chesney was very good, he decided, as the ship spun and dodged without, as far as Joshua could see, any warnings of detection.

"Always well," Chesney grunted, "to be careful. Touch-down, six minutes . . . ."

There was a city below. He extruded spoilers, killed the drive. "Don't want to go *too* slow," he said. "Or some traffic cop'll throw a rock and knock us down. One minute sixteen. Here we are."

He put reverse thrust on as the *Resolute* shot over long rows of housing into open country, then towers and great buildings loomed ahead, gold and red brick in the dawn's light.

"And here we be," he said, braking sharply. The *Resolute* bucked and fell a few feet, and Chesney moved the slide-pots of the antigrav system up, and the ship stabilized. "Just on time."

The *Resolute* settled toward a huge cement pad, marked with regular lines. Beyond was a large stadium. The *Resolute* touched down with never a jar. "I'll keep it just grounded, so we don't punch a nice easy-to-spot ship-sized crater in their parking lot," Chesney said. "Perhaps you'll see to the niceties, then? Do take a gun. Freedom-lovers can prove most unreliable."

Wolfe picked up his heavy blaster, went to the lock, opened the inner and outer doors, and looked out. On one side was the stadium, on the other a low building, on a third a large grove.

He extruded the gangway as a small gravsled came from behind the building and shot toward the *Resolute*. There were two women and a man aboard, and, in the back, a large case.

The lifter grounded ten feet from the *Resolute*, slewed sideways, its skids striking sparks from the tarmac.

"Freedom," one of the women shouted as she jumped out.

"Or death," Wolfe replied dryly, wondering if enough starships grounded on Bulnes' campuses for a password to be needed.

"I'm Margot," the woman said.

"And I don't have a name, and hope that isn't your real one, either," Wolfe said. "Never give away what you don't have to."

The woman appeared angry, then perplexed.

The other two lifted the case out and staggered toward the *Resolute*. Margot glanced at Joshua as if expecting him to help. Wolfe didn't move, but kept the gun ready. She gave him a dark look and helped the other two.

"All right," she said when the case was in the lock. "You'd best lift, before the Inspectorate makes a sweep over us."

"You're forgetting something," Joshua reminded her.

Her eyes flickered. "Oh. Yes. Sorry," she said. "Sorry I forgot, but my mind was on security."

Joshua decided she was a rotten liar. The other woman brought a packet from the gravsled. Wolfe opened one end.

"It's all there," Margot said. "Don't you trust us?"

Wolfe made no reply, shuffling notes. "Good," he said at last. "Now get away from the ship. We're going straight up and out."

The three ran to the gravsled, and the driver lifted it away.

"Go!" Wolfe shouted to Chesney and hit the close sensor on the lock.

It slid shut as the *Resolute* went vertical. Wolfe grabbed for a handhold and fell against the lock door as the secondary came on, then gravity shifted as the ship's own system went on.

He looked out the tiny bull's-eye port at the shrinking parking area, the suddenly tiny gravsled, and, from the copse of trees, two gravlighters lifting out of concealment.

"Hit it hard," Wolfe called. "Our customers just got stopped!"

*

Wolfe let the radiation counter clatter for a moment, shut it off, and set it down beside the case. "Whatever's in there is hot," he said. "I have no intention of opening it, even in space wearing a suit. I'll take their word it's what the rebels want."

"Good," Chesney said. "What about the money?"

"It's real, as far as I know," Joshua said. "But I'm

hardly an expert on Bulnes' coins of the realm. Here, give me a hand."

He and Chesney lifted the case down the passageway, lashed it down in the small cargo hold, and returned to the control room.

"I need a drink," Chesney said. "You?"

"Maybe later."

Wolfe waited until Chesney had the cork out of the bottle, about to pour.

"How much did the Inspectorate pay you to rat them out?"

The bottle jerked and wine spilled across the table. "What *are* you talking about?"

"Come on, Merrett," Wolfe said. "When I came out of my room, before we went in-atmosphere, you were talking to somebody. You heard me, jumped like a goosed doe, then came up with a cockamamie explanation that the rebels were the chatty sort. How much?"

Chesney eyed Wolfe. Joshua took a small pistol out of his shirt, laid it down on the table, put his hand on top of it.

"Half a mill," Chesney said reluctantly.

"Where's it to be delivered? I assume you're not planning to go back to Bulnes and collect?"

"I have a number-call account. They're transferring funds now."

"Good," Wolfe said. "You can com your banker right now, and transfer 250K to an account number I'm going to give you. Remember, the split's equal, right?"

Chesney blinked, then a smile creased his face. "You don't care about them any more than I do."

"Why should I?" Joshua said. "I'm no more political than you."

Chesney picked up his glass, drained it, refilled it.

"You know," he said, "I might have found myself a real partner."

"Maybe," Joshua said. "But don't think that game works twice. Not on me, not on the people we're making the delivery to."

"Of course not," Chesney said. "For openers, their security—the Inspectorate I heard you call it—wouldn't have any reason to pay me if they had both sets of baddies and the geetus as well, now would they? This way, they've already made the transfer, and now they're waiting for me to tip them the wink once I reach Osirio to get the rest. They'll be waiting a *very* long time. Partner."

* CHAPTER THIRTEEN *

NOT FOR PUBLIC RELEASE

DO NOT DISTRIBUTE BELOW EXECUTIVE LEVEL

The management of Hykord Transport GmbH has determined we will no longer accept cargoes either directly or for transshipment from companies who are part of our Galactic Efficiency Group for the following sectors:

Alkeim, Garfed, Montros, Porphyry, Q11, Rosemont, Saphir, TangoZed, Ullar, Y267, and Yttr.

In addition, no cargo intended for any of the so-called Outlaw Worlds will be accepted.

Finally, we no longer accept shipments to any scientific or military presence in the worlds formerly part of the Al'ar sectors.

This decision has been reluctantly reached not because of various distressing rumors, which are utterly absurd to anyone who takes a moment to consider their probability, but due to the hugely increased insurance premiums leveled.

Management hopes that this situation will change shortly, and Hykord Transport GmbH will be able to return to its proud motto: "You Crate It, We Carry It. Anywhere, Anytime."

* CHAPTER FOURTEEN *

"It looks tropical down there," Chesney said gloomily.

"The gazetteer agrees with you," Wolfe said. "I quote: 'Most of the planet is tropical to subtropical, with extensive rain forests which have been heavily exploited by the Osirians. These forests are the home of many interesting fauna, including the primeval and exceedingly dangerous tarafny, click here for holo, many species of snakes, including the aggressive, dangerous-to-man . . .'" Wolfe let his voice trail off.

"*This* is the motherworld," Chesney said in amazement. "They're not decadent—you have to have accomplished something for it to get rotten. And why am I always going to places where the bugs are not only bigger than I am, but carnivorous?"

"You must've been lucky in another life," Wolfe said.

"Ah well," Chesney sighed. "Here we go. In-atmosphere. Ring up our clients if you would, and see if they've got the soup on."

Wolfe touched sensors, opened a mike. "Freedom," he said.

There was a crackle of static. He tried again.

"Or death" came back.

"Inbound per your instructions," Wolfe said. "ETA . . ." he glanced at Chesney.

"Fifty-eight minutes," the pilot said.

"In five-eight. Will monitor this freq. Do not broadcast except for emergencies," Wolfe said.

There was the acknowledging click of a mike button.

"Well," Wolfe said. "Perhaps a professional. Or at least someone who's read a book or two."

"Here's the plan," Chesney said, and his fingers touched points on the map on a secondary screen. "I'm bringing it in over this ocean, hopefully without being noticed. I'll low-fly to shore, then ground it here, which is the grid location they gave us, on what looks like a beach, next to this river here. If anything goes wrong, we withdraw gracefully, leaving big black streaks. Remember, my finances have been a little close lately, so the missile tubes are for show only. The only armament the *Resolute* has are the chainguns, so we shouldn't play the bravo. Comments?"

"Other than it looks easy, which scares me, none."

"Buckle up."

Osirio swallowed their screens as they closed, and Joshua dimly heard atmosphere-roar. The screen went to gray for an instant, then came back with a real-time visual: thick cloud cover below, blanking everything. Chesney switched to infrared.

"Nothing much down there," he said. Wolfe examined the blotches along the shoreline, saw nothing change, flipped the scanner through various spectrums.

"I've got a little wiggle about where we're headed," Joshua said. "Signals within the ninety-one-point-five megahertz range."

"Diagnosis?" Chesney's voice was tense.

"Don't know."

"Must be a village. I'd guess they'd have some kind of com to civilization. Just like amateurs to pick a place they can sit and drink beer in while they wait."

"Maybe."

"Wolfe," Chesney said worriedly. "I've got a—"

Alarms roared as the com blared: "Ambush! The Inspectorate's holding the town! Break off! Go for—"

"Strong radar signal," Joshua said. "We are being tracked." His voice was cold, emotionless, very clear.

"Understood," Chesney said. His voice could have been a duplicate of Wolfe's.

Another alarm shrilled.

"We are targeted," Joshua said.

"Your call."

"Maintain flight pattern . . . Stand by for evasive action . . ."

A third alarm gonged.

"I have a SAM launch," Wolfe said. The alarm rang twice more. "I have two more launches." He could have been talking about the weather.

"Give me music. We're blown," Chesney ordered.

Joshua touched two sensors, skipped two, tapped three others.

"ECM broadcasting."

"Results?"

Joshua waited.

"Results, dammit!"

"Negative on one and three—I have a lock on two—two is wavering—he's lost contact with us . . . Two self-detonated."

"Your call."

"Stand by—wait—wait—roll right, dive 300 feet, jink left," Joshua ordered. "On my command . . . four . . . three . . . two . . . NOW!"

Chesney's fingers swept the control board, and the *Resolute* dove sideways, corrected, banked left.

"One toppled . . ." The slam of an explosion rolled the ship.

"That was three," Wolfe said. "A bit close. Stand by . . . I have another launch—max evasive action—jink left—left—right—climb five-zero . . ."

Breathe . . . breathe . . .

"Two more launches," he said.

"They're trying to pin us against that ridge." Chesney's voice cracked.

"Continue evasive maneuvering." Wolfe's voice was quite calm.

Breathe . . . breathe . . .

"Christ," Chesney moaned. "What I'd give for one lousy little air-to-air—"

"Missile closing—jink right!"

Another explosion rocked the *Resolute*.

"Missile one—miss."

Joshua *felt* death, *felt* the second missile, remembered a time he'd used his mind to warp a countermissile into a target, remembered the fear, *felt* death once more, and hurled a rocket, a ghost that never was, at the image onscreen.

He *felt* the power of the Lumina in the compartment behind him, *felt* it glow into life, *felt* its colors whorl around the empty room. He *felt* the missile in his hands, closed them like talons, and the missile image was gone.

"Missile two self-detonated," he said, and again *reached* for the third. He *felt* nothing, there was nothing, there was no power within, nothing reached out. "Dive," he ordered, and the *Resolute* dove toward the sea not 200 feet below.

Then there was nothing onscreen.

"Missile three missed," he reported. "Evidently lost its target." He touched a sensor, saw an exhaust flare. "I have it headed toward space."

"And we're going after it," Chesney said. "This is too much like dangerous."

"Negative," Joshua said.

"I said—"

"Remember the deal, Mister," Wolfe snapped, and his tone had the long-disused sharpness of command.

Chesney caught his breath. "Sorry. Your call."

"Over the village full-tilt and straight for those mountains," Wolfe said. "Right over the SAM site."

"Understood."

A screen showed a cluster of buildings rushing at them, with gray-green lifters and three mobile launchers, two low-altitude chainguns that started yammering as they passed overhead. Then they were over the village and there was nothing but jungle onscreen and the rising mountain ahead.

"Take her over the ridge crest then the nap of the earth until I say. Then we'll look for a hiding place to put her down on, and figure out what to do next."

"Understood," Chesney said, then the habits of the past took hold, and he automatically added, "Sir."

*

The *Resolute* sat in dimness, sixty feet underwater. The lock slid open, and a man in a spacesuit floated out. There was a long, sealed roll tied to his shoulders. He unspooled a wire from a reel at his belt, opened a small door beside the lock, and plugged the reel in.

"Am I communicating?" Wolfe said.

"Very clear," Chesney answered. "I still think you're overcautious in wanting a wire for a com. They can't be monitoring *every* freq."

"Nobody had a SAM site in that village, either."

"Strong point."

"Stand by," Wolfe said, and pushed away from the lock. The river's sluggish current took him away from the ship. He activated the suit's antigrav unit and came to the surface.

Fernlike trees reared high on either side of the river, with smaller growth below them and some brush on the ground. Water churned as the antigrav unit sent him toward a climbable bank. Half a dozen loglike objects lay along it. One of the logs slithered off into the water as Wolfe approached.

"There are some *really* big snakes in these parts," he reported.

"Man-eaters?" Chesney asked.

"I'm not going to give them my arm as an experimental hors d'oeuvre." Wolfe clicked on an outside mike, and jungle sounds poured in. One of the snakelike creatures opened a long, toothed slit of a mouth, and the booming roar deafened him until the mike automatically cut the volume.

"That was your friend the snake," Wolfe reported. "He's wondering whether he wants to fang me . . . He just decided it wasn't worth the bother and went swimming."

Wolfe waded ashore, unsnapped the roll, and took out a small cylinder. He moved to one of the trees, activated his antigrav to maximum power until he weighed no more than ten pounds, and climbed hand-over-hand up the trunk to about a hundred feet above the ground. Clinging to the trunk, he used his gun butt to tap a spike into it and hung the box from the spike.

"I hope," he said, "this jerry-rigged bastard works."

"No reason it shouldn't," Chesney said. "If it locates from a suit in space, it should work fine by itself with all this thick, smudgy atmosphere to go wading in."

"I would've thought, after all those years playing sojer boy, you would've learned the basic rule that when it's something you need, it's guaranteed to break."

"I'm a romantic," Chesney said. "Speaking of which, I assume the air's perfumed and smells of exotic spices."

"Hang on a minute," Wolfe said. He cut power a little, let himself drop down the tree from limb to limb until he thudded into soft, decaying leaves at the base. "Now I'll satisfy your curiosity," he said, unsealing his face plate.

"Well?"

"Not exactly attar of roses," Wolfe said. "Try old armpit, shit, and stale beer."

"Typical jungle."

"Typical jungle," Wolfe repeated. "One down, one to go."

He went back into the river and drove toward another tree, a few hundred yards downstream.

*

"Freedom," Wolfe said patiently into the two microphones in front of him. He heard nothing but dead air.

"Ah, the romantic life of a soldier of fortune," Chesney murmured.

Wolfe waited fifteen minutes then tried again: "Freedom."

"It appears the Inspectorate scooped our clients up," Chesney said. "We've been doing this for three hours now. Do you know anybody else who might need a do-it-yourself bomb?"

The speaker suddenly crackled. "Or death."

"They're on freq one," Chesney reported. "And their password's not only stupid, but it's now got a long gray beard."

"I receive you," Wolfe said.

"Name yourself," the speaker said.

"Your supplier," Wolfe said.

"Give name of person providing materials."

"Almost enough for me to get a location," Chesney said. "And what they want's still crappy security. The Inspectorate could've pulled that woman's toenails out by now."

"Margot," Wolfe said.

"Good," the voice said. "Are you still onworld?"

"Perhaps," Wolfe said.

"Are you still willing to make delivery?"

"Affirmative."

"If you're onplanet and close to where the meet was blown today, give us your location and we'll come to you."

"I have him," Chesney said. "Lousy triangulation, but he's broadcasting from—" he looked at the onscreen map, and where two red lines intersected, "—about one ridgeline over, if this map is correct. They could get here in what, two hours?"

"You've obviously never hiked the bush," Wolfe said, and keyed the mike. "Negative on your suggestion. Somebody's leaking on your side, in case you hadn't noticed. We'll come to you."

There was a long silence, then the voice came back. Even on the tinny FM band, it reeked suspicion. "We don't know *who* betrayed us. Dislike idea of giving present location. You could be Inspectorate on our frequency."

"True," Wolfe said. "But I already know where you are. If missiles don't start incoming in the next few seconds, suggest your paranoia unjustified."

Again, a long silence. "Very well. We have no choice, do we? We'll await your arrival. ETA?"

"Sometime day after tomorrow. Probably in the morning," Wolfe said. "Out." He shut off the com.

"Whyn't you get behind the controls and ready for a fast getaway," he suggested. "Just in case we're the ones who got located and we weren't chatting with noble freedom fighters."

Chesney obeyed. "So we're going to go for a walk," he

said. "And you're right, I've done very little forest-crawling. Do we go in nice, air-conditioned spacesuits so we don't have to get close to the local fauna?"

"Nope," Wolfe said. "Too bulky, too slow, too easy a target."

"I'd rather be an armored target than a naked one," Chesney complained. "And how'll we navigate? I understand a satellite positioning system can be a double-edged sword."

"It can," Wolfe agreed. "I've booby-trapped a few myself. We'll print out the map, and I'm going to invent a brand new device you might've never seen. It's called a compass."

"Christ," Chesney groaned. "The things I do for greed."

*

The ship surfaced at dawn and slid to the bank; the lock opened. Wolfe and Chesney got out. They carried Wolfe's two packs and pistol belts. Wolfe had a blast rifle slung over his shoulder. In the lock was the bulky case with the radioactive materials, a suit antigrav generator strapped underneath it. Joshua activated the generator, turned it to high, and picked up the case by a cargo strap as if it weighed no more than a pound or so.

"I wish I had a better arsenal," Chesney complained as he stepped onto the bank. "Why is it, every time I take an assignment, I think I've got everything I could conceivably use, and the only things I don't have are what I really need?"

Wolfe shrugged. Chesney took a small box from his pocket and pressed sensors. The *Resolute*'s lock closed, and it slipped underwater. "I always feel naked outside the ship," he said.

"Good," Wolfe said. "Naked men stay scared. Scared men stay alive. Let's hoof."

THE DARKNESS OF GOD

*

An hour later, they passed through the ruins of a village. The wooden huts had been burnt, and there were blast holes in some of the roofs. Three trees had rotting, sagging ropes looped around them, and a few bones scattered nearby.

Wolfe *felt* screams, agony, prolonged death.

"How long ago did this happen?" Chesney asked.

"Maybe a year, maybe a little longer."

"Who did it?"

"Maybe rebels, maybe soldiers. As a guess," Wolfe said, "I'd go for the government. The farmers would've come back if it'd just been 'revolutionary justice.' "

"Nice people," Chesney said.

"Would it have been any more civilized," Wolfe said, voice harsh, "if they'd razed the village from the air? Or is it worse because somebody had to look in somebody's eyes as he killed him? Or her?"

Chesney didn't answer. They went on.

*

Wolfe counted paces, consulted the map, and stopped regularly to pour water from his wine-bottle canteen into its plas cap and float the tiny needle he'd magnetized atop it before going on.

*

They stopped when the glow that was the barely visible sun was approximately overhead. Chesney let the case down to the ground, and wheezed. "Gad. Weight-schmeight. It's the mass somebody ought to figure out how to eliminate."

"Einstein did," Wolfe said. "And our customers are going to use his cookbook."

"I meant—never mind what I meant." Chesney opened his pack, took out two ration paks, and tossed one to

174

Wolfe. He lifted out a small bottle of wine, looked at it longingly, but put it back. He touched the heater tab, waited a few moments, opened the pak, and grimaced.

"I've *got* to learn to not buy things just because they're a bargain. What is this glop, anyway?"

Wolfe had his own pak open. "Interesting," he said. "I'd guess some centuries ago it was intended for soldiers that might've been Earth-Japan émigrés. This would be bean paste, this pickled cucumber, this, well, some sort of mussel, shellfish, which you put on the rice. The small plas pak's soy sauce."

"What's this green stuff?" Chesney said, sampling.

"Wait! That's . . ."

"Hot—hot . . ." Chesney managed in a strangled tone, and unsealed the wine bottle that now served as a canteen and gulped down water.

"Some sort of ground-up root," Wolfe continued. "Wasabi, I think I remember hearing it called."

"Sadistic bastards!" Chesney moaned.

*

"Doesn't—this—damned hill ever end?" Chesney panted.

"It'll be downhill tomorrow. And think how easy it'll be on the way back."

"I can't—I keep thinking about the other side of this goddamned ridge that we'll have to climb before then."

"It's easier if you don't try to talk," Wolfe advised.

"I'm a pilot, which means anything but a ground-pounder," Chesney said, ignoring the advice. "Why I ever—"

Underbrush rustled; horror rushed them. Wolfe saw pincered legs, claws, a glaring multifaceted eye as he pinwheeled sideways, blast rifle flying away. The beast clawed at him, missed, spun on its own tracks.

Chesney had his gun out and snapped a shot. The bolt blew off two of the creature's legs, and it shrilled agony and rage.

It reared, segmented body towering over Wolfe.

He *felt* for its brain, found nothing but raw savagery as his pistol came up, fired twice, and dove away as the creature screeched once more, and came down. He put another bolt, then a third into its side as it writhed, then, forcing himself to stay calm, aimed and blew its single eye into spattering gore.

The nightmare flailed and thrashed about.

"Get around it," Wolfe shouted, and Chesney, moving very fast for a man of his size, pushed through the brush to the uphill side.

"Come on," Wolfe ordered, and the two men went uphill at a run.

The creature's death agonies—if that was what they were—continued as they pushed on.

"Gods—no. That thing doesn't deserve a god," Chesney said. "What was it? That taradny or tarafny you were reading about? We should've looked at the holo."

"Hell if I know," Wolfe said. "But I surely don't want to run into its big brother if it isn't."

Chesney nodded.

"I—notice," Wolfe managed, "you're not panting any more."

"Too—scared."

*

"Can we build a fire?" Chesney asked. "I assume you know how to rub two wet sticks together, and all that woodsy lore."

It was dusk, and they'd just finished another ration pak. They'd crested the ridge an hour earlier, and Wolfe had found a campsite on the far side, where a spring began the long run down into the valley below.

"No," Wolfe said.

"But what about that tarantula's brother?"

"I'd rather worry about him than somebody from that village who might be airborne with a snooper and an air-to-ground. Bugs are maybe—heatseekers are for sure," Wolfe said.

"Oh well," Chesney said. He took the rather fancy coat that was the only rainproof he had out of his pack, and rolled himself up in it. "Mrs. Chesney's favorite son wasn't meant to sleep rough," he complained. "I'll be tossing and turning till dawn."

Wolfe found a rock, zipped into his waterproof coat, and put the rifle across his knees. Moments later, Chesney's breathing grew into a whiffling snore, his beard ruffling like a sail. Wolfe grinned wryly.

Breathe . . . breathe . . .

He *felt* the Lumina, back in the *Resolute*, *felt* it flame. He *reached* out, around them, *felt* nothing, no one. He let his senses flow, like lava, over the next crest, down the long slope to the sea, toward the village where the SAMs had been, far distant.

He *felt* people, *felt* warmth, warmth of their homes, their fires. He tasted hard cold metal, like blood, and knew the Inspectorate and its missiles were waiting. He *felt* its outposts, *felt* men worried about the morrow, worried about the patrols that would range into the mountains, looking for enemies.

Joshua brought himself back and listened to Chesney's measured snore. He *felt* the night around him, *felt* no menace.

He *felt* another presence, *felt* fright somewhere below, somewhere in the valley they'd traverse in the day. His hand drew a line toward it in the dirt. He tried to *feel* how many there were, what they looked like, what they thought—he failed.

He opened his eyes and looked at the line he'd drawn. It followed the same azimuth he was trying to hold to, toward where the two lines from the radio-locator on the map came together.

Suddenly exhausted, he sagged back against the rock. Rain pattered on his head, and he pulled the hood of his coat up. The rain grew harder. *Sleep now,* he told his body. *Feel nothing.*

*

Joshua came fully awake, hearing a voice. The rain had stopped. He didn't move, but his finger slid the safety off the rifle. Then he realized the speaker was Chesney. He was speaking clearly, in a low voice, but in a strange, affected accent: "My dear chap . . . I have utterly *no* idea what you're talking about. No, I can't say I see any resemblance to me and this horrid boy, so stop waving that holograph in front of me. Absurd to so accuse a Federation officer!"

Wolfe was about to shake him awake, but *felt* no danger, no threat in the surrounding blackness. Chesney sighed, rolled over, snored twice, then spoke again: "Certainly not! I've been too busy, what with the peacetime closures around this base, to even breathe. I certainly didn't know she'd taken a—a lover. I'm completely shattered. Good heavens, man, can't you recognize the obvious? It must've been some back-alley goon that tried to rob them, and things went terribly awry. I must say I object to this entire line of questioning, and wish to notify my commanding officer I seem to be in need of legal assistance."

Once more a long silence, then: "Certainly not guilty, Admiral."

Now his voice went low, became a conspiratorial mutter: "Yes. Yes, of course. It'd be an utter disgrace for an innocent man like myself to be a convicted—disgraceful for the service, as well. You have no idea how I appreciate this. Yes, yes. And I thought you didn't believe me, when I told you what must've happened to her and that man . . . Of course I'll make sure I never come back here, or have anything to do with the Navy. Why should I? These fools have tried and convicted me."

Then, in a gloating voice: "Trevor? You were wrong. Quite wrong."

Chesney laughed chillingly, then his breathing choked, and Wolfe knew he was awake. Joshua took in a slow breath, let it rasp against the roof of his mouth, and exhaled noisily.

"Wolfe?"

Joshua snorted, coughed. "What?"

"I—just wanted to know if you were awake," Chesney whispered. "Sometimes my—my snoring bothers people."

"Not me," Wolfe said, in a carefully sleep-filled voice. "I can sleep through the crack of doom."

"Good," Chesney said. "Goodnight again."

Wolfe knew he wasn't sleeping, but listening.

Finally Wolfe's mind, drunken monkey that it was, gave him what he'd been looking for on Merrett Chesney. There'd been three separate tabloid sensations. First a war hero, a special operations veteran of many close-fought engagements, was accused of murdering his wife and her lover.

Then a second scandal broke. The hero had been keeping a terrible secret. His real name wasn't Chesney, but . . . Wolfe's mind sought for the name but couldn't bring it up. A rich youth, parents near the top of their planet's social set. The boy had been unhappy, but seemed to settle down once he was placed in a military school. During one summer leave, there'd been an explosion at the family's mansion, an explosion that was at first blamed on a faulty power grid. Further investigation had found the blast came from a land mine stolen from a military depot that'd somehow been set off in the house.

Wolfe tried to remember how many had been killed. He couldn't, but he was sure the family had been obliterated, except for the son, who'd been out with a girl that night. But he had refused to name her, refused to soil her reputation. There'd been a trial, but the jury couldn't quite convict him of murder in the first degree, and it settled on a secondary charge. The boy would have served five E-years or so before he was released and disappeared.

That had been the end of that—until that highly decorated Federation Navy commander, Merrett Chesney, had been accused of murder. Investigation revealed he'd fraudulently enlisted at the beginning of the war. He'd been a model sailor, quickly commissioned and volunteered for special operations, although there'd been whispers he wasn't averse to enriching himself if it didn't interfere with his duties.

Chesney had married well during the war and, as soon as the Al'ar vanished, set to work spending his wife's inheritance. When the money began to run out, both developed wandering eyes. Then the wife and one of her lovers had been murdered—beaten to death, as Wolfe remembered.

The third sensation was after Chesney was convicted. Before the penalty phase of the trial was completed, he'd escaped, with the connivance of at least one fellow officer. That officer's body had been found next to a hangar where a patrol ship had been kept, a ship that was now missing.

No one had much time to look for Chesney: The postwar interregnum was swirling chaos. Everyone assumed he'd fled to the Outlaw Worlds and hopefully met a deserved fate.

Nice choice of partners, Wolfe, Joshua thought wryly. *Maybe I should have stayed on Ak-Mechat VII.*

*

"Do not move," the voice said.

Joshua stopped in midstep, let his boot ease to the ground.

The woman came out of the brush. Her clothes were worn but clean, her face dirt-streaked, although that might've been an attempt at camouflage. She held an old sporting rifle ready, and Joshua noted it was very clean.

He'd sensed someone ahead for about five minutes, just after they'd struck the path they were following. "Freedom," he said.

"Or death," the woman answered, but the gun stayed leveled.

"We have what you've bought," Chesney said, moving a hand toward the case he was lugging, freezing when the gun barrel was focused on the middle of his chest.

"Put down the rifle, and unfasten your gun belts," the woman ordered.

They obeyed. A man came from the other side of the path and picked up their weapons.

"Are they carrying any communications gear?"

The man patted them down hastily, eyes meeting Wolfe's nervously, then looking away. "Nothing," he said. "But in that case . . ."

"'Don't open it," the woman and Chesney said in near unison. Wolfe grinned, and a smile almost made it to the woman's lips.

The man shrank back as if it were a tarafny.

"You," the woman said, indicating Wolfe with her gun barrel. "Carry it. You go first."

Joshua picked up the case, slung the strap over his shoulder, and started off.

Ten minutes later, the woman pushed aside brush, and they went up a narrow, skillfully camouflaged side track. The ground had been planted with a tough grass that didn't show bootprints.

They came to a creek about five feet wide and crossed it on the flattened chunk of alloy that served as a bridge. There was a sentry on the other side, young, alert. He looked at Wolfe and Chesney with an expression somewhere between hostility and awe.

They entered the camp. There was a rocky cliff, with a protruding rock shelf that covered the entrance to a low cave that went back for almost fifty feet. There were at least twenty men and women in the camp. A man came out of the cave. "You can call me Andros."

Joshua's lips quirked. "I'm tempted to introduce myself as Homme. But I'm John Taylor. This is—Archibald Tuesday." Chesney frowned for a minute, then recovered.

"Good," Andros said. "No one needs real names until the war is over."

"Sometimes not even then," Wolfe said.

"True. But we do not plan on taking our planet in the direction of Messieurs Dzhugashvili and Ulyanov."

Chesney was puzzled, not understanding what Wolfe and Andros were talking about. The woman had a faint smile on her face.

"I assume that is what we are paying so dearly for?" Andros indicated the case.

"It is."

"Very, very good. Now the tide will be on the turning."

*

It was just after dark. The rebels had prepared a meal while Chesney and Wolfe washed at the creek. For guerrillas, Chesney said, they ate like gourmets. Fish wrapped and baked in an aromatic leaf, three kinds of unknown vegetables, a meat that tasted like pork dipped in a fiery sauce, then fruit. They drank a cool herbal tea. Their plates and utensils were military-issue plas.

Joshua and Chesney sat just outside the cave mouth with Andros and the woman who'd been introduced as Esperansa. Their guns and packs had been returned and now lay beside them. The other rebels were farther back in the cave, talking quietly over the remains of their meal. There were around forty now, about half of the band, Andros said. The others were out on patrols or staked out on ambushes on the other side of the ridge. "By rights," Andros said, "we should have had a roaring fire and a feast. But infrared detectors have taken the romance out of being a guerrilla."

"Never mind," Wolfe said. "Neither of us believe in parties when we're working." He looked around the cave.

"Something I'm curious about. You're not planning on assembling the—device here, are you?"

Esperansa laughed aloud. "No, Mister Taylor. Not here. But I shall not tell you where I'll work."

"Don't want to know," Joshua said amiably. "The only thing I'd like to know is the recipe for that pig we just ate."

"Pig?" Andros looked puzzled. "Oh. You mean the baked tarafny?"

Chesney sat suddenly upright, eyes wide.

"We think it's quite fair. The tarafny tries to eat us," Andros said, pretending not to notice Chesney's dismay, "so we eat it first."

"Never mind about the recipe," Joshua said. "I don't think, assuming the tarafny is the same charmer we encountered on the trail, it'd be very practical to keep a cageful aboard a starship. Now, perhaps we should talk business?"

Andros poured himself another glass of tea. "Certainly." He turned. "El-Vah," he called. "Would you bring me that brown envelope that's in my bedroll?"

A young man came out of the cave carrying the fat envelope. He was armed with a pistol. He gave Wolfe and Chesney a cold look and sat down a few feet to the side.

"Let me ask something first," Andros said. "You two are quite a team. When the Inspectorate sprung their trap, we were just outside the village. We saw your ship and knew you were doomed. But you escaped their missiles and came back through their midst, showing your contempt for the swine. I've never seen or heard of such piloting, such skill. Our cause would be greatly helped if we had an attack craft such as yours, with you two piloting it. We could strike real terror in the pigs we've sworn to destroy."

"How much?" Chesney asked flatly. "I come expensive, especially since there'd be only one of me, which makes it easier for them to pick a target. And my friend here isn't cheap, either. I won't tell you who he really is, but he was a high-ranking commando officer during the Al'ar War, and has great skills fighting on the land as well as in the air."

"Ah?" Andros considered Wolfe. "We could certainly use a master tactician, someone to train our recruits, perhaps lead us in raids until our own officers gain greater experience."

"Is anyone planning on asking me if I'm interested?" Wolfe asked.

"I don't know if you would be," Andros said. "For I must tell you what we're paying for that package you brought from Bulnes practically bankrupts our treasury here on Osirio. You would have to wait for payment until our coffers are replenished from Bulnes, or from some of our out-system supporters. Not that we would be ungenerous. We would pay what we could now, and give ten times that once the Inspectorate has fallen."

"I've got other commitments," Joshua said. "Sorry."

"I don't have anything in the fire right now," Chesney said. "But one thing a freelancer can't do is fight on the if-come. People have a tendency to forget about what they owe once they've won. Wasn't it Machiavelli who suggested a lord who actually paid his mercenaries any other way than by the sword was a damned fool?"

"I understand," Andros said. "And I am sorry we could not afford your further services. So here are the credits we were able to raise." He held out the envelope.

"*Able* to raise?" Chesney said, disbelief becoming anger.

Andros shook his head. "It would have been so much simpler if you'd been interested in joining us," he said, reaching behind him. "As it is, I'm truly sorry . . ."

Joshua's small hideout gun snapped from his sleeve and he shot Andros in the face. The man rolled on his side, his half-drawn pistol falling into the dirt.

El-Vah drew his pistol. Wolfe shot him in the chest. The boy made a surprised sound in his throat and tumbled backward.

Wolfe heard shouts from the cave as Esperansa brought up her rifle, fumbling with the safety. Two blasters crashed simultaneously and she fell forward onto her face.

Blast rifle up, Wolfe sent a burst into the cave. He tossed Chesney his gun belt, stuffed the brown envelope into his shirt, and shouldered his pack.

"To the trail," he snapped. "Back the way we came. Stay just ahead of me."

Chesney nodded, buckling his gun belt on, hefting his pack. "What about the case?"

"Leave it. They almost paid for it."

Somebody shot at them, and the bolt smashed into the ground nearby. Wolfe sent another burst at random and started running, pistol belt slung over his shoulder.

The sentry in the middle of the path looked bewildered. "What is happening? What—"

Chesney shot him in the head. He spasmed, throwing his rifle high overhead, fell back into the creek. They went over the bridge, and Wolfe kicked the length of alloy down into the water on top of the sentry's body.

He caught up to Chesney. "We walk like hell for a count of one hundred," he ordered. "Then you keep walking for another hundred count, and go off into the brush and wait for me."

"What're you going to do?"

"Double back, ambush them, then join you. For pity's sake, don't shoot somebody coming up the path whistling. It'll be me."

"Right."

"Especially since I still have the envelope with the money."

"Let's go," Chesney said. "I can hear them coming."

They went on. It was just light enough to dimly follow the path. Wolfe counted carefully, calmly: ninety-eight . . . ninety-nine . . . one hundred.

He ducked to the side, and Chesney kept moving.

Wolfe *felt* out, *felt* them coming. But he didn't need the Lumina. He saw figures in the dimness, pelting up the trail. He stepped out and fired a long burst.

There were screams, wild shots. Another burst followed the first, then Wolfe went uphill once more. *Damn, but I wish I had some grenades,* he thought with the part of his mind that wasn't counting.

At fifty, he stopped, frowning. He thought for a brief moment, then turned off the path.

*

Chesney lay prone, pistol pointing back down the path, ready to fire. He shrieked involuntarily as a hand came down on his shoulder, and Wolfe crouched beside him.

"God, god, gods," he almost sobbed. "Don't *do* that, man. My heart's not up to that. Why didn't you—"

"Wasn't sure there might not be a mistake," Wolfe said.

"I heard you shooting them up," Chesney said, voice nervous. "Did you get them all?"

"Nope. I'm not that efficient a killer."

"So what's next? Are we going to have to keep running?"

"We are—but I've got a way to slow them down, or anyway give them somebody else to worry about." He dug into his pack. "I brought these along in case we needed a diversion," he explained, holding up two space-suit emergency flares. He took the end cap from one, inverted it, and put it on the other end.

"Wolfe, everybody on the goddamned planet'll see that!"

"Hope so," Joshua said, and slammed his hand against the cap. White fire hissed upward nearly a thousand feet, and blossomed into a series of red-green-red-green flashes.

Joshua sent another one after the first. Chesney was still utterly bewildered.

"Now we turn left," Wolfe said. "We'll move parallel with the ridge crest until dawn. Then we'll turn uphill again, and cross into our own valley. Up and at 'em, soldier."

*

Minutes after they started moving, they heard the whine of gravlighters and saw lights in the sky.

"Down, and hope the Inspectorate's shitty with people-sniffers," Joshua ordered.

Explosions boomed, and the ground shuddered around them.

"Good," Joshua said. "Bomb that old jungle. Always do it the easy way."

There were high screams from the sky, and a pair of scoutships dove down. Fire blossomed from their bellies, and rockets slammed into the mountain.

"They'll keep that up all night, if I know my amateurs," Wolfe said, "then land troops on top of the mountain and sweep down. When—if the Inspectorate discovers the cave, they'll have something to keep them busy, and they won't be looking for us."

*

Just before dawn they heard gunfire and explosions. "They found them," Chesney said.

"Maybe," Wolfe said. "Or maybe they're shooting up each other or a really offensive tree."

"I hope they get the bastards."

"Why? They did something stupid," Wolfe said, "and it seems to me they've already paid for it."

"I don't like people who try to kill me."

"An understandable emotion. I frequently share it."

*

Chesney was staggering by the time the sun came up. Joshua found an impenetrable thicket, and they pushed their way into it. Chesney went immediately to sleep, not offering to stand guard.

Wolfe let his senses float out but *felt* nothing. He calmed himself, breathing steadily, and let his body relax while his mind watched.

Around midday, Chesney grunted and woke up. He saw Wolfe sitting cross-legged, counting money. "How much do we have?" he asked.

"A little less than half a million," Joshua said. "Again,

it appears real." He shook his head. "They should've bargained instead of going for the guns. Two-thirds isn't bad soldier's pay."

Chesney nodded agreement. "You're right," he said. "Lord knows I've taken less and not cried all night. But why the hell can't people stay honest?"

Wolfe looked at him without replying.

Chesney had the grace to turn away.

*

They moved slowly, quietly, following the mountain crest, until almost midnight, then they holed up until just before dawn. Aircraft constantly passed overhead, scoutships, lighters, gravsleds. But none slowed, so Wolfe paid no mind.

They crossed the few open spaces at a trot, listening carefully first. "We're making a big circle," Wolfe explained. "We'll have one more night in the open, then make the *Resolute* not long after first light."

"Oh Lord, a consummation devoutly to be made," Chesney misquoted fervently. "I never knew I could smell so bad. I'm going to *live* in the fresher until further notice. Is that what it's like being a soldier?"

"Nope," Wolfe said. "It's when you don't know you stink and don't care either that you start soldiering."

*

That night, when Chesney slept, Wolfe slid over beside him. He picked up Chesney's pistol and pushed its bell mouth firmly down into the ground they lay on. He wiped the dirt from the outside of the barrel, and set it back down near the pilot's hand.

*

Chesney touched controls on the tiny box and waited.

Brown water roiled, and the *Resolute* surfaced. Its secondary drive hummed, pushing it close to the bank. Its lock door opened, and the gangway slid out. Wolfe started down the bank.

"Joshua."

Wolfe stopped.

"Turn around, Wolfe. I don't like being a back-shooter unless I have to."

Joshua obeyed.

Chesney had his pistol aimed in both hands at Wolfe's chest. "I really don't think three-quarters of a mill is enough for two people," he said, and his voice gloated as it had when he told Trevor he was wrong. "And I don't think I'll be sharing it with our mutual friend, either."

"You don't want to do that, Merrett," Joshua said.

"Oh, but I have to," Chesney said, and his voice had a tone like the ring of cracked crystal. "I know you weren't sleeping. I know I was talking in my sleep. No one must know about me. No one."

"I said, don't do it," Wolfe said calmly.

The dirt-clogged barrel of Chesney's gun was aimed steadily at Wolfe. "But I'm going to," Chesney said.

Wolfe turned, started up the *Resolute*'s gangway.

Merrett Chesney laughed again, convulsively jerking the trigger.

*

"Chesney's dead," Wolfe said into the blank screen.

"How?"

"He didn't believe people tell the truth sometimes," Joshua said.

"What does that mean?"

The transmitter hissed for a while.

"All right," the voice conceded. "He was a strange one at best. I suppose you knew about him?"

"I learned."

"He was so afraid of anyone finding out, and I think everyone knew. Oh well. So what next?"

"No changes," Wolfe said. "I've got nearly three-quarters of a million credits. I take my cut, drop the rest off with you."

"What's the split?"

"I'm going to take my fifty percent of what we agreed on, plus half of his fifty percent for general aggravation," Joshua said. "You get the rest."

"Pretty damned generous," the voice said.

"Why not? I've got a ship now, so I can afford to keep up the old ties."

"Good. Nice doing business with you," the voice said. "Stand by to record."

Wolfe scanned the control panel of the *Resolute*, found the recorder, and switched it on.

The voice reeled a set of coordinates, then: "Got them?"

"I do."

"Good." There was a moment of silence. "Wolfe . . . I'm sorry about what happened—but you understand how business works."

Wolfe lifted an eyebrow.

"Clear," the voice said, and the contact was broken.

*

The coordinates were for open space, far between systems, near the fringes of the Federation. During the war a great battle had been fought here, and the shattered hulks of starships, Federation and Al'ar, still spun in aimless orbits.

A medium-size, ultramodern starship hung in space at exactly the specified points.

Wolfe opened his com. "Unknown ship, this is the *Resolute*."

"Go ahead, *Resolute*. You have the credits?" It was an

unfamiliar voice. Wolfe shrugged. He hardly expected his contact to meet him personally.

"I have."

"Come on across, then."

Wolfe breathed, *felt* across the distance. There was nothing. No warmth, but no threat. He tucked his hideout gun into his waistband, put on a spacesuit, buckled on a heavy blaster, went into the lock, and cycled himself into space.

It was dark, except for the far-distant glimmer of forgotten suns. Wolfe turned on a suit spotlight, jetted across the short distance to the other ship, and touched down next to its lock.

The outer door was open. Wolfe went into it, closed the lock door, and let the lock cycle.

The door opened into luxury. Stepping out of the lock, Wolfe saw three men with guns. They wore strange helmets that fit snugly from the base of the neck over the top of the head and down over the forehead. Reflecting goggles hid their eyes.

They held blast rifles leveled.

Joshua slowly lifted his hands, grimly cursing his carelessness.

A man came out of a compartment. He also wore a helmet, but instead of a suit he wore a uniformlike tunic with a jagged crimson streak on the chest.

"If you move, you're dead," said a voice in Joshua's speaker.

The man took Wolfe's gun, gingerly unfastened his helmet, and lifted it away. His hand came back very quickly with an air-hypo against Wolfe's neck, and he pressed the stud. Wolfe jerked aside, but not in time.

"There." The voice came from another room. "That's got you."

A door slid open. Out came Jalon Kakara. He walked over to Wolfe. His eyes were alive with rage, hate. "I warned you," he said, and smashed his fist into Wolfe's face. "I warned you," he said again.

* CHAPTER FIFTEEN *

SECRET

By the authority of Federation Military Regulation
267-65-909, the following INACTIVE RESERVE
UNITS are REACTIVATED and will participate in
Federation maneuvers as soon as they are at full
TO&E strength:

783rd Military Police Battalion
43rd Starport Security Detachment
12th Public Information (Active) Detachment
7th Long Range Patrolling Unit (less 17th Troop)
96th Logistical Command
21st Scoutship Flight
78th Scoutship Flight
111th Scoutship Flight
831st Heavy Transport Wing
96th Field Headquarters Support Company
4077th Field Medical Unit
3411th Field Medical Unit
9880th Field Medical Unit

All members of these units are to report IMME-
DIATELY, and are permitted to use any civilian

transportation necessary, and are authorized the highest priority in reaching their units.

Members of these units should advise their dependents they will be on extended active service and, at this time, there is no capability for dependents to travel with them, nor will their new posts allow dependent housing.

This activation is a purely routine test of the Federation's ability to mobilize.

There is no cause whatsoever for alarm or false rumor.

FOR THE COMMANDER:

> Tara Phelps
> Vice Admiral
> Federation J-1

* CHAPTER SIXTEEN *

"I told you," Kakara went on, "to sleep with one eye open—but you didn't. You just went on about your merry way, as if you could steal my wife and there'd never be any paybacks to worry about."

Wolfe tried to speak, couldn't.

Kakara grinned. "Can't talk, can you? Just so you know, you've been hit with about two hundred cc's of HypnoDec. Your automatic body controls function, but that's about it. Go ahead. Try to walk."

Wolfe's sluggish mind tried to work, tried to reach out, tried to *feel* the great Lumina a few hundred yards away in the *Resolute*.

He was empty, drained, half-stunned.

"You see," Kakara gloated. "You see? Now here's the way things are going to work. You've gotten a preliminary dosage. So right now you're suggestible. I'm programming you now, just like a frigging computer." He turned to his aide. "Hit him with the rest of the dose."

The man obeyed.

"Good," Kakara said. "Now I can tell you to kill yourself, if I wanted to. But I don't. We need you, Wolfe. Go to sleep! Sleep!"

Wolfe's eyelids drooped, he sagged, fell forward.

"Catch him," Kakara ordered, and two of the suited men had Wolfe's suit by the utility belt.

"Good," Kakara said. "Very, very good. Move him into the lab, strip him, and body-search him. Check his body cavities, make sure the son of a bitch doesn't have any surprises. If there are any, it'll be your asses."

"What about his ship?" one of the suited men asked.

"Destroy it," Kakara ordered.

Somewhere, deep in some distant ocean, Wolfe's mind stirred, felt red panic, horror. Somehow he pulled himself up, pushed toward the surface miles away.

Somehow he *reached* out . . .

Or perhaps the Lumina *reached* for him.

"Never mind," Kakara said. "I changed my mind. Don't waste the energy. Let the ship rust with the others."

*

Joshua heard words, repeated over and over.

"Wake up, wake up, come on, man, wake up. Dammit, something's wrong!"

Wolfe floated toward the sea's surface.

"Nothing is wrong," a calm, sterile voice said. "We possibly gave him too much HypnoDec, and he's taking some time to come back to awareness.

"Do not fret, Kakara. All worry does is shorten your life."

Wolfe heard an inarticulate snarl of rage, was just below the surface.

"Yeah," Kakara said. "Yeah, he's back with us. I saw his eyes flicker. Can you hear me?"

"I can hear you," Wolfe said.

"Can you understand me?"

"I can understand you."

"Is he telling the truth?"

"He is," the calm voice said. "Perhaps he's not fully able to analyze what you say, but your speech, your orders are absorbed, and will be retained in his memory."

"Good," Kakara said. "I want to give him something

that'll eat at him. Listen to me, Wolfe. I know who you are, I know everything about you. Joshua Wolfe, prisoner of the Al'ar, commando hotshot during the war, worked for Federation Intelligence, fell on hard times like most soldiers when there's no public tit to suck on, ended up in the Outlaw Worlds as no more'n a bounty hunter. Freelanced for FI, got on their wrong side, is currently hotter'n hell, though there aren't any wanted posters up yet.

"How about that shit?

"When you stole Rita—I don't know why, but you're going to tell me—I told you not to make any long-range investments, didn't I? Jalon Kakara gets what he wants. *Always.* So I started looking for you. I started by backtracking. There's some dead people around, thanks to you. I started with that bitch at the employment agency who sent you to me. She didn't know shit—that resume you mickeyed up fooled her good. But she's dead. I don't like people who play games with me.

"But then I had a dead end. I figured I'd been had by a pro, and there aren't many slick ones. So I had my security people—I've got real good ones, you know—start looking in the sewers people like you live in. One name kept coming up. Joshua Wolfe. But the holo I got didn't match the one on your employment record, so I set it aside.

"But your damned name kept appearing again and again. And most of your compatriots could be accounted for: dead, working, or with good alibis. And this Joshua Wolfe liked working as either a gambler or a barkeep when he was undercover.

"So I took a chance. I play poker like that, too. Get a feeling about things—and I'm damned seldom wrong. And I remembered the number of crooks who've had their faces rebuilt when the heat was on. I went looking for you. Looked hard. Posted a big reward. Real big.

"Nothing for a while, and I was starting to think I was wrong, when I got a call from somebody you know. He said you were doing a job for him, but he'd be willing to hand you over for a price I was willing to pay, if you got out alive. He even left a message for you. 'Like I said, it's only business,' he told me to tell you. Nice friends you got, Wolfe. I would've cleaned up his loose end, but he's a very cagey player and hard to locate. Sooner or later, though, I'll get a lead, and wrap him up, too. Doesn't all that make whatever brain's not doped up squirm, Wolfe? Make you finally realize who you went up against?

"Now I'll tell you what I want you for, but I bet if your mind was working you would've figured it out by now. You're going to tell me where Rita is, and, since I assume you didn't take her for yourself, who the bastard is who's got her."

Wolfe's breathing came fast, and his fingers clawed.

"No, you fool!" the sterile voice came. "You just alerted one of his compulsion modes. Continue and he's not un-likely to have a brain hemorrhage or even suicide!"

"All right, all right," Kakara's voice went. "Forget what I just said about Rita."

Wolfe's breathing eased.

"This is like walking through a minefield," Kakara complained. "All right, Brandt, what do I do now? And don't ever call me a fool again. I only give people but one warning."

"My apologies," the voice said, undisturbed. "Tell him to come fully awake."

"Wolfe, wake up. See, hear, feel," Kakara said.

Wolfe surfaced. He felt the table he was lying on, and the restraining straps. He opened his eyes.

THE DARKNESS OF GOD

Standing next to Kakara was a slender, balding rather friendly-looking man in his early sixties, wearing old-fashioned glasses. He was dressed a bit formally, in an expensive lapel-less jacket and pants and tip-collared shirt.

"Joshua Wolfe," the man said, "I am Doctor Carl Brandt. Have you ever heard of me?"

"No," Wolfe said.

"That is good," Brandt said. "For I've always despised the limelight." He surveyed Wolfe with a smile. "You must forgive my pride, but I consider you my creation. For quite some time I worked for Federation Intelligence. I am the one who devised the various mindblocks and suicide programs that you've been conditioned with so you wouldn't have to worry about torture, drugs, or prolonged interrogation. Very seldom have I had the chance to examine one of my field operatives, particularly one who's been through as much stress as you. While you were unconscious, I ran a battery of mechanical tests, and I am certainly impressed with your mental stability, at least as far as physiological means could determine. I would dearly like to have some time with you, and perform a complete analysis, but Kakara said that's impossible. Since I'm now working for him, I'll just have to watch from the sidelines, I'm afraid."

"You see, Wolfe?" Kakara said. "You can't even escape by dying. Somebody warned me all of you hotshot spooks were loaded for bear, and if anybody fooled around with your mind, tried to interrogate you or use heavy drugs, you'd kill yourself. Shut your brain off permanently, cause a heart seizure—they said there could be a dozen ways you'd been modified to suicide. So I went looking for a good headsplitter, and got lucky. I've found the harder you work, the luckier you get. I ended up with

the guy who put you—or anyway the people like you—
together.

"Another precaution I took. I kept hearing stories
about how you could do things other people couldn't, and
I remembered how you managed to hypnotize me, and
some other people so we thought you were invisible. Or
maybe you even *can* make yourself invisible. The reality
doesn't matter much. A couple of people my men talked
to said it was because you spent so much time with the
Al'ar. They said you were about half Al'ar yourself. Jesus, no wonder I get the skincrawls around you. You're a
goddamned monster like they were. That gave me some
problems. Then Doctor Brandt told me about something
you probably never heard of."

"The Federation was well aware of the Al'ar's mental
abilities," Brandt said. "They mounted a crash program
to find a way to keep the Al'ar from exerting their powers
against men. They tested several versions in combat, but
none seemed to work, except for those helmets you saw
Mister Kakara's men wearing. They were tried out in
a raid just before the Grand Offensive, and appeared
to make men invisible to the Al'ar, or at any rate the
postaction report said the Al'ar were confused at their ap-
pearance. There wasn't time to put the helmets into pro-
duction before the Grand Offensive, and then, when the
Al'ar vanished, there wasn't any need for them. I had
read the preliminary reports, and was able to find a handful of the experimental models. It would appear the reports were correct, wouldn't it? You certainly weren't
about to do anything to prevent your capture."

"You see?" Kakara said, "we've got you fore and aft,
as they used to say. All right, Doctor. Enough talk. How
do we get this bastard to do what we want?"

"Quite simple," Brandt said. "You cannot ask him to
reveal his secrets. But you can order him to take us to

wherever your wife is. And you can order him to make sure she expects friends, not enemies. Ask simple, direct questions, and you'll receive a direct answer. Don't ask for any interpretations or extrapolations. Even with the drug, he has enough free will to avoid answering those. Or else his avoidance mechanisms will be activated."

A slow, dirty smile spread across Kakara's broad, battered face. "All right, then. Take me to Rita."

The sea was a tempest above. Wolfe sank deeper, deeper.

"Set your nav coordinates for the deep space settlement known as Malabar, in the Outlaw Worlds," he told Kakara.

*

Kakara poured himself another drink, lifted it in a toast to the rigid figure of Joshua Wolfe. They were alone in the ship's luxurious captain's suite. "Let me tell you what's going to happen," he said, "once I get Rita. First, I'll kill you, because I don't want any chance of a slipup, and I'm still not sure what you are, a man or an Al'ar. But you won't die easy.

"I thought I'd kill this man, whoever he is, next. But then I considered . . . I think I'll have some fun with Rita first. Show that bastard what I used to like to do to her. But this time, I'll let it go further than I did. Then I'll kill him. Slower than you died.

"As for Rita . . . I thought for a while I'd kill her last," Kakara said, breathing heavily. "But there's worse things than death. After I finish with her, maybe let some of my men have their fun too, I'll leave her alive. Maybe I'll drop her on a world I can think of, with some supplies. Put a bird with a camera on her, and watch what happens. There's—things, I've never been sure what they are, might be interested in her . . . I'd like that."

Kakara wiped his mouth with the back of his hand. "Yeah," he repeated. "I'd like that." He sat for a time, just staring at Wolfe. There was a tap at the door. "Come in."

A man wearing Kakara's jagged crimson flare on a uniform tunic came in, with a sheaf of printout. "I have some preliminary data on Malabar, sir."

"Give me a verbal," Kakara ordered. "Wolfe, this is Pak, one of my analysts. He's helped make Kakara Transport what it is. I use him for the cute details that I'd just as soon nobody know I need. Like what shipping line president likes to hire cute young men for traveling companions, or who grafted who during the war. I set him to work finding out about Malabar. Go ahead, Pak."

"Malabar's the name for the biggest planetoid," the man said. "It's not much more than a moonlet in an asteroid belt, system bap-bap-bap, coordinates thus-and-so, one-time Special Operations Naval Base during the war. After the war it was turned into a parking place for parts of the mothballed fleet."

"Huh! We ever arrange to get a ship from there, back when we were getting started?"

"No, sir. It's pretty well on the fringes of nowhere. It's got a reputation for being a smuggler's base, an illegal shipyard, a transshipment point, and so forth. Not much shows on the surface—most everything's underground. No estimates on current population. Somehow it's been converted to private property, even though the mothballed ships are evidently still there."

"Any government?"

"None I could find. The official caretaker for the scrapheap is someone named Cormac. An ex-Spec Ops pilot, highly decorated, frequently reprimanded. That's the only name he uses now, but his full name is Cormac Pearse. Discharged with the rank of commander."

"Rita was a pilot during the war," Kakara said. "I got the idea she was involved with that stupid commando shit, too. Wolfe, is he the one?"

Joshua said nothing.

"Shitfire," Kakara said in exasperation. "Do you know this man Cormac?"

"Yes."

"Did he know Rita Sidamo?"

"Yes."

"Well, well. So Malabar's where we're going, and it's a real den of thieves, eh? Pak, is that something for us to worry about?"

"Negative, sir," the brown-skinned man with the calm face said. "I've never known criminals, or anyone on the wrong side of the law, to stick up for anyone other than themselves . . . or possibly for an immediate gain."

"And there surely isn't an advantage going up against Jalon Kakara. Still . . . Send in Captain Ives. I think we'll visit Malabar with a little muscle."

*

Five ships broke out of N-space. One was Kakara's liner, two were converted troop transports, two more were scoutships. All wore the jagged crimson insignia.

About three E-diameters distant floated dead starships, warships, liners, freighters, and yachts, orbiting close to the largest planetoid in a scattered asteroid belt.

In the liner's main salon and in the two troopship holds, armed men stared at tall screens, listening to Jalon Kakara:

". . . the bastards have been very happy here on Malabar, taking a ship of mine here, a cargo there, for five or six years. It's taken us that long to track them down, but finally we've found their little den of thieves. The Federation doesn't seem interested in intervening, although I've requested support half a dozen times or more.

"Most of you know Jalon Kakara, and know he doesn't stand interference, and if pressed he has a way of taking care of things in the most effective way possible, if maybe not the way bleeding hearts would prefer.

"That's you, men. Some of you have worked for me in

the past on ticklish little jobs like this, and you know how you're taken care of. You've already seen the insurance policies, no questions asked if anything happens to you, seen the weapons you're issued, and know how promptly you're paid if the mission is successful. This whole operation will be on the same level. All I want is no more Malabar. Not ever. When we pull out, we'll set blasting charges so no other jackals will be able to use this den. And as far as what happens to the men—and women— who're down there . . . They've cast themselves beyond the law, haven't they? Now the law—*my* law—has winkled 'em out. We'll deal with them the best, most permanent way we know, won't we?"

There were hungry roars of approval.

Jalon Kakara motioned, and the pickup went dead. "That's as much as they need to know." He walked across the bridge of the liner to another com, where Wolfe sat. Joshua wore a tiny receiver in one ear, and Brandt, standing to one side, out of pickup range, wore a bonemike. Kakara picked up another mike, positioned it on his breastbone.

"Go ahead," Kakara said. "Make the call."

Wolfe sat motionless.

"*Mister* Kakara," Brandt said in reproof.

"Sorry," Kakara grudged, then said, precisely, "Wolfe, contact Malabar without arousing alarm."

Far down, Joshua fought for control of his mind, his lips. They moved silently, then spoke aloud: "Malabar Control, Malabar Control. This is the—"

"*Corsair.*" Brandt's whisper was loud in Joshua's ear.

"This is the *Corsair*. Request approach and docking instructions."

Wolfe waited, not patiently, not impatiently. Finally: "*Corsair,* this is Malabar" came from the com. "We're a private port, and don't grant approach or landing permission without reason."

Wolfe sat motionless, as if the information had no meaning.

Kakara pursed his lips angrily. "Go ahead," he whispered. "Contact your friend Cormac. Tell him it's all right. Tell him who you are. Just like the last time you talked to him."

Just like the last time . . .

"Malabar, this is *Corsair*. Request you contact Cormac. Tell him I shackle Wilbur Frederick Milton unshackle. Sender Ghost."

"*Corsair,* wait."

Time passed, then: "Ghost," a different voice said, "this is Cormac. Golf Alpha."

"This is Ghost India," Wolfe said.

A few seconds passed, then: "Welcome back to Malabar, Joshua. I assume everything's well with you."

Wolfe made no reply.

"Joshua," Cormac said, "are you all right?"

"He's got a virus," Brandt whispered. Kakara nodded, keyed his mike.

"You have a virus."

"I'm all right," Wolfe said. "I have a virus."

"Well, come on down, and tell me where you acquired that fine fleet I see. Evidently times've been good."

Wolfe made no response.

"You're doing fine," Kakara prodded.

"I'm doing fine," Wolfe echoed.

"Guess it doesn't hurt to be warmish with the Fed, eh? Good. Tell your ship captains to switch to channel 643, and I'll have Control give them individual docking instructions. As for you, you rogue, I've still got the De Montel you didn't finish last time."

"Good," Kakara said. "Why don't you and Rita meet me?"

"Good," Wolfe said. "Why don't you—you and Rita meet me?"

"That's what we planned," Cormac's voice said. "See you in a few, Ghost India."

"Ghost India. Out."

"Now," Kakara gloated, "now it'll all come paid."

He turned to the bridge.

"Captain Ives. Take the deck. Have two men with rifles meet me in the forward lock."

"Yes, sir."

"I'll disembark first with Brandt and Wolfe. Stay linked with me, and I'll give the word for the main attack. We've got a chance to nip 'em in the bud now, and if their leaders are down our job'll be even easier."

"Yes, sir."

"Let's go, Wolfe. This is what they call the hour of reckoning."

*

Kakara was suited up, except for his helmet. He took an expensive live-mask from its pouch, pulled it over his head, and tugged at its earlobe on-sensor. The mask took a moment to warm up and mold to his features. Kakara now was a balding, bearded, benevolent-looking man who might've been a banker. "Like I said, I think of everything," he said, and pulled his helmet on, sealed it, and closed the faceplate.

"Cycle the lock," he ordered. "Entering Malabar. Go first, Wolfe."

Joshua obeyed, walking carefully, one alloy-suited foot in front of the other.

His mind clawed, spat like a caged catamount, *reaching* out, swirling as the deep ocean currents swept him helplessly around.

Then he *felt* another wave, far distant, growing from

nothingness, from another ocean, one that held everything, held the "red virus," held the Al'ar Guardians.

He remembered long years ago, on a gray shore, being very small, and watching someone he loved dive into a cresting wave, and he felt fear for that person. Then the person's hand waved, and he was swimming safely on the far side of the wave as it curled, broke, smashed into shore. Another wave loomed, and feet kicked, and the man—it was a man, his father—swam forward, was swept up by the wave, lying in it, cradled like Joshua's mother cradled him, one hand jutting out, the other along his side, and the wave held him, and he was using the wave, letting its power carry him toward . . .

"Come on, Wolfe," Kakara ordered. "On through."

The outer lock of the liner closed, then the outer lock of Malabar.

Joshua felt the whir of machinery, then heard it dimly as air filled the lock and the inner door slid open.

The five men went into a bare room.

"Where's your friend?"

Wolfe made no response.

Kakara hesitated. "We'll unsuit," he ordered, and twisted his helmet off. "Take off your suit."

Wolfe slowly obeyed. As he stepped out of the lower half of the suit, a speaker crackled. "Joshua, this is Cormac. A slideway was stuck, so we're running a little behind. Be there in a moment."

Kakara smiled thinly. "I like a man who's in a hurry to get what he's due," he almost-whispered, then started as a wall panel slid away, revealing a long, dimly lit hall. "What do we do, Wolfe?"

"Go down there," Joshua said. "He will meet us."

Kakara motioned them forward, his other hand near his holstered gun.

They started down the corridor, first Wolfe; then

Brandt, beside and a little behind him; then Kakara and the two gunmen.

The great, friendly wave was roaring, coming closer, but still far, far away...

A panel slid open about thirty yards distant, and Rita Sidamo and Cormac stepped out. Rita wore a close-fitting tunic, Cormac his familiar khaki pants, faded shirt, and old sleeveless sweater. Neither appeared armed.

Wolfe fought to cry out, to strike, but he could do nothing.

"It's nice seeing you again, Rita," Kakara said, stripping off the mask and drawing his pistol.

"It is you," Rita said, her voice cold with loathing, but utterly unsurprised. "I thought you might have changed, might've been able to let go of things, but—"

"Neither of you move," Kakara said. He keyed his bonemike: "Ives, send in the men."

Cormac leaned back against the passage wall. He shook his head sadly. "Kakara," he said, "you're just about a thorough utter damned fool and someone should have put you out of your misery years ago."

"The only one who'll be doing any killing is me," Kakara said. "Both of you, get your hands up. Now! Connors, Amtel, take them!"

The two men drew their guns, walked forward.

The wave was closer, much closer, its hissing promise of danger loud, very loud...

Rita started laughing.

"Jesus God, but Cormac's right. You're so damned *dumb*." The two holo images vanished as a door panel slid away, and the real Cormac shot Amtel and Connors. The panel closed as Kakara snapped a shot, and the bolt crashed harmlessly into the nearby wall.

The wave broke...

Now everyone was underwater, and Kakara's shout of

alarm was blurred. Wolfe was in no hurry, had all the time in the universe. The drug still flowed in him, but there were antibodies, leukocytes surrounding each molecule of HypnoDec, isolating it, eliminating it . . .

Wolfe was turning, hands, feet in the reflexive attack stance . . .

Kakara spun, almost falling, pistol coming up . . .

Brandt's mouth was open. He was shouting.

Wolfe sidekicked him forward as Kakara fired. The bolt smashed away Brandt's lower jaw and upper cheekbone. He shrieked, clawed at himself, fell.

Kakara's gun bucked with the recoil. He pulled it back on target, and Joshua was crouched, spinning, then up, and his foot caught the blaster, sent it whirling ten feet away to clatter against the deck of the passageway.

Joshua *felt* out, *felt* behind the passageway wall, *felt* Cormac and Rita. Cormac had his gun in one hand, his other on a panel-opening sensor. Joshua *felt* inside the sensor, *felt* its tiny parts. One of them bent, and the lock was jammed. He turned to Kakara. Now there was all the time in the world.

Kakara's eyes were wide in fear.

"You told me once you were good with a knife," Joshua said softly. "There's a blade in your pocket. Get it."

Kakara's eyes never left Joshua's face. His hand swooped into a pocket, came out with a long folding knife. It snapped open with a click.

"No Al'ar secrets," Joshua mocked. "No games. Come to me, Jalon Kakara. You're mine."

Now Joshua was riding the wave, part of it, its power his, spray and foam, and he saw his father laughing from the shore, a woman beside him, his mother, young, alive . . .

Kakara came in cautiously, left hand extended at chest level, right about a foot below, behind the left, holding the knife like a fencer holds his foil, moving sideways, circling, moving toward Wolfe's weak side.

He slashed, and Joshua wasn't there, ducking under the slice, then coming up. Wolfe's right hand blurred, and the back of his fingernails whipped across Kakara's forehead, just a touch but drawing red lines, and then blood poured.

Kakara lunged from a crouch, forefoot sliding out. His knifepoint touched Wolfe's breastbone, then glanced away.

Joshua spun inside him, drove his elbow back into Kakara's shoulder, had his forearm in his left hand, yanked him down toward his knee as it snapped up, and Kakara's ribs smashed. Kakara screamed, fell. Joshua sprang away, waited for him to recover.

The man came halfway to his feet, charged, knife hand slashing, back, forth. Wolfe jumped to one side, struck down with a claw hand, and Kakara's ear ripped, tore, dangled down on his cheek.

A very faint smile came to Wolfe's lips, stayed there.

Kakara lunged once more, and Wolfe's left hand shot out palm first, smashing into Kakara's face below the eyebrow. Kakara's eyeball split as if it had been smashed with a hammer, and clear fluid poured down his face.

Kakara backed away, half-blind, bloody as a bull after the picadors, knife weaving a steel blockade against Wolfe.

"Enough," Wolfe said. "Let's finish it."

Joshua snapped a block with his right hand, kicked into Kakara's armpit, turned inside Kakara's guard, and struck the knife from his hand almost delicately.

Kakara balled his hands into fists, but it was too late.

Joshua shouted and struck Kakara full force in the solar plexus with a right spear-hand. He didn't have time to scream as Wolfe recovered and drove his palm into Kakara's forehead.

The big man's skull smashed like a thin-skinned melon as Joshua reached with his right, tapped four fingers sharply against Kakara's heart, denied it permission to beat, and let the corpse slump to the deck.

The wave was nothing but foam, and there was sand gritting under Joshua's knees, and he rolled sideways, came to his feet in the shallows, laughing, tasting the ocean's salt.

Wolfe stood in an empty corridor, the taste of salt strong in his mouth, four bodies at his feet. There was a smashing sound, and a door panel ripped off its slide, and Cormac and Rita came out, guns ready. When they saw the bodies, both relaxed.

"For a man with a virus infection, you seem to have done all right," Cormac said.

"The bastard ambushed me," Wolfe explained. "Had me under a hypnotic."

"You did fine, Ghost," Cormac said. "But why the hell didn't he screen you, make sure what you were going to say meant . . ."

"He told me soldiers weren't worth anything once they were off the public tit," Wolfe said. "A man who thinks like that isn't going to care about one phonetic letter instead of another."

"I figured something was wrong when Control told me the shackle code you gave him. You never were the kind of slob who uses the same one twice, so that was enough to put my boys in motion. But thanks for the second warning, Ghost India instead of Actual," Cormac said.

"He was always like that," Rita said. "Bull your way through, and everything'll fall into place." She looked at the body. "Didn't work this time, did it, Jalon?"

"I assume you can lumber to our quarters under your own power and let the rest of that hypnotic wear off," Cormac said. "Rita'll escort you. I'll go make sure Kakara's goons are policed up."

"They shouldn't be much of a bother," Joshua said. "One of Kakara's toadies said thieves never fight together. I think their morale is being shaken right about now."

"So he thought he was coming into a nest of thieves, eh?" Cormac laughed humorlessly. "Didn't anybody suspect I anticipate visitors and have a welcome committee on standby? Kakara was a long way from being the first to want to pluck this ripe, dangling fruit called Malabar. Who was it who said a man must be moral to live beyond the law?"

"I forget," Joshua said. "Jesse James, maybe. Or Tamerlane."

Cormac went back through the panel into the hidden passage and was gone.

Rita was still staring down at Kakara's body. "You probably hurt him a lot worse than I would've," she said. "But you should've let me kill him."

"You weren't around," Joshua said blandly, thinking of the jammed lock.

"I didn't mean now," the woman said. "I mean back when you pulled me away from him. Back aboard the *Laurel*."

Joshua grimaced. "Yeah," he said. "I guess I should have."

*

The five men, all experienced at reconning hostile artificial worlds, entered the big, empty chamber cautiously, keeping low, guns moving, pointing like searching eyes.

Small gunports opened behind, above them.

"Now?" a scarred man asked.

"Now," said a woman who, but for her hard, knowing eyes, could've been his daughter, and gunfire spattered.

THE DARKNESS OF GOD

*

A trapdoor opened as one of Kakara's officers stepped on it, the antigrav generator at the bottom of the shaft activated at full reverse thrust, and he fell screaming. The dozen men behind him shrank back and huddled against the walls.

A voice spoke: "The rest of the passage's on hinges too, boys. Better throw away the guns."

The men looked at each other, then threw their blasters down the hall.

"That was sensible," the voice said. "Just stay where you are. There'll be somebody along to collect you in a while. Maybe if you're good we'll feed you a beer."

*

The room was circular, opulent, with scarlet drapes hanging from a high ceiling. There were tables with half-eaten meals, half-empty glasses. It was deserted.

The seven men entered. One picked up a glass and was about to sample its contents.

"Don't," his leader hissed. "Poison!"

The man dropped it. It smashed on the marble floor.

Then the room was full of laughter, rich, amused, female.

One man tried the door they'd entered through and found it locked. The other doors were locked as well.

"What do we do now?" one whispered.

Echoing laughter was his only reply.

*

The two scoutships hung in space just off Malabar, "above" the docked liner and troopships.

Two missiles floated from the back side of the planetoid, and fire hissed from their tails as they went to full drive. Alarms shrilled on the scoutships, and one managed a countermissile launch. The second was too slow, and vanished in a ball of greasy flame and quickly vanishing smoke. A third, fourth, and fifth missile arced around the planetoid's surface, overloading the first scoutship's sensors.

It too exploded soundlessly.

*

"This is Malabar Control," came through the speakers on the bridge of Kakara's liner. "We have taken or killed all of your men. Jalon Kakara is dead. Surrender, or we shall launch missiles against your ships. Reply immediately on this frequency."

The voice was Cormac's.

On the bridge, Captain Ives looked at Pak, who avoided his gaze.

"You have thirty seconds," Cormac's voice said.

Ives picked up a com.

*

"We'll sort through them," Cormac said cheerily, "then arrange for one of our ships to dump them somewhere not too far from civilization, on its next run with the goodies . . . Not that I'm sure what's still civilization. Things have been getting decidedly strange."

"I know," Wolfe agreed. He picked up the snifter, swirled it, sipped, and set it back down. "I better not have any more of this before dinner," he said. "I've been leading a clean life lately, and I'm sort of out of training."

"Just as well," Cormac said, draining his beer. "I'm starving. Rita, where are we going to eat?"

"Fifth Level," she said. "They're doing a victory banquet. I already accepted."

"You want company, Joshua? I can think of a couple of lovelies who wouldn't mind meeting the Hee-ro of Malabar."

Kristin's face came to Wolfe, was pushed away.

"Like I said, I'm living a clean life lately." He stood.

THE DARKNESS OF GOD

"Joshua," Cormac said, "you said you knew that things were weird out. Did you have anything to do with that?"

"In a way."

"Are you away from it now?"

Joshua slowly shook his head. "Now I'm about to dive straight into the middle of things. Let's go. If this is likely to be my last meal, it might as well be Trimalchian."

* CHAPTER SEVENTEEN *

FEDERATION URGES CALM

Martial Law Temporary Measure to Quell Rioting

Press for More

NEW DJAKARTA, EARTH— Federation spokesperson Lisbet Ragnardotter announced today that the martial law recently proclaimed on many Federation worlds should be considered strictly a "temporary measure."

She cited the recent rioting on Starhome and Ganymede as justification for the extreme measures, and said the emergency proclamations will be withdrawn as soon as what she termed the "currently unsettled situation" is stabilized.

"Those Federation worlds we have been forced to temporarily withdraw from will be strongly supported, and as soon as the current military buildup reaches proper strength, they will be reinforced."

She stressed there is no cause for alarm by any Federation citizen, and said that the current flood of rumors are "palpably false to any logical man or woman, and should be ignored. Those spreading these wild tales should be reprimanded for attempting to destabilize the situation and, if they persist, reported to the proper authorities."

No questions were allowed at the conference, and no information was available about the reported loss of Federation units somewhere near the Outlaw Worlds.

* CHAPTER EIGHTEEN *

Michele Strozzi looked out at the workmen swarming over the scaffolding that marked where the new Residence was rising. *His* Residence, he thought with quiet satisfaction. He waited until the whispering died, then turned. Twenty-seven men and women looked back at the slender, quietly dressed man.

"Very well," he said. "Is it agreed that, in the present state of emergency, I speak for the Order, and shall continue to do so until peace has returned and a proper consensus may be found?"

There were nods, quiet yeses.

"Good. I could practice false modesty and thank you for the honor, but I truly believe I am the best suited to represent the Chitet at this time and possibly in the future. Hopefully you will continue to agree with me. I have been made Master Speaker because I have argued we must take immediate action, rather than continuing to moil about in the shock and distress caused by the death of Master Speaker Athelstan and most of our hierarchy."

"I think most of us here agree on that," a man with a neat goatee said. "But what, exactly, should this action be? There's been the conflict."

"I do have a plan, one which I think will be the best for the Order. However, indulge me for a few moments, and consider history. A bit more than three hundred years ago, we attempted to bring order to Man's worlds and replace the Federation, or, at any rate, install our brightest minds at its head. Obviously we were premature, and Man had not yet developed his fullest logic, for we were defeated, and our leadership either imprisoned or sent into exile. We bided our time, knowing that the battle had only begun.

"A hundred years later, on consideration of the Al'ar phenomenon, our then-Master Speaker realized we had erred in assuming we could continue at leisure to develop our culture, our society, and allow Man to recognize our superiority when it became obvious.

"Further analysis was done, the process and records of which seem to be lost, and our Master Speaker determined, for the ultimate good of Man, that we must seek an alliance with the Al'ar, since it was clear to him they possessed talents superior to Man's. With such an alliance, we might learn these talents and continue assisting Man in his progression toward rationality. We were rejected by the Al'ar, and our envoys destroyed.

"We returned to our normal passive ways, and time passed. Perhaps this was an error in our logic, and we should have pressed matters. I believe it was, but my synthesis isn't complete. Eventually, as we had predicted, war broke out between the Al'ar and Man. We firmly backed the human cause, having come to the realization that if there could be no cooperation between Al'ar and Chitet, they must be unutterably destroyed. The manner of their destruction is still unknown, but they vanished from our known universe, just before the final attack was to be made. Whether this was some sort of mass suicide or an interdimensional shift is unknown. Certainly since the Al'ar seemed completely alien to this spacetime, the second theory seems the most probable to me.

"In the midst of the celebration over the war's end,

THE DARKNESS OF GOD

our new Master Speaker, Matteos Athelstan, made a remarkable jump in logic, using techniques and sources that are still being sought. He decided that the Al'ar had not only fled the threat of destruction by Man, but that they also recognized a greater threat in the offing, one which they would be unable to defeat and hence refused to confront. He did not know what it was, or even what form it might take, but determined, as you all know well, to recover any and all Al'ar artifacts that seemed pertinent to their weaponry and thinking and turn their benefits to our Order. This included the Lumina stones and, when the existence of the ur-Lumina, the Overlord Stone, was discovered, that became the prime area of concern.

"At this point our matrix of events intersected Joshua Wolfe, who we quickly realized was our most dangerous enemy, the one who's brought greater destruction to the Order than anyone in its history. Master Speaker Athelstan captured this man, if he is indeed just a man, and attempted to use him in our quest for the Overlord Stone."

"*Just* a man, you said?" a very old man asked.

"Wolfe spent time among the Al'ar," Strozzi said. "He was supposedly their captive at the beginning of the war, although I privately wonder if that is a fact or a cover-up Wolfe or his sometime superiors in Federation Intelligence promulgated.

"I personally believe that Master Speaker Athelstan erred slightly in his thinking about Joshua Wolfe, accepting that he was truly a renegade, rather than an agent in deep cover working for Federation Intelligence. Certainly it's absurd to think one man could wreak the havoc he has managed." Strozzi glanced reflexively at the ruins of the Residence.

"At any rate, Master Speaker Athelstan met his death attempting to use Wolfe to find the Overlord Stone. As you all know, Master Speaker Athelstan was very careful about security. Perhaps he was too careful, since we still have no idea exactly what happened on Rogan's World. All records of the event appear to have been destroyed with Master Speaker Athelstan's ship. However, we have sent skilled operatives to Rogan's World, and they have analyzed the situation. We have some tentative appreciations:

"1. Joshua Wolfe was not killed in the debacle, but survived the destruction of Master Speaker Athelstan. Whether he was a causative factor is unknown.

"2. He managed to secure the Overlord Stone from the traitor and murderess who had possession of it, and he fled, possibly with the connivance of those Chitet who had been ordered to guard him closely. That last is a mere theory, though. But it is absolutely known that he has possession of the Lumina and that he killed Token Aubyn and destroyed her political machine that controlled Rogan's World.

"Where Wolfe went from Rogan's World is unknown. What he intends to do with the Overlord Stone is unknown. What Joshua Wolfe has to do with this present emergency in the former Al'ar Worlds, the so-called Outlaw Worlds, and the settled systems close to them within the Federation is also unknown.

"My belief is that Wolfe is indeed connected with the strange events that have come upon us, strange events foreseen by Master Speaker Athelstan. It is my belief that *all* of the events I've discussed, this possible alien entity that is wreaking so much havoc, the Overlord Stone, the Al'ar, and Joshua Wolfe are inextricably linked. It is also my belief that we are being invaded, that there is a new alien race no one knows anything whatsoever about, and they are infinitely more hostile than the Al'ar. We must act immediately to save Mankind."

"I would like to see an analysis of your thinking, Brother," a woman said.

"I cannot provide it at the moment," Strozzi said frankly. "There are some quantum leaps I'm not yet able to justify mathematically. But I *know* I am right, just as Master Speaker Athelstan *knew* he was right, and events bore him out."

"Accepting for the moment your thesis," the woman continued, "have you a course of action?"

"I do," Strozzi said. "The place where the ur-Lumina was found is, I believe, a locus. The ship where the Overlord Stone was found had been deliberately placed where it was by the Al'ar, and they did nothing by accident or without considerable deliberation. I also note that the earliest reports of the current phenomena came from sectors close to that point.

"I propose we send two or three of our finest reconnaissance craft, manned by the most skilled and experienced crews, to that sector, and, just within range of communication, our most powerful battlefleet, ready for the most immediate response to any eventuality. To prevent any errors, I shall accompany that fleet."

"What do you expect to happen?"

"I don't know," Strozzi said.

"Isn't there considerable risk to the recon ships?" someone else wondered. "And, conceivably, to yourself? We do not wish to sacrifice another Master Speaker."

"There is," Strozzi said quietly, "considerable risk to all Mankind right now. We must not delay. I feel the Overlord Stone will once again return to where it was found, and it will be returned by Joshua Wolfe. And when it does, we shall, we *must*, be ready to strike."

* CHAPTER NINETEEN *

"Well?" Rita asked. Cormac was at the ship's controls; she leaned back in the navigator's seat.

"Phew," Wolfe said. " I thought I knew how messed up things have been lately. Not even close, was I?" He handed back the three fiches of recent newswires. "The world hasn't become a better place in my absence."

"And you're going back into it? You sure?" Cormac asked.

"I don't have any choice," Wolfe said flatly.

"You could always give up the Saint George complex and get into a deep hole with us," Rita suggested, "at least until things shake out a little and you can see through the mud a bit more clearly."

Joshua smiled politely.

"It was worth a try," she said. "We'll be breaking out of N-space in—four ship-hours."

*

Joshua turned end for end and touched down on the *Resolute*'s hull. He keyed the lock door sensor's pattern. It slid open, and he pulled himself inside the lock, looked back.

Cormac's ship, a former Federation deep-space scout, hung about half a mile distant. Its signal lights blinked.

G-O-O-D L-U-C-K S-E-E Y-O-U N-E-X-T T-I-M-E T-H-R-U.

"Not in this life," Joshua said, waving a hand in farewell before he entered the *Resolute*.

THE DARKNESS OF GOD

*

Wolfe smelled tangerines, heard the long wail of a saxophone; a memory came, went, too brief to do more than make him smile, and the *Resolute* came out of N-space.

The ship hung in the darkness between stars. Joshua checked all screens. "Nothing but nothing out there," he said to himself. "Now to see what we shall see."

The Lumina sat in a padded case in the center of the control room. He picked it up, carried it to an empty storeroom, and put it in the middle of the floor.

Joshua stripped and took a hachiji-dachi stance facing the Lumina, legs spread, body straight, relaxed, hands curled into fists. He took slow breaths in, breathing from his diaphragm, held them, exhaled. Breathe five . . . hold seven . . . exhale seven . . .

Wolfe bowed deeply to the Lumina, sat cross-legged on the deck without using his hands.

Breathe . . .

His mind reached for the Al'ar stone.

The Lumina flared, colors flashing across the walls as if it were a spinning multicolored mirror-ball, but the head-size stone stayed motionless.

Then very slowly it rose into the air and hovered at Wolfe's eye level.

Joshua's breathing came faster, and the colors swirled around him.

Then he was in the control room, and his presence moved from sensor to sensor. Screens blanked, showed new displays. The navigation computer whined for an instant, then stopped, and its screen lit.

SET FOR JUMP

A sensor was depressed, with no finger, no hand visible. The *Resolute* vanished into N-space.

Joshua "returned" to the storeroom, but did not "enter"

224

his body. He moved outward, beyond the hull of the ship, into the confusion of hyperspace.

But there was no confusion now. He was in a constantly changing cage, a lattice that moved, enlarged, shrank, dipped around him. Beyond it were the objects of conventional space as they moved in their orbits, so many clockwork mice.

He heard sounds, the hiss of suns, the crackle of radiation, the hum of quasars.

Wolfe saw his ship as a loose assemblage of various atoms, then, more deeply, as a spaghetti-heap of vibrating "strings." He let it go far past him, then he was in front of it as it flashed past.

Wolfe laughed. He felt like taking the *Resolute* in his hands, remembering the toy ship he'd had as a child; he wondered what had happened to it, but stopped himself.

He shifted until he was floating above the *Resolute*, keeping it company as it went from one point to another to a third, following the irrational logic of its computers. To Wolfe, it made perfect sense. Perhaps he could jump "ahead," await the *Resolute* when it left N-space—but he hesitated.

In that instant, he returned to the storeroom, and the Lumina settled to the deck. It was now a small gray boulder, with only a few flecks of color. Joshua stood without using his hands and went out of the storeroom. There was no sweat on his forehead; his face showed no sign of strain.

"If I can do that again," he said, "I might be getting somewhere."

*

The dead voice whispered dry words:

. . . They all go into the dark,
The vacant interstellar spaces, the vacant into the vacant,

. . .
And dark the Sun and Moon, and the Almanach de
    Gotha
And the Stock Exchange Gazette, the Directory of
    Directors
And cold the sense and lost the motive of action
And we all go with them, into the silent funeral.

Wolfe turned the audio off, stared out into the silence
between the stars.

*

The *Resolute* flew low over the planet that was dead
without ever having been born, empty, desolate.

He *felt* the missiles tracking him, the metallic death
one grasping-arm sensor-touch away, *felt* the strangeness, the terror under the world's dry, silent stone.

"This is the One Who Fights From Shadows," he
broadcast in Al'ar yet again.

There was a faint crackle on a speaker.

"You are received," a voice answered. **"Welcome
back. We feared you had gone beyond, had met the
real death when you ordered us to flee and you remained behind to fight those you said were the
Chitet."**

"I live," Wolfe said, and fatigue showed in his voice.
"But Taen met his doom at their hands."

"That we knew," the voice said, and Wolfe recognized it as that of Jadera, the Al'ar who was the head of
the tiny handful of aliens who'd chosen not to make The
Crossing with the rest of their race, but remained behind
as Guardians to hold off the "virus" that had driven them
from their own universe into Man's. **"We felt him pass,
feared you had gone with him, for we are not able to
sense your life as we could an Al'ar's."**

"He died well," Joshua said, "as the warrior he was."

"Of course," Jadera said. "There could be no other possibility ... Or for us. The time is very close now. Our mutual enemy has gained a foothold in this galaxy, and is ready to transfer its center, its nucleus, here. We were preparing for an attack, knowing that we could not succeed without the Great Lumina, which I sense you have."

"I do."

"And do you know how to use it?"

"I am learning."

"Enter your home, then, One Who Fights From Shadows, and we shall ready ourselves for the last battle."

A radar screen flickered, showing movement on the ground below. Wolfe zoomed a forward screen to its highest magnification and saw a rocky hillside yawning open—the entry port to an underground Al'ar hangar.

*

Once before, Joshua had eaten Al'ar foods in this shadowy great cavern, with light-sculptures flaming on the walls. But then it had been as much of a banquet as the Al'ar were capable of, welcoming Taen. But if they weren't capable of much celebration, Joshua thought, their mourning was equally nonexistent. Half a dozen times the half dome on the table in front of him opened, and he took the plate it held and ate. Jadera sat across from him, equally absorbed in his meal.

Finally replete, Joshua made no move to accept the next plate offered. Jadera did the same. They sat in silence for a time, as was the Al'ar custom.

"I have a question," Joshua said. "When an Al'ar dies, like Taen did, does his—spirit, I suppose it should be called, make The Crossing?"

THE DARKNESS OF GOD

"A good question," Jadera answered. "I do not know. That was the hope of some of our more romantic brothers."

"Utterly impossible," an Al'ar at a nearby table said. "No one who died in our previous galaxy appeared in this one. Dead is dead."

Joshua half smiled. He recognized the alien, Cerigo, who had lost his broodmate and offspring during the war and carried his hatred for Man close, like a favorite garment.

"I thank you for honoring me with your presence, Cerigo. Last time, you refused to eat with me."

"I would do the same this time," Cerigo said. "But we shall fight together soon, and only a worm allows enmity to one who will share the blooding."

"Thank you."

Cerigo made a noise Wolfe took to be an acknowledgment.

"Cerigo reminds me of an admiral I served under," Wolfe said. "He always spoke in an animal-growl, too. But very few of us could fight as hard as he did."

"Cerigo was a great ship leader once," Jadera said. "An admiral, in charge of what you call a *battleship*. He was one of our best commanders."

"Not good enough," Cerigo said. "For I did not kill enough Men for it to matter."

"Cerigo has been selected to be in command of our attack," Jadera said.

"Good," Wolfe said. "A man who hates well generally fights well, as long as he does not allow his animal side to rule."

"There is no worry of that," Jadera said. "Cerigo is far too experienced a warrior to succumb to any ... what you call *emotion*," he finished, then changed the subject. "None of us have seen the Overlord Stone for a great time," he said. "Some of us have never witnessed it at all. Would that be possible?"

"You hardly need ask permission of me," Joshua said, "for it is your property."

"No longer," Jadera said. "We discussed the matter while you were gone, and agreed that if you succeeded in returning alive with it, you would probably be the most capable to use it against the invader."

"You assume much of my capabilities," Wolfe said.

Jadera made no response.

Wolfe opened the case that sat at his feet and lifted the Lumina out.

Around him other Guardians stirred, and lifted their grasping organs.

Wolfe *felt* their power, took it into him, let the Lumina lift from the floor, float in the room's center, its kaleidoscope colors flaming.

He looked around, at the corpse-white long faces, their attention fixed on the Lumina.

"Will this tool, this weapon, suffice?" he asked.

Jadera turned to him. "We do not know. But we have other devices prepared which might help. Come."

*

Wolfe couldn't see the far walls or the roof of the hangar. But it seemed small, barely large enough to house the monstrous battleship that loomed over their heads.

Its fuselage was a flattened cylinder, reminding Joshua of a shark. It had two thick "wings," one curving forward, the other aft. At the tip of each wing were weapons stations, and other podlike stations were studded irregularly along the ship's body. It was commanded from another pod, located just under the shark's chin, where a remora might hang. Its stern bristled with ungainly antennae for the ship's sensing and ECM capabilities.

The ship was a mile long, perhaps longer, greater from wingtip to wingtip.

"I never—thank the Powers Beyond Myself—" Joshua said, "saw or even heard of anything like this during the war."

"It was still in final testing when the war ended," Cerigo said. "Our Command On High was trying to determine where its deployment would be most effective. It was intended to be able to deal with an entire Federation battlefleet by itself, needing escorts only for its antimissile screen."

"Taking this ship out against the invader is very noble," Wolfe said carefully, making sure he would give no offense.

"But one single ship cannot ever succeed in a mission, and all aboard it will be doomed, without coming close to accomplishing their task."

He remembered history, remembered a doomed great ocean-ship called the *Yamato*.

"We realize that," Cerigo said. "However, the final reports from those who stayed behind in our home universe suggested that fusion weapons appeared to set this—this entity, whatever it is, back. These we could deploy successfully. We also have a sunray, such as you used against us from your planetary fortresses. The ship is also armed with countermissiles, in the unlikely event it encounters any Federation ships before it reaches the target zone. Perhaps not enough, but there was no other option, besides curling in our burrows waiting to be spaded out and skinned. The Al'ar were never burrowing worms."

"All this is meaningless noise," Jadera said, "since you have recovered the Mother Lumina. Now we are capable of fighting on an equal plane, or so I believe."

"I feel," Wolfe said, "like an aborigine who's just been

given a machine gun without an instruction manual and told to take care of those bastards who're wiping him out."

"Not a bad comparison," Jadera said, also in Terran, then reverted to Al'ar. **"Do you actually think *we* know anything ourselves?"**

*

The Lumina floated in the middle of the room. Joshua sat cross-legged underneath it. Al'ar, either in the flesh or in projection, were clustered around him. Occasionally one or another would wink out as other duties called.

"Our strategy," Jadera said, **"will be to fight from the great ship, which we have named the *Crossing*. We have other ships—three for each Al'ar—which have been roboticized, so in fact we have a fleet of more than 160 craft, including the *Nyarlot*. Each is capable of launching missiles into the invader when we close. We suggest that you attempt to strike the invader with the Lumina's force. Perhaps you may hurt it, more likely you might be able to force it back, through the rift into the universe it came from, once the Al'ar home."**

Joshua sat thinking.

"Do you have a better plan?" Jadera asked.

"I do not," he said.

"We should begin our strike from where the Lumina was positioned, in its satellite," Jadera said. **"Perhaps, even though the Al'ar are gone, such positioning may increase its power."**

"Very well," Joshua said in Terran, and rose. **"Let us go to war."**

* CHAPTER TWENTY *

"You may or may not be pleased, Admiral Hastings," Cisco said, "that I specifically requested the *Andrea Doria* and its battlefleet for this mission."

"I'll be honest," the officer said. "I'm not. I'm not sure, with everything else going wrong around us, this is the most important mission my ships and men should be used for. We've pulled back from who knows how many worlds in the past few months. Others have evidently fallen into chaos, anarchy. Entire sectors aren't reporting. We've lost at least sixteen fleets . . ."

"Eighteen," Cisco corrected. "That's confirmed. More likely twenty-three."

"To what? To something nobody can even see?"

"That's also been corrected," Cisco said. "Although the information won't make you feel any better."

"What the *hell* are we fighting?"

Cisco motioned him to a corner of the bridge, away from the other officers. "You don't have the proper clearance," he said. "No one else aboard the *Andrea Doria* does either, but I was advised by my superior I should inform you of the Federation's current explanation for these events, so you'll understand the importance of your orders. It appears our universe has been invaded by some sort of single-cell—although 'cell' is not the right word—

being, an entity that's capable of making interstellar flights, jumping from star to star."

"That's impossible!"

"It certainly is," Cisco agreed. "And I'll give you an even less possible truth: This being, this alien, appears to be able to alter the very nature of matter, to make it disassemble itself, then reassemble in the form of the alien's structure."

Hastings looked at Cisco. "That violates every single principle I have ever learned," he said. "This alien is capable of altering string, of altering its vibrations, its resonance, into—into what?"

"Into its own form of matter," Cisco said. "Into itself. Not matter, not antimatter."

"So everything will become part of it eventually? Stars, planets, space, people?"

"If that theory's correct," Cisco said, "yes. Maybe not people, though. I assume you've heard the stories of the 'burning disease'?"

"I have, and they're as utterly unbelievable as what you just told me. Preposterous!"

Cisco didn't reply.

Hastings' shoulders slumped. "I'm not a fool, Cisco. Obviously there's *something* out there, something utterly unknown that's slowly destroying everything. So how do we fight it?"

"No one knows yet," Cisco said. "The Federation has anyone and everyone working on every possible solution."

"With obviously nothing but theory so far?"

"As far as I know," Cisco said. "Needless to say, none of this is to be discussed with anyone until I personally advise you differently."

"I wouldn't anyway," Hastings said. "I don't need to be in command of sailors who think me mad." He took a deep breath. "But how is destroying this Chitet fleet going to solve matters?"

"First, the Federation hardly needs traitors among its own," Cisco said. "Second, the Chitet have attempted to league themselves with other aliens in the past. The Al'ar. Now we've gotten word that they've assembled their warships and moved them into the Al'ar Worlds."

"Why?"

"We don't know," Cisco said. "But we know where they are. We have a highly placed source within the cult, someone who recently recognized his patriotism." Cisco's lips twisted into a smile. "Or else no longer wanted to back a loser."

"I have the coordinates but little else," Hastings said. "What are your orders, once we emerge from N-space, assuming the Chitet are there?"

"We can expect around a hundred ships," Cisco said. "All Al'ar War vintage, but well reconditioned. None bigger than the battlecruiser you drove away when we recovered Joshua Wolfe from them. They're to be given one chance to surrender, and if they do not accept, they're to be destroyed in detail. The Chitet must *never* be allowed to work against Man again."

Hastings nodded, managed a smile. "At least it'll be good to have a nice, simple battle to fight," he said, "instead of nothing but confusion."

* CHAPTER TWENTY-ONE *

"Are we ready to lift?" Joshua asked.

"All systems go," the *Grayle* reported.

"Did you miss me?"

There was a silence. Joshua was about to withdraw his question, then: *"By 'miss,' analysis indicates that I am supposed to provide an emotional response, that is, your absence created a negative condition in me. Further consideration suggests you are intending what is listed in my files as a 'jest' or 'joke.' However, I do admit a preference for being used, for being active, rather than being in a state of nonbeing, such as I have been since landing on this planet."*

"Well dip me in a bucket," Joshua said in some amazement. "Cormac ought to change his name to Viktor. Okay, Monster. Take it on out of here."

"Understood."

The *Grayle* came clear of the hangar floor, and the door opened. The ship moved slowly out over the wasteland, then climbed for open space.

"Lifting clear," Joshua reported. **"Time until entering N-space, approximately twelve ship-minutes."**

"You are heard," Cerigo's voice came over a speaker. **"We will lift in approximately five of your minutes, enter N-space approximately fifteen of your minutes afterward. We will therefore emerge at the desired point**

235

in exactly eight of those minutes after you. Is that correct?"

"Correct. This is the *Grayle,* clear."

*

The contact alarm gonged as Federation ships came out of N-space. Michele Strozzi heard someone swear, ignored it. "We were betrayed," he said calmly to his admiral, Ignatieff.

"Yes, sir. Should we attempt to withdraw?"

"No," Strozzi decided. "They'll pursue us, and we do not need to have an enemy at our back. Eventually we'll have to confront the Federation, to make them realize we're right in what we're doing. How many of them are there?"

Ignatieff asked an electronics officer and relayed the answer: "About 160, sir."

"They outnumber us," Strozzi said. "But the Federation's ships are mostly manned with recruits, and ours with veterans. They've been subject to peacetime economics; we've kept our men fully trained. Admiral Ignatieff, destroy this Federation fleet. Perhaps this is our beginning, even though it was not in my projection of coming events."

"Yes, sir."

*

The Federation ships came out of N-space in battle order, a huge crescent, sweeping toward the Chitet fleet.

"As I promised you, Admiral," Cisco said. "The Chitet. Do you wish the honors?"

Hastings took the mike his aide held out. "This is the Federation battleship *Andrea Doria,*" he said. "I order all vessels not under Federation command to immediately signal blue-white-blue as a signal of surrender. You have five minutes to comply, or you will be attacked."

"Captain," a weapons officer reported, "one of the ships has launched missiles. I've activated countermeasures."

"There's your answer," Cisco said.

"Very well," Hastings said, switching to another frequency. "All ships. This is the *Andrea Doria*. Authentication Witnal. Attack!"

*

Missiles spat from the Chitet ships at the oncoming Federation fleet, and countermissiles flashed back. Explosions dotted space and quickly vanished. Other, greater blasts came as the Federation took hits, and ships pinwheeled out of formation or drove "down" or "up" in senseless directions.

The Chitet launched a second wave of missiles as they closed on the Federation.

*

Too many Federation weapons crews were inexperienced, but there were still veterans of the Al'ar War among them.

Aboard one Federation ship a warrant officer in his sixties pushed a lieutenant out of his way and crouched over a launch station, cursing as his prosthetic leg creaked.

"Target acquired," he said, his voice level. "Launching— One launched—Two launched . . . Now, goddammit, Lieutenant, watch how I'm trying to spoof 'em. The first one goes for the incoming missile . . . closing . . . Got the son of a bitch! The second goes right on through the debris, uses the crap to mask itself against their countermeasures—don't go to autopilot but keep the controls and you ride it right on into the . . ."

*

The Federation missile smashed into the bow of the *Udayana*, into its electronics bays, and explosions tore at the battlecruiser, ripping the bridge decking three floors above like an ancient tin can.

Michele Strozzi was sent spinning into a control panel, blood spattering the screens beside him. He sprawled motionless for an instant, then stumbled to his feet. He saw Admiral Ignatieff's head lying next to him, looked for his body, saw nothing.

An aide was beside him, arm around his shoulders. "Sir, lie down," she shouted.

He looked at her, opened his mouth to say something reassuring, inspiring. Blood poured out, drenching her tunic, and his eyes went dull and he went down limply.

The aide knelt, keening in loss, and another missile smashed directly into the bridge. The *Udayana* exploded in a long sheet of flame.

*

The Federation forces swept forward, the ships on the ends of the formation following orders, trying to bend the vast C around the Chitet to encircle the fleet. But the center of their pattern was already broken, and the battle center was a swirling catfight.

"All Federation ships," someone—no one ever admitted to the command—ordered, "break formation and choose your own targets. I say again, go for their throats!"

*

The *Grayle* left N-space for Armageddon. Wolfe gaped at the madness, keyed his com.

"Nyarlot, Nyarlot, this is the One Who Fights From Shadows. There's some kind of battle going on here."

"Who is fighting?"

Wolfe took a moment to examine his screens, calm himself. "It appears to be a Federation fleet . . . I don't know who they're against—maybe Chitet? Maybe civil war?"

"What should we do, One Who Fights From Shadows?"

"I don't know," Wolfe said.

"Whose enemy are they?" Cerigo said. "Should we stand aside? Will they leave us alone, let us fight our own battle, fight the battle for them as well? Can we explain in time, and would they believe us? Would they join us? We stand by for your will."

Joshua took a deep breath, gave an order.

*

On the bridge of the *Andrea Doria*, the ship's executive officer glanced at a master screen and screamed in utter horror, seeing something out of a nightmare vanished long years before.

*

The Al'ar ships came from nowhere, sweeping forward in a *grasping hand* formation, a phalanx of corpse-white death.

It seemed to some watchers they came slowly, instead of at their light-second-devouring real speed.

At their head was a monstrous winged shark, scimitar-shaped, beyond any memory of the Al'ar terrors. It was flanked by the robot ships, flying in fours, two abreast, two slightly behind the first pair, as the Al'ar held their grasping organs in combat stance.

Shipskins bulged, split, and birthed slender missiles that trembled once and homed in on their targets. Some Federation or Chitet ships had time for countermissile launches, but too many didn't see the doom from nowhere.

The Al'ar formation lifted "above" the spinning pandemonium, swept past, reversed course, and came back in a second attack.

A Chitet frigate spat four missiles at the *Nyarlot*; five countermissiles launched and closed on the missiles.

There were three explosions, then a fourth, larger one on one of the *Nyarlot*'s fighting pods.

Guardians died, and the ships they controlled veered away from the fight, uncontrolled.

Wolfe *felt* their deaths and flinched. He saw the out-of-control ships and reached for them, as he'd once taken and crushed a missile. The ships were his. Wolfe didn't notice that the ships broke formation and regrouped—not as the two-two they'd attacked in, but as five fingers, four ships almost parallel, the fifth guarding the rear, human fingers reaching for human throats.

He sent them into the madness, controlling them as they fired their missiles. Federation and Chitet ships were there, past, gone. He came back, dimly aware of the *Nyarlot* somewhere behind, volleying its own killers toward the human ships.

A ship he knew, a ship he'd been aboard, was close to "him," but he veered his fighting formation away, away from the *Andrea Doria*.

Wolfe's face had a tight, skull-like grin.

*

"Whiskey element, engage Chitet vessels at 320-12," Hastings ordered. "Hotel, please respond to this station. I say again, Hotel, respond if you are still capable. Quebec, regather your elements." He was as calm as if he were on a peacetime exercise, or moving models on a map.

Cisco stood beside him, trying to stay out of the way, trying to make sense of the madness that englobed them.

Then there was something else on the bridge. It was an Al'ar, an Al'ar nearly fifteen feet high.

Someone shrieked, and a blaster smashed through the Al'ar and blew a hole in the deck above the apparition. The Al'ar stepped forward, and its grasping organ reached. Cisco shrank back, but the organ came on, came on.

His hand fumbled in a pocket, came out with a gray

stone, the Lumina he'd taken from Joshua Wolfe, and brandished it like a talisman. The Al'ar brushed it aside, and it smashed to the deck and shattered.

The alien changed, and for an instant Cisco saw Joshua Wolfe reaching for him. Then the grasping organ touched Cisco's chest, and he screamed, flung back as if smashed by a blaster bolt.

The Al'ar vanished.

Hastings had time enough to manage, "What in Mithra's holy name was . . ." Then three missiles hit the *Andrea Doria*, and it broke in half. The rear half exploded, the forward section spun away from the battle, into an orbit without end, vanishing into emptiness.

*

Then there were fewer ships and fewer still as Chitet ships broke and ran for hyperspace, and Federation ships went after them, or fled on their own. There were no more than a dozen of Man's ships left in that outer darkness.

"End contact," Cerigo commanded, and Wolfe obeyed, pulling his "fingers" back, away. He sat on the bridge of the *Grayle*, panting as if he'd fought a tournament.

"The way is clear," Cerigo said.

"Yes," Joshua agreed. **"Slave all ships to mine. Now we must approach our real enemy."**

*

The *Grayle* emerged in the depths of what had been the Al'ar Worlds. Joshua *felt* redness, death, change, all around him, and his body burned, as if too close to an all-surrounding fire. The stars were dim, the planets indistinct, their shapes blurred, red around them, consuming them, changing them into itself.

The *Nyarlot* and the robot-ships were there.

Joshua *heard* hisses of rage from the Guardians aboard the *Nyarlot* as they sensed their ancient enemy.

No commands were given, none were necessary, and the ships spat heavy missiles at the entity, at what should have been empty space, but Wolfe saw it as red-speckled, pulsing like a diseased organ.

Nuclear fires blossomed, died.

Joshua's burning pain ebbed, returned more strongly, ebbed once more.

He *saw*, aboard the *Nyarlot*, a fighting pod, as Al'ar flesh smoked, curled, and blackened, and Guardians fell, dying, dead.

A small sun was born in nothingness as the Al'ar sunray activated, and fire ravened at the alien.

Joshua felt it shrink, writhe.

The sunray burnt itself out, and the alien gathered its force, its power.

Suddenly the *Nyarlot*'s drive went to full power, and it drove away from the *Grayle*.

"Die well, One Who Fights From Shadows," came Cerigo's last broadcast. **"Die as we die. Die as an Al'ar."**

The *Nyarlot*'s engines, fuel, and missiles exploded as one. Flame seared at Wolfe's eyes, and his screens blanked for a moment. He *felt* the Guardians, the last of the Al'ar, leave this spacetime.

"May you be on The Crossing," he said without realizing it. The pain was gone momentarily, and he *felt* the invader recoil. He took the deaths of the Guardians and threw them at the "virus" as he'd once hurled Taen's death at his murderer to slay him.

The Lumina floating behind him was a flare of solid white, starlike, flaming hot.

Now he saw the invader not as the "red virus," but, in flashes, as the Al'ar might have, great writhing fanged crawlers, worms, the monstrous worms that had forced the ground creatures who became the Al'ar from their burrows to the surface and then to the stars.

The worms became the serpent of Midgard, gnawing at Yggdrasil for an instant. But Wolfe's "eyes" went beyond, saw the bits that composed the "virus," reached below the molecular, the atomic levels, and *felt* the resonance of its ultimate bits.

He allowed the resonance for an instant, absorbed it, then forbade it.

The alien strings/not-strings hummed down into silence, and there was a vortex of nothingness, absolute nothing, not matter, not energy, not antimatter, at the core of the invader, spreading, eating, a not-cancer.

Far away, Joshua *felt* the rift in space, then was standing in the huge cavern, hearing the dripping of liquid from its walls, and the monstrous stone door, carved with strange symbols, was in front of him.

The door to the universe the invader had come from yawned open. Behind him, coming toward him, he *felt* the invader, trying to flee, trying to return to its own place, the universe it had created that became itself.

Wolfe stretched out a hand, and the door boomed shut, and the sound of the booming echoed through creation. He reached up, pulled rock from the ceiling, and it cascaded down with a rumble, burying the passage to the door that his mind had created from a different reality, sealing the rift between universes.

The "virus," the invader, was around him, and he *felt* it, had it cupped in his hands. He considered it coldly, then denied it permission to exist.

A soundless scream came, like the tearing of dimensions, and the invader was gone.

Joshua Wolfe hung in space. He was enormous, he was subatomic. He *felt* the rhythm around him, normal, strange, warm, cold, dark, light.

THE DARKNESS OF GOD

Stars were above, below, next to him. He studied them for a long time. Some he knew, others were strange. Far in the distance was a familiar yellow star. He approached it, saw its nine worlds. He leaned over one, blue, green, and white, and knew it for his birthplace.

Wolfe stretched out a hand to touch Earth.

His nose tickled.

Joshua Wolfe was on the bridge of the *Grayle*. Behind him, the Lumina rotated, sending its comfortable, familiar colors around the control room. Wolfe thought of a ceiling, of an artist. His nose still tickled.

He scratched it.

Then he burst into laughter, great, booming waves of total amusement.

* CHAPTER TWENTY-TWO *

The *Grayle* orbited a system that had lived and died long before Man, a system without a name, only a number. Its planets had been devoured when the sun went nova, and now there was nothing but the dying star and a tiny starship.

Wolfe relaxed in a chair, gazing at the screen in front of him. He poured the last of the bottle of Hubert Dayton he'd husbanded in the ship's safe for years, savored its burn, tasted the grapes of Gascony, remembered a winding road, a girl's laughter, the acrid smell of woodsmoke as the pruned vines burned, a cold wind coming down from the massif, a storm minutes behind, and the welcome flicker of the fire in the tiny cottage ahead.

"A long time ago," he said, lifting the snifter in a toast. "Quite a run," he said. "They gave me quite a run indeed."

A line from the long-dead poet came:

"In my end is my beginning."

He said the words aloud in Terran, then again in Al'ar. Something that might have been a smile came and went on his lips. He drained the snifter.

Wolfe stood. He gave a series of coordinates.

"Understood," the *Grayle* said. *"Awaiting your command."*

The flames of the red giant reached for him, welcoming.

"Go." The ship's drive hummed to life.

THE DARKNESS OF GOD

He crossed his arms across his chest, brought them slowly out, palm up, as his breathing slowed. The Great Lumina roared life, incandescent as never before. The bits of matter that had been Joshua Wolfe stilled, were motionless.

Joshua Wolfe's corpse slid to the deck. The slight smile still remained on his lips.

The *Grayle*, at full drive, plunged into the heart of the dying sun.

✎ FREE DRINKS ✎

Take the Del Rey® survey and get a free newsletter! Answer the questions below and we will send you complimentary copies of the DRINK (Del Rey® Ink) newsletter free for one year. Here's where you will find out all about upcoming books, read articles by top authors, artists, and editors, and get the inside scoop on your favorite books.

Age _____ Sex ❑ M ❑ F

Highest education level: ❑ high school ❑ college ❑ graduate degree

Annual income: ❑ $0-30,000 ❑ $30,001-60,000 ❑ over $60,000

Number of books you read per month: ❑ 0-2 ❑ 3-5 ❑ 6 or more

Preference: ❑ fantasy ❑ science fiction ❑ horror ❑ other fiction ❑ nonfiction

I buy books in hardcover: ❑ frequently ❑ sometimes ❑ rarely

I buy books at: ❑ superstores ❑ mall bookstores ❑ independent bookstores
   ❑ mail order

I read books by new authors: ❑ frequently ❑ sometimes ❑ rarely

I read comic books: ❑ frequently ❑ sometimes ❑ rarely

I watch the Sci-Fi cable TV channel: ❑ frequently ❑ sometimes ❑ rarely

I am interested in collector editions (signed by the author or illustrated):
   ❑ yes ❑ no ❑ maybe

I read Star Wars novels: ❑ frequently ❑ sometimes ❑ rarely

I read Star Trek novels: ❑ frequently ❑ sometimes ❑ rarely

I read the following newspapers and magazines:
   ❑ *Analog*   ❑ *Locus*   ❑ *Popular Science*
   ❑ *Asimov*   ❑ *Wired*   ❑ *USA Today*
   ❑ *SF Universe*   ❑ *Realms of Fantasy* ❑ *The New York Times*

Check the box if you do not want your name and address shared with qualified vendors ❑

Name _____
Address _____
City/State/Zip _____
E-mail _____
                                          darkness of god

PLEASE SEND TO: DEL REY®/The DRINK
201 EAST 50TH STREET NEW YORK NY 10022

DEL REY® ONLINE!

The Del Rey Internet Newsletter...

A monthly electronic publication, posted on the Internet, GEnie, CompuServe, BIX, various BBSs, and the Panix gopher (gopher.panix.com). It features hype-free descriptions of books that are new in the stores, a list of our upcoming books, special announcements, a signing/reading/convention-attendance schedule for Del Rey authors, "In Depth" essays in which professionals in the field (authors, artists, designers, salespeople, etc.) talk about their jobs in science fiction, a question-and-answer section, behind-the-scenes looks at sf publishing, and more!

Internet information source!

A lot of Del Rey material is available to the Internet on our Web site and on a gopher server: all back issues and the current issue of the Del Rey Internet Newsletter, sample chapters of upcoming or current books (readable or downloadable for free), submission requirements, mail-order information, and much more. We will be adding more items of all sorts (mostly new DRINs and sample chapters) regularly. The Web site is http://www.randomhouse.com/delrey/ and the address of the gopher is gopher.panix.com

Why? We at Del Rey realize that the networks are the medium of the future. That's where you'll find us promoting our books, socializing with others in the sf field, and—most important—making contact and sharing information with sf readers.

Online editorial presence: Many of the Del Rey editors are online, on the Internet, GEnie, CompuServe, America Online, and Delphi. There is a Del Rey topic on GEnie and a Del Rey folder on America Online.

Our official e-mail address for Del Rey Books is delrey@randomhouse.com (though it sometimes takes us a while to answer).